NERVE DAMAGE

YOU CAN'T OUTRUN THE PAST

By J.L. MYERS

A Chilling Psychological Thriller that will have
you Covering Your Eyes and Turning the Pages
Faster at the same time

MORE BOOKS BY J.L. MYERS

THE BLOOD BOUND SERIES

What Lies Inside

Made By Design

Web Of Lies

Born To Die

~

OTHER BOOKS

Fallen Angel

ONE

KASEY

I trudged along a scenic, tree-winding road that saw at most a few cars every hour. In gray jeans and a black hoodie, I blended into the dreary surroundings, just another shadow below the early morning ashen clouds.

A deep ache settled in and I shrugged my clanking backpack higher once, twice, three times after a few more steps. My gloved hand on the strap kept the heavy load from sliding back down. My car was well out of reach now. Out of sight too, down over the steep drop-off to the right in an isolated parking lot no one used in these colder months of the year. Safe and hidden...until I needed it. The rain that fell was ignored, the crunch of wet gravel under my combat boots lost to the sway of wind-battered trees.

Though I stared ahead, what I saw was not the hardening downpour or the flying of loose leaves.

Instead, I saw a girl's face. Young. Innocent. Twentyish with forest-green eyes and long, almost black hair. Her smile had been infectious and the words from her pretty mouth had set my course. "…Saturday morning. At the crack of dawn. My dad doesn't believe in waiting for sunrise. Not when the whole day is waiting. That Kananaskis Trail…"

Now I was here. Soon I'd be the one waiting.

Right before a hairpin bend on this less-traveled road, my booted strides stopped. Anticipation filled me with a flood of warmth, but a deep breath of brisk air tightened my chest. I ignored the discomfort as raindrops trickled down my brow and cheeks. After days, months, and years this was it. There was no turning back now. This was my only escape, my only way to make the past right.

Dropping my backpack with a clatter and quick stretch of my back, I bent over. A flash of cold metal came free, long like a chain but not as smooth. The long length jangled as I stretched it out over the asphalt and then the weedy grass beyond before tucking the end behind a bush.

Road spikes.

A quick jog delivered me back across the road and I reclaimed my lumpy backpack. Then I was back at the bush and crouching behind it. A quick grab and click cemented the scene as my Polaroid camera hummed out a happy snap. A memento. As I tucked the device back out of the rain, a set of headlights shone around a smooth bend back down the road and brought my head up.

"Shit!" I spat from beneath my hood as an old sedan sailed too fast up the rain-slicked road. My gloved hands tugged the length of metal back just before the sedan's tires could claim those sharp spikes. Heart pounding like a drum, I muttered as I watched the red taillights disappear around the bend. Wrong car. Then I ran out to string those spikes back in place. An approaching white glow had my hood snapping up to see another car coming.

Right on time.

Racing back over the road, I dove for cover behind the bush. The headlights of the approaching white Merc flashed on highs for two beats.

I'd been spotted.

And then the front tires hit the spikes. With a hiss of released air, traction was lost. The man driving yanked the steering wheel and anchored on the brakes, the tires barely squealing on the wet asphalt. But it was too late. The drenched road provided a slippery passage as the sedan fishtailed then spun, sliding sideways over the edge too fast to stop. It tipped on the sudden drop-off, tumbling guts over roof, guts over roof.

The tall cypress tree that halted its descent with a deafening clap wasn't a Godsend. Metal cried out as it curved around the tree, reshaping the driver's side and shattering the windshield.

And then there was a moment of pure quiet, nothing but the sound of peaceful whooshing wind as the rain eased off.

Tugging back the spikes and concealing them behind the bush, I hoisted up the backpack and unhurriedly made my way down the slippery path to the wreck. The next part to come was a means to an end. My anticipation lied in the aftermath but not in this act. And yet with each step, I felt nothing. No uncertainty. No regret. Those feelings I'd shed long ago. I'd had no choice.

Reaching the wreckage, red was visible beneath the mud-caked windows. My backpack was dropped to gain a closer look. The middle-aged female in the front passenger side was out cold, with cuts that leaked blood down her face to her blouse. In the driver's side, the man's features were unrecognizable, covered in glossy red. There was a creak of movement. It wasn't him. In the back, there she was, her perfect lips no longer smiling and dark bruising puffing up her pale face. With a blink of her lids over her bloodshot green eyes, she wasn't dead.

Unfortunate for her…she was coming around.

I tugged the car's back door open and reached in, taking hold of the young woman and dragging her out. She was pretty out of it, eyes dazed and lids twitching. She was injured too, with multiple cuts and bruises on her face and arms. A bump on her forehead was ballooning beneath the skin. Her feet trailed as I dragged her by her arms across the mushed-up ground.

Then I noticed the object she somehow clutched in her tight fingers. A phone. Relieving her of the device once we were well out of reach, I positioned her to face the wreck.

"Don't worry. I've got you now."

My combats squelched through the mud back to the car, and with a lean over the dead man, a click sounded as I unlocked the fuel tank. Back around the Merc, I found the fuel lid open and unscrewed the cap. My black Zippo lighter came free of my pocket along with a long rag. A minute or so after soaking the rag and I was yards away, the Zippo's flame fighting the wind and rain and losing.

"Cassidy..." The woman still in the car—the young woman's mother—was waking up. Still alive. She moved as her hand came up to her head. "Cas...talk to me." She groaned, and then sucked air as she twisted to get a better view, seeing her husband and the empty back seat. "Cas!"

The girl's eyes fluttered then went wide. Her voice was a painful rasp. "Mom…"

"Time to say goodbye." There was a crunching scrape as the Zippo sparked back to life. The flame met the material's end and I returned to the girl, turning to see the fire retreat.

"Mom!" The girl's voice was shrill, and she swayed as she scrambled to get up. Her eyes rolled *like marbles, bringing her back down. And then it was too late. With a whoosh the soaked rag below the sedan ignited in a fiery ball, climbing up the metal walls and curving inside the dry cab. The woman's shrieks cut through the dying rain as my camera immortalized this moment in time. But the sounds of her death faded all too fast, the fire taking her pain away. Taking her life away.*

As the girl I'd saved from the wreck whimpered, I readied what I needed before returning. Standing over her, the small boulder in my hands blocked the view of my face. The hefty weight of the rock returned that ache to my tired shoulders. "Don't worry, Cassidy. This isn't the end. I need your help...to bring them all to me."

TWO

THIRTY DAYS LATER

A click followed by a creak tore me from my nightmares: the fire that engulfed our family car, my mother's screams the second before the inferno claimed her too, and the hooded figure over me with a boulder ready to crush my head.

I ratcheted upright and rubbed my eyes, scrambling back until I hit a hard metal rod. A bed frame. Vision hazy, I cowered at the blue-clad figure that neared. His closing-in strides and jangling ring of keys made sweat bullet all over me and stuck my clothes to my body. He stopped at the foot of the bed and threw down a flat-pack plastic sleeve. "Time for your interview, Cassidy Lockheart. Knock when you're ready."

At the sound of his retreating steps and the close of the solitary door he'd come through, my eyes finally cleared. So did my head. I knew where I was. Not a hostage in some dingy wet basement. But in a cell. Minimal of much of anything except a white-linen bed, a table with a single chair, paper, and a pen. And a two-foot-square window nailed shut and screened with thick wire. A wellness hospital, which was a nicer way of saying *mental institution.*

Sliding my legs over the edge of the bed, I turned my arms inner-wrist-side up over my lap. The two scars down the middle of either forearm were long, no longer covered by bandages though still raised and bright pink. My attempt to join my mom and dad after the 'accident'—*because that's what it had been.*

I squeezed my eyes shut, refusing to cry. Not today.

What a crock.

Slippery road, gas leak, and no seatbelt to hold me back from being thrown free of the fiery death my parents had suffered. That's what I had to tell the doc now...if I wanted to escape this prison I'd been in for the last thirty days. If I wanted to have the chance to visit my parents' graves finally. No person darting across the road. No one to drag me from the wreck. No figure setting a gasoline-soaked rag alight. I sniffed, even now smelling the accelerant. No one concealed by a hood as they stood over me in dark jeans and muddy combats. No large boulder blocking my view of their face and ready to pancake my head.

There'd been no trace of them or foul play. The

gas had come from the punctured tank below the car.

"Never happened," I muttered, pushing up and ripping into the plastic sleeve of clothes to get dressed. The sooner I got out of here, the sooner I'd be able to make it up to them. The sooner I'd never have to tell that story—fact or delusion—again.

Loose pants and plain white hospital johnny off, I tugged on the black jeans and plain gray blouse. Nearing the door, where the back of the guard's head was clear through the wire-laced peering window, I knocked lightly. "I'm ready."

As the door opened and I stepped out, I didn't look back. There was nothing to remember from this place. And so much I wished to forget. More than the stifling smell of this place would always be a part of me now. Like it along with everything here had absorbed into my skin to take up a form of permanent residence.

Without words, I kept in toe with the guard as we passed more cell doors down the long hall and a new guard every fifteen feet. They didn't like it when you fell behind. A cry of anger punched from further back up the hall. When a girl banged into the next door I passed, fists bashing on the glass, I let out an involuntary yelp as I flinched. I'd never get used to this place. The Calgary Wellness Centre, or CWC, was always full, and with much worse cases than me. The institution wasn't just protecting patients from themselves. It didn't even mostly do that. Mostly it protected outsiders from the admitted residents. And for the sane, non-homicidal ones of us, it was made as safe as it could be. As secure too. The four wings were broken down into categories, with red for the worst of the worst, and green for the short stayers like me. Green lockdown was every night for the duration until morning. Red lockdown was permanent, except for when a guard escort was arranged for meals and exercise times.

When we reached the wing junctions, the locked glass door buzzed and automatically slid open, and then I was deposited into an interview room. The same one I'd sat in every day for the past month to recount my ordeal and be told what had really happened.

Without wall hangings—because some patients would see anything framed especially with a glass cover as a possible weapon—the room was bare. One metal table with obscenities scraped into the top, and a metal chair screwed to the linoleum-covered concrete. An anchor was bolted to the table too, but I sat without worry that I'd be chained to it.

The woman sitting opposite me was in her white coat, as usual, red hair pulled back in a bun, and black-framed glasses edging down her nose as she looked up from my file with a grin. Doc Bethany. "Hello, Cas. How are—"

"Just Cassidy. *Please.*" I couldn't stop the words. My parents called me Cas. Or they had. My mom when she'd screamed out to me…for the last time. But I guess the doc's tests were already beginning. Had I failed before I'd even begun?

"Very well." With a nod, she eyed my clothes. "So today is the day, I hope. How did you sleep last night?"

My eyes flicked to the side and the door where the guard who'd woken me stood. He'd tell. They always did. Lying would just prove I wasn't ready, and their bribe of 'outside clothes' would yet again have been wasted. "Same nightmare."

"And when you went to sleep, you remember that?"

Another test. Because a head injury had resulted in an internal brain glitch, one that would have me blackout at times without warning. A glitch the doc believed remained as a form of self-preservation, by stripping the clarity of my memories before the crash from my mind. A glitch that also stalked me with unrealistic nightmares. In the past I'd lied about them, claimed I'd had none in a single day, only to be told a guard had needed to haul me up and return me to my bed from the place I'd lost consciousness in.

I rubbed at my forehead, sighing deeply. "No, I don't."

Her smile unnerved me, not because it was cruel or expecting, but because I'd never seen it like that before. "Then you've made progress. You're accepting the truth and not trying to hide behind the fear of change."

Mumbo jumbo crap. I was taking Einstein's theory of insanity literally: *Doing the same thing over and over and expecting a different result was the definition of insanity.* Lying about those questions hadn't worked in my favor, but the truth, at least in this instance, had. And now would come the clincher. I knew it as the guard slipped from the room at the doc's nod, and as she turned a page in my file—revealing photos of the scene.

My heart almost stopped, then it raced as if trying to escape what it felt; the torture of reliving that day again right now in this moment in my mind. Like every other time, I closed my eyes. I coughed, wincing at the pain I had no control over, blinking back tears as I forced myself to look at the photo she turned around. Blackened car, broken windows, two burned bodies in the front. I gulped down the rise of vomit that spiked my throat.

"Tell me how this happened."

It was almost thirty seconds before I could choke out a sound. My hands shook so bad, but I kept them in my lap where she couldn't see. As the sun rose above the estate's tall treetops into a powdery blue sky, its creeping rays through the barred window warming my shaking legs, now was the time. Honesty 101. Fake it until you make it. Or be locked up forever.

"I…" I had to take a few deep breaths before I could speak, before I could look up from the gruesome photo the cops on scene had taken. "I was in the car with my mom and dad. They were arguing. I was. We must have hit something. A rock. A pothole. Dad lost control. The car went over the edge. It rolled. I was thrown free. Then I smelled gas. The car burst into flames. I heard my mom scream…and then…nothing. I don't remember blacking out. Then I was at Rockyview General in a hospital bed. The cops took my statement." The one that made them stare at me like I'd sustained more than just superficial cuts and grazes. The one they'd made me repeat over and over for the next few days. "Then the fu—neral," I choked on the word. "It was set for the day after my release. All prearranged by our account's executor. But I couldn't…I didn't want…to live without them." I absently rubbed at the raised scars running up my wrists. "I tried to join them. After that, I woke up here. To you."

Doc Bethany tilted her head as she regarded me, eyes narrowing ever so slightly. She closed the cover on my patient file and folded her arms across the top. "What about the 'figure', the one you saw crossing the road? The one who dragged you from the car and lit the fire? What about them?"

Now I had to sell it, to make her believe that I believed my own bullshit words. That I knew that figure had been a figment of my fear rather than something that could come back to warp my reality again.

Sliding my shaking arms from my lap I lay them across the table, wrist-side up to show my scars. The tears I'd held back came forth and fell, pat-patting on the metal table. "I…I couldn't accept that they were dead, that fighting with them had been the thing that had killed them. I needed to blame someone. To believe that an evil person had singled us out and done this on purpose. I…" I spluttered before sucking it back in and wiping my tears away. "I killed them. It was my fault. That's why I tried to…" I looked at my wrists, unable to see the scars through thick tears. "To end it."

"It was your fault?"

I shook my head and gulped. "That's how I felt. Still kinda feel. But it wasn't just me. I wasn't driving. I didn't make it rain. I didn't put that rock or whatever it was on the road. I know that now. I mean, I can't stop the guilt I feel, but I can see the reality of what happened." I sighed long and hard, seeing fire behind my eyes as they slid shut for a second—an eternal second. "It was a horrible accident. One I survived. And I'm not giving up the memory of my parents to bail out because it's easier. I'm going to get through this." I nodded now, feeling the first truth I'd said in the past few minutes. "I have to. Failure is not an option."

There was a screech as Doc Bethany's chair was

pushed back and she stood. Unlike mine, hers wasn't bolted down. She fished into her white coat pocket, making a tic-tac sound as her hand came free with a white-capped orange bottle of pills. "The things you dream are not real. They are figments of your traumatized mind trying to process the tragedy of your parents' deaths." Placing the bottle on the table she slid it over the metal toward me. "These pills will help with your nightmares and the blackouts. Now that you're not in denial. And as you allow yourself to heal and re-experience places and activities from your past, they will help alleviate your fuzzy memories."

"You mean…?"

With a smile she bent, a crinkle sounding as she straightened to hold out another clear plastic pocket. Inside were the clothes I'd been wearing when they'd brought me in here. My funeral clothes. The smears of blood were now ruddy brown on the long gray sleeves of the black dress I'd had on while cutting myself. A black-tagged key with the number sixteen sat atop the neatly folded pile. My lucky number, and the key to my dorm at the University of Calgary in Alberta Canada. And lastly… I snatched up my phone, tears welling at the instant sensation of having a piece of my parents back. A piece I thought I'd lost forever. The one thing apart from me that had survived the 'accident.'

"You're free to go, Cas…I mean Cassidy." Doc

Bethany's smile stayed warm. "I hope I don't see you again."

THREE

My slow footsteps over the lush grass between headstones was a quiet *brush, brush, brush,* kicking up that freshly mowed scent as damp cuttings stuck to my black shoes. Every slow blink of my cried-out eyes sent flashes of color up behind my lids. A soaring church with a depressing organ belting out morbid funeral music. A back room with a tall freestanding mirror. A reflection of me in my black dress with long gray sleeves and mascara smears down my face…and a knife slicing down the length of my inner forearm. And then blood, pouring, falling, collecting in two puddles on the ground.

I shook the memory of my suicide attempt away and sucked in a breath. The cool afternoon air held too much of a chill, numbing my nose and burning as it filled my lungs. Or was it just the fact that I couldn't take a full breath in without feeling like I was going to break apart. That day I'd missed their funeral. I'd wanted to join them.

Now I was here. Queen's Park Cemetery.

God, each slow step as I followed the directions the ground's keeper had given me made this all too real. Too raw. One hand clenched tighter around my phone, scared I might lose my last piece of them, the last piece of my parents. The other strangled two bouquets of pretty white and yellow flowers.

And then I saw it. Their final resting place.

It was obvious in the change from vibrant green blades to two side-by-side dirt patches with healthy grass shoots spearing out in random thick and sparse patches. *Phil Lockheart* and *Jean Lockheart* were etched into the two tall rounded marble headstones with *Loving Husband and Father* and *Devoted Wife and Mother* in smaller stylized print below.

I swallowed, feeling like my hand now clutched around my throat was a fist stuck inside. Dropping to my knees, I didn't care that dampness soaked straight through my jeans. Didn't care that the flowers I'd switched to hold with my arm against my body fell to the ground. Didn't care that I could hear movement way behind me at the older and larger headstones and tombs. Still clinging to my phone, I pressed it and my hand against my father's marker and my other open palm to my mother's. My head hung, tears I had no control over falling in silent grief.

"I'm sorry," I whispered. The chattering of wind-swept trees beyond the cemetery's stone barrier kept my apology private, keeping this moment in time eternal and undisturbed.

Minutes passed, it could have been an hour for all I took in around me. The afternoon sun dipped lower, its gentle warmth across my back fleeting as shadows grew from surrounding headstones. Finally, I sat back on my haunches, but I didn't look up. Instead, I kept my sight down on my phone, my heart starting to rush as I thumbed the screen, bringing up the last recording of the people I cared most about in the world. Rolling the start time to seven minutes and twenty-two seconds in—to the seconds that had changed my life—I hit play.

"Mom, Dad...I'm dropping out."

The patter of rain was clear through the speaker as it battered the windshield, and as I closed my eyes I saw with vivid clarity the exact moment of this part of the recording. Me staring out the car's rear window at the shifting gray sky above wet trees— because I didn't want to see the disappointment on their faces again. My shoulders had hunched in preparation of what was about to come.

The vocal silence finally broke with my father's rebuttal. *"Absolutely not. You wanted this. Like every other choice that you've backed out of before this one."* His face had been fierce as he'd scowled at me in the rearview mirror. *"We're not a bank to fund your entertainment."*

Mom's hand had come across the center console

to rest over my dad's strained arm as he squeezed the steering wheel. She turned far enough to face me in the backseat. *"What your father means to say is that we believe in you, in your interest in becoming a psychologist. In helping others. I know you want to do something meaningful with your life."*

"I do. I just don't think I'm cut out—"

"No. This time it's no." Dad's head craned to glare at me over his shoulder, his eyes diverting from the slippery road while rain obscured the view beyond. *"We've paid out the semester. You'll see it throu—"*

"Look out!" I cried suddenly as something dark darted across the road.

The sudden noise through the speaker made my blood run cold: my father cursing, sounds of movement, the soft screech of tires, Mom crying out, *"Cassidy, your belt!"* then grunts, a scream, metal creaking and squealing as we tumbled down the hill. A sudden thump ended the marriage of noise that had my teeth grinding together with the vivid memory. Now my only vivid memory.

The recording stopped.

Slipping my phone into my back pocket, I tried to regulate my breathing from hitched back to normal. I didn't quite make it, but despite the shaking that attacked my body and limbs, I managed to speak. "I had to come and see you both. I'm okay now. I…I'm going back to university. You're here because of me, because of that day. But I won't let you die in vain. I'll be everything you ever wanted me to be. Mom…" I sniffed back tears that fell anyway and my hands came together like I was praying. "Daddy, I promise you. I'll make you both so proud."

Gathering up the strewn bouquets, I laid one ribbon-tied bunch at the foot of each glossy headstone. Then I kissed my fingertips and pressed them over my father's name, then my mother's. I was about to get up when a moving shadow crept over me, striking out the waning sun's warmth with a sudden chill down my spine.

I glanced over my shoulder to find someone in a black hoodie loitering a few headstones back. They weren't looking my way, but the hairs on the back of my neck prickled in warning. Average height and build, dark jeans, and combats on their feet. I looked away, fighting not to hyperventilate. It couldn't be. I'd imagined that person. Made them up to blame someone other than myself for my parents' deaths. And yet I felt fear racing in, an ingrained sense of protection that screamed at me to leap up and run.

I stood slowly, starting to glance back out of the corner of my eye…

"They deserved to die, you know. Just like the rest of them do."

Terrified but suddenly furious, I whirled fully. My chest pumped with quick breaths and my hands came up as if they were enough to protect me from the deranged cemetery lurker. "How dare—"

My tongue froze, my heart skipped, then resumed its slowing race. There was no one there. Not where I'd seen them standing, not down the row of headstones, not beyond the stone border. I was alone—in so many ways.

I wrapped my arms around my body, feeling an unrelenting chill that had nothing to do with the wind. My eyes were playing tricks on me again. My ears too. Either that or I was losing my mind, letting the guilt I'd promised to overcome eat away at me from the inside out. But I couldn't do it. I had to pull through. For them. For my parents. "Get your shit together, Cassidy."

I owed them a full and productive life.

~

I skulked down the hall to room sixteen, the tagged key in my hand ready, but my mind totally not. I felt like a fraud. Like I didn't belong. I'd given up on my life here and my future. A decision I'd regret for the rest of my life. Pausing only long enough to glance down either length of the hall, I saw no one. Not a surprise being winter break. Most students had returned...*home*. My heart clenched like it was being squeezed by a forever tightening vice. *Home*...a place I could no longer face returning to without the people who'd made it that.

A single twist of the key had me pushing inside

my dorm room and closing the door to slump against it.

My drooping lids shot open and I breathed in deep. Smoke. Not strong and billowing from fire—like the worst day of my life—but dull and sooty.

I blinked as I scanned, searching as if seeing the room for the first time. Single bed with plain yellow linen. A closet with the door ajar. A shelf of textbooks and folders beside a wall of posters with sayings from famous theorists. Bare wooden floors and a cracked open window with wind-rippling white-and-yellow curtains in front of a darkening sky. I left it open? I wondered as my gaze settled on a large piece of furniture. A desk against the wall that doubled as a dresser with a mirror…topped with skewed photo albums.

My grip on the plastic bag of my stained clothes tightened. I wanted to see their faces. To remember with total clarity what they'd looked like. Even now as I tried to picture their features, I saw only the necessary: brown hair, hazel eyes, the features that made up their faces…but even that already seemed fuzzy. Like it was slowly disappearing. And even as I ached to bawl over the life's memories in those albums, my heart just couldn't do it. Knowing they were gone, I couldn't bear to see how happy they'd been. How happy they could still have been…if not for me.

And then I saw the source of the smoke

remnants. A solid wastepaper basket—full of black ashes. All the photos that had once filled those albums.

I felt myself shatter apart on the inside. Knowing that what I hadn't been ready to see was gone hit me again like the day of their funeral. I swayed on my feet but locked my knees in place. I had no memory of this, but the scene was like a story being told. The day I was supposed to say goodbye, I'd done so much more than try to end myself. I'd tried to erase the pain first. Erase their existence in my heart by removing the proof of my lost memories.

I may not be ready to remember them properly yet. But to have taken this vital source away forever...

Tears streaming, I dumped the bag of clothes on the dresser. I threw the closet door open, glanced up then down, *there*, and grabbed an empty box. Falling to my shaking knees at the desk, I dumped the empty albums inside. I couldn't bear to see what I'd so recklessly done. I could barely breathe. As I lifted the last one and tilted it to fit it sideways in the remaining space, something slid free. A photo.

My breath caught. I froze.

I flicked through the remaining pages, but it was the only one. Now staring up at me from the carpet, it had landed face-side up. A color photo of my parents, a selfie, both smiling, my dad's arm around my mom, both of them dressed in puffy jackets, scarfs, and beanies with goggles atop their heads. Dressed for the snow, with a whited-out background and two sets of skis in my dad's hands. As I picked the photo up, date-stamped for last year, I couldn't remember being there. I couldn't remember them going away.

My chest tightened with the truth I hadn't wanted to admit to myself, let alone my doctor at CWC, a truth I hadn't been able to hide. Before the accident, I couldn't remember my life, at least not clearly. I'd thought being back here might help, that visiting their graves would. But despite the grief of loss I felt, my memories were like a thick fog, patchy at best. And this sole surviving photo…stirred *nothing*.

Picking up the photo, I closed the box and placed it in the bottom of the closet below my hanging clothes and my own snow gear. I stared at their features as I walked numbly to the dresser and sat down behind it. The orange pill container caught my eye from the plastic bag and I unzipped the plastic slider to pull it free. I hoped once my nightmares and blackouts were under control, my memories would come flooding back. At least that's what Doc Bethany had promised…so long as I engaged in familiar activities and visited old haunts.

I began to unscrew the lid—and paused as I heard a *swish* sound to my side. Something had just been slid under my door. An envelope.

Pills dropped, I was out of my chair and opening my door that creaked as I peeked out. Down the hallway, I saw someone walking away in a hoodie with their hands buried in their pockets. *"Not real."* I blinked hard and then opened my eyes.

The hall was empty. No noise. No person.

"It's all in your head," I muttered, edging back into my room. But as I looked down, the envelope was *real*. I frowned as I picked it up and lifted the flap.

WINNER! was printed in big letters at the top, and the white landscape with clear blue skies and chairlifts painted a picture before I even read the finer print. *Cassidy Lockheart you have won the trip of a lifetime. An all-inclusive weeklong snow trip to the Fernie Alpine Resort with free lift pass, equipment hire, and transport. All meals included.* Inside the envelope, everything was there: itinerary, the ticket, the bus pass.

My mouth was already gaping. One: Because aside from a sudden flash of memory of someone slapping a stack of flyers in front of me, I couldn't remember entering the competition. Two: Because this was an escape from winter break when I couldn't bear to go to my family home, especially with Christmas less than a week away, and my birthday even sooner. Three: Because this was exactly what the doctor had ordered to prompt my memories. Four made my jaw drop even further as I scanned the itinerary.

Departure was tomorrow…

My mind was already made up. To save being alone here. To take my mind off everything I could and couldn't remember. To get my head in the game so I'd be ready when next term started. To live a full life—because I'd promised them I would. To take the leap to a place I'd likely been to with my parents to gently jog my memories. I already had some of my own snow gear. It was win-win, a glimmer of good out of the hell I'd lived through. A ray of sun in my lonely future. An escape as much as a hope of healing.

I was going. For me. For them. To believe there was a point to all my promises.

Glancing up, I saw my reflection. CWC hadn't allowed mirrors for obvious reasons. Seeing myself now still unnerved me, even though it wasn't the first time since my release. The scars I'd felt with my hands after the accident, the ones I'd had trouble looking at in the hospital mirror before their funeral, were where they should be, and haloed by my long, dark hair. Mostly small ones, tight lines that were already healed white remnants of the 'accident.' A larger one crossed my forehead, just as remarkably white as the others. They'd been mostly superficial, like the rest of the ones that covered various parts of my body and legs. Cuts from the tumble and being thrown from the car.

Because that's what had happened.

The one thing though that held my stare was my eyes, the left one in particular. Aside from my blurry sight after the 'accident' and for the first week after waking at CWC, I hadn't known—hadn't remembered, more likely—until a bathroom trip before visiting my parents' graves earlier. Blunt force trauma had left one of my green eyes with a pupil that looked like it'd been pricked with a pin to bleed out just enough to reach the rim of the iris.

Now knowing what I looked like, that every time I'd see myself, this especially would be a reminder of what had happened, I'd taken action to make it go away. I pulled a plastic container from my pocket and unscrewed the cap from one side. The contact lens came free, green to match my eyes and cover up the proof of what I'd done and could never take back. Already wet, I pulled my lower and upper lids wide and placed the tiny little disc over my eyeball, blinking at the discomfort as it shifted into place.

Glancing back up, I breathed a sigh of relief as I unscrewed the lid from my meds. No one would ever pick it. And I hoped these little white miracles would do what Doc Bethany had promised. I popped the pill and dry swallowed, sending out a prayer, putting my every determination into who I was and who I would continue to be. "I am Cassidy Lockheart, daughter of Jean and Phil. And I will survive. I will keep my promises."

FOUR

At the Calgary Airport bus stop the next day, I was packed and ready to go. A duffel bag was stuffed with my snow gear and a backpack held an extra jacket, my gloves, and a scarf for easy access when the crisp snowscape temp would greet my arrival at the Fernie Alpine Resort in three hours time. Hugging my arms around myself, I felt—well it wasn't excitement. I couldn't feel that knowing what I'd lost so recently. Though it was heavily laced with guilt, I guess I felt anticipation for taking charge of my life, for making good on my promise, for being strong enough to face a location that could return the past in all its detail—and heighten the devastating grief that had me tearing up even now.

I sniffed, rubbing the back of my hand across my nose. A torn newspaper page tumbled by with a blast of wind. Hitting the legs of a commuter, I saw part of the headline. ESCAPE. As a stronger gust carried it away into the crowd, another emotion took over.

Not anger. Not even a deeper burdening guilt. They were there, but there was something else.

Jolting statue still, the hairs across my nape prickled. My discomfort grew. I shot a glance at the passengers milling around up and down the long pickup lane with briefcases, handbags, and suitcases: the working class, a few elderly, parents with kids, a group of dodgy-looking teens. Yet the feeling wasn't a result of any of them—because not a single one of them was watching me.

But someone was.

I could feel the weight of someone's hard and unwavering stare that pressed down on me like a physical force. I could sense it in the tingles that kept riding up and down my spine, which had nothing to do with the gustily wind that came and went with the passing of another fully loaded bus. Someone was definitely watching me, *here*, on this platform.

I whispered under my breath, *"You're imagining things."* Yet I couldn't turn off the sudden and drowning need to take flight. To run. My lungs felt like they'd shrunk to the size of tennis balls.

Headlights from my ride flashed in the distance and neared, lighting up the gloomy morning and everyone waiting. Another larger bus was following right behind. I dared to glance back through the gathering of people who edged in for a closer spot while others picked up their belongings or children. Nothing stood out. No one person, young or old.

The bus rolled to a stop with a screech of brakes. Pulling my ticket from my backpack, I became part of the mass, being ushered forward to the doors as they clapped open. I glanced over my shoulder, left then right—my heart skipped a beat. *There.* Peeking out from a pillar behind a mass of waiting people. Someone in a black hood, bathed in shadow from a raked shelter—staring right at me. I twisted to get a better view and was shoved by a guy I didn't look to see. Almost tripping I stumbled into the bus and dropped my duffel. Swooping it up, my ticket was snatched. But I wasn't staying. I turned back to the exit, eyes darting to the now empty space beside the pillar.

Real? Delusion? I didn't know, but I needed to. The pills had been helping, or at least I thought they had—

I slammed right into a tall guy, tipping back with the weight of my duffel to take me down—until his broad hand flung out and caught my forearm in a firm but gentle grip. In my fear and my need to escape, I was breathing hard. He was too as he steadied me on my feet. "Oh, shit. I'm sorry. I didn't see you."

I glanced from the empty pillar to the many stragglers on the platform, none of which were wearing hoodies.

When I focused on the guy still holding my arm, he let go and grabbed a pole for support as the bus began its jerky forward motion. He brushed a hand through his slightly wavy, blond hair, his blue eyes full of sincerity and hesitation—or was that surprise?—as they met mine. "I—I um…was missing the ride. I…you… Did I hurt you?"

"Ah, no. I'm fine," I said as I scanned over his plain V-neck—no hood—and dark jeans over running shoes. Not the hooded person I'd seen. Yet as I glanced back up to his face, with its sharp lines, full lips, and sparkling blue eyes, I kept looking at him for another reason. And not because he looked like he was in his early twenties and was seriously handsome. Something about him was strangely familiar. I frowned at the bag slung over his shoulder. An army green duffel similar to the black one I'd dropped. "Do I know—"

"Hey, let me grab that." The guy bent to pick up my bag and motioned with it to the empty back row on the bus. With a brilliant smile, he began walking. "It's the least I can do."

I followed slowly behind, fighting the bus's movements to keep vertical. When the guy had placed my bag down on the central seat and dumped his beside it, he stood back for me to sit. As I hesitantly did, scooting into the far-side window, he held out his hand. "I'm Jeremy, by the way."

I clenched my hands, then released, leaning forward just enough to take his hand. "Cassidy." I let go too quick, unable to place his face or where I knew him from as I dumped my backpack on top of my duffel. I nodded to his bag. Maybe interrogation would shed some light. "You moving or something?"

Jeremy glanced at his bag then back to me as he took a seat on the other side of our fort-worthy luggage. "Nah. All my crap wouldn't fit in this bag. I'm off for vacation. Going to the snow for a week."

Coincidence? "I guess it's that time of year. Winter break." Fishing much.

"You're off that way too?" He eyed me with curiosity as I nodded. "I got the sweetest deal though. Fully paid for. Everything included. Didn't cost me a cent."

I froze and my stomach dropped.

Jeremy noticed. "What? Oh, I guess it's rude to brag. Especially if you forked out for your vacay."

"But I didn't…" I tugged down the zipper on my backpack and pulled out my winning ticket, the one that had even covered this exact bus ride with a shuttle change toward the end. The one Jeremy had been rushing not to miss. "Fernie Alpine Resort. All expenses paid. Everything included down to lift pass and food."

Jeremy's eyes bugged, the cornflower blue in them seeming to darken with genuine surprise. "This is weird as." From his back pocket he pulled an exact winning copy of my ticket, except with his name in the winning line. *Jeremy Peters.* "I received this a week ago. Bit short notice, but I had nothing better planned." He shrugged as if over the shock and perfect alignment of our introduction. "Wonder if there are any other winners."

I read the detail on his card. *Alpine Creek Lodge?* "We're…we're staying at the same place."

Jeremy tucked the card back into his pocket and tilted his head, more in anticipation than the confusion I could feel morphing my expression. "Then I guess we'll find out when we check in."

~

I was well on the way to the Fernie Alpine Resort when I felt a change creeping in. Warmth hummed behind my eyes and my skin came alive as if every inch was suddenly riddled with crawling bugs.

"Oh, no. Not now."

My voice was lost to the chatter of passengers as panic set its hooks in me. I didn't want to blackout. I didn't want to dream. But the bus's gentle rocking and padded seats worked against me. The farming landscape blinked out of view once, twice, then permanently as my lids slid shut. Weightlessness overcame me as external darkness welcomed, my link to consciousness lost. But like every other time I closed my eyes and feigned sleep, the serenity of having no thoughts or interruptions, no clear memories, didn't last.

As if out-of-body, scenery took shape, morphing into crystal clear clarity. Ashen sky. Wet slope of weed-riddled grass and mud. The sound of pattering rain was soothing—until a dying screech of tires broke the false calm.

The white Mercedes swerved as it appeared over the road's edge. The front tire got air, and then came down as gravity took control. Screams peeled through the rain as the sedan tipped and rolled like a giant metal tumbleweed.

Before the impact, the scene skipped forward. Now on my back, stunned and body aching, unable to move, I heard the crackling first. Fire. Blazing red and orange flames and black smoke that stole the smell of burned rubber and billowed up in a swelling mass. Through the blaze, I saw two figures. My mom and dad stuck in the car. Already singed black and way past any ability to scream. Dead. Burned alive.

I knew what came next. My false memory of that day. My delusion to lay the blame on someone but myself.

I tried to speak as a shadow crept over me, as that hood came into view. Too shadowed to see, just like every other time, I couldn't make out their features. Then that boulder came up, blocking what little I could see anyway.

Thank God. It was almost over. Even in my blackout dream state, I knew that. The suffering, the real and fake memory, was almost played out.

"Don't worry, Cassidy. This isn't the end." The

voice I heard from behind that boulder was a rasp, and it frightened the hell out of me. I'd never heard them speak before, not since that first—not real—time. "I need your help…to bring them all to me."

Terror paralyzed me even more than my injuries that kept my body from responding to my internal plea to leap up and run. No, this wasn't right. Why wasn't this ending?

And then that boulder came down—right on my face.

Before I could wake from the shock of it all, the scene continued. Gloved hands grasped my pant legs and hauled, dragging me down the hill over muddy weeds, rocks, and then through tall trees. I felt none of it, seeing the events as if I was a ghost watching from the sidelines. And then we arrived. The overgrown, puddled parking lot concealed a beat-up old sedan that had a huge barrel dominating the back seat. My legs were dropped and the trunk was flung open. My attacker wrapped my pancaked head in plastic and grunted as he hauled me up to dump me inside.

The trunk slammed shut over my corpse and everything turned black.

Sudden trees shot up like spears to the night sky, whispering in the breeze as if spreading secrets. A sudden whirring sound grew alarmingly louder. A crack and a tear followed by a repetitive sawing sound highlighted the horror I saw from a distance.

With their back to me, the hooded guy dragged a battery-powered hacksaw back and forth over…

If I'd been awake I would have hurled. Even standing here now, somehow seeing but not really present, I felt nausea turn my stomach and squeeze like a fist around my throat.

My body was laid out before my hooded attacker in the dirt, as my leg—my second leg—was sawn through. Because the other parts were already in the rusted barrel beside my remains, one pale hand peeking out next to my blood-spattered and muddy running shoes. That sickening sawing kept up as the jagged teeth were forced faster and faster back and forth. When my last limb was thrown like meat in a cow-butchering shed to join the others, my neck was worked on…to sever my head. *Back and forth. Back and forth.*

It kept on going, the wet slurping and cracking filling the forest. But this wasn't real. This horror. This sickening act. I was alive. Safe. On a bus. And yet I didn't wake up. Which was bullshit. Isn't that how nightmares worked? If you figured out you were in one, its hooks no longer held you, the understanding that what you were experiencing wasn't real always brought back consciousness.

And still I remained, seeing my head sail up like a gruesome basketball to swish in the barrel. The guy hefted my slick torso up with a grunt, and wedged it down into the barrel, fighting with my dismembered limbs—no, *the* dismembered limbs, because this wasn't real, this wasn't me. Once in as far as it would fit, a can was retrieved from behind the barrel and its liquid contents emptied over the headless body and protruding hands and feet. Space was gained before a lighter encased in their hand was lit, and then *whoof!* A ball of flames engulfed it all like the barrel was a giant candle and my—*the*—body parts were the wick.

I came awake with a wheezing gasp, hands going to my throat as my eyes flung wide. *Not real. Not real.* Though my heart raced at the vivid memory of what I'd just dreamed, the fact that my arms could move—because they were still attached and could grip my neck that was still holding my head in place—made me believe my words. My vision cleared, seeing my shaking legs where I sat in my seat as I heard shuffling. People sitting before me on the bus had spun at my noisy waking and were now turning back around. Damn PTSD. They all pretended they hadn't been gawking, except for one.

That Jeremy guy.

Still in his same seat across the bus, he openly watched me, eyes narrowed and lips pressed into a thin line that made me uncomfortable. The bags between us looked...*different*, like they'd been opened or shifted. He didn't say a thing, either, which made the staring all the more weird, though he looked like he wanted to question me.

43

No way in hell.

I looked away quickly, peering out the window as farms rushed past. My warm breath fogged up the glass, and finger-drawn letters appeared, growing with every breath. *Whitmore.* The sight made me freeze, but I was just working myself up even more for no reason. People defaced public transport all the time, and a quick wipe with my sleeve brushed the messy letters away. I had something so much bigger on my mind anyway, and after a minute or two of catching my breath, of repeating *not real* in my head, I snuck a glance back.

Jeremy was facing forward again, a frown on his face as if he were trying to figure something out. His head twisted slowly like he felt my gaze, and I quickly looked away.

I didn't look back for the rest of the trip.

FIVE

KASEY

Amongst the slopes of steep white snow, my hoodie beneath my ski jacket kept any discernable features from being seen. Not that obscurity mattered. Not on this closed trek that was no longer printed on any of the resort maps. And especially not with the whiteout that blanketed the air and blocked out the blue sky.

But the lack of visibility didn't stop me. I knew this trek better than I knew my own mind.

Now on foot, my ski boots sank into the powdery snow with each step; a set of skis were strapped to my back, the ends caked with snow from recent use. The backpack over my shoulder was held in place with one hand as I forged a curving descent through the few exposed rock clusters and obstacle-causing trees. Nothing deterred me or slowed my pace.

"An avalanche couldn't even stop me." I chuckled to myself, being the only one around and the only one in on the joke.

When the passageway narrowed, turning into a path between a rising cliff face and sheer drop-off into the snow-covered brush, I glanced left to right. A clear patch of white was vacant and secluded down between a thick semicircle of trees. If anyone had been here, not even the whiteout could have hidden the slow smile that widened my chapped lips. "Perfect."

Crouching by the base of the thin clustered trees edging the drop-off, I placed my backpack down in the snow. My gloved hands shoved in deep, and then a little—but not that little—black box came out. A green light lit up with the press of a button as I wedged the plastic rectangle down into the snow, leaving only the top half exposed. With a scramble across the snow an identical box was placed right up against the rising cliff, buried just enough to be almost out of sight with a thin dusting over the top to conceal the black. With one gloved finger, I pressed down and an identical green light shone. Another press had a beep-beep *echoing off the reflective slope and rough cliff face as the lined-up box across the descent registered the setting.*

My smile broadened in fond memory. An Internet chat room. A sex-starved prisoner with a sentence of ten-to-life. A sexy photo of a smiling young woman in preppy cheerleading clothes doing a high kick that I'd snapped from my Polaroid camera when she wasn't looking. My claim that she had a thing for guys behind bars. And the message he'd gotten out to his fake lover—really me.

Not for the first time, I was glad I wasn't one of those pent-up guys. Sex had never been my thing. Revenge would taste so much sweeter.

A small controller came free of my ski jacket with a red wire hanging from one end. Pushing one of the two buttons on the flat top resulted in the two boxes responding simultaneously, beeping once each. Their green lights turned off. The controller was replaced in my waterproof pocket that I zipped shut before folding down the Velcro flap.

Again that slow smile crept over my sheltered face, pulling more on one side than the other. Not a word was said as I pulled the skis from my back, threw them down, and clicked my boots into place. Ski poles came next as the backpack was looped around both my arms. A glance back at what I'd left behind was matched with a "Ready, set, boom!" as I let gravity take control.

Pointing my skis downward, I navigated the winding, rising and falling slope dotted with never-ending obstacles without fall or concern. Rocks were dodged, boulders too. The quick tree that rushed at me through the white haze was anticipated even before it came into view. I knew this track like the back of my hand and was as sure of its dangers as I was the steady beat of my heart.

Covering distance at speed, the way back was

faster than the way up. When resort rooftops bobbed in and out of view, I veered off the track. The thicker cover of trees that were easily navigated connected with a mainstream slope. Now that the visibility was clearing out as the white haze thinned, a few stragglers ventured out onto the not-so-challenging terrain. I sped past them with ease. Before the base was reached, where the chairlifts were warming up as the whiteout cleared completely, I slid to a stop, unclipped, hoisted the equipment onto my back, and took off on foot.

Through the trees, a footprint-free path led around the back of one of the hotels. Alpine Creek Lodge: three stories of bare wood with balconies caked in snow. A place with nice facilities, which had a range of middle to lower-class rooms that were more affordable than the flashier resorts on the slope.

Reaching the back entry, my equipment was dumped on the rack beside two other sets of skis and poles and one snowboard. My warm ski jacket was unzipped as I ducked inside, but my hood remained in place. Down a hall and a few steps, I retrieved a tagged key with room thirty-four from my pocket. I threw a glance back up the hall. Clear of movement, of people and noise.

Clear of witnesses.

The door ending the hall unlocked without fuss to reveal a small room. One bed, a side table, a door to a minuscule bathroom...and a black duffle bag taking up most of the non-existent floor space. The winning ticket with Cassidy Lockheart was haphazardly laying on the bed among a few brochures: the usual welcoming advertisements for spas, massages, dining and shopping, along with a map that I snapped up and pocketed. A replacement was pulled from inside my unzipped jacket, detailing the main slopes and highlighting a certain track that was a not-to-be-missed opportunity of ski fun, challenge, and beautiful views. I tucked it neatly behind the winning ticket and in front of all the other advertisements. Then the stack was moved to the bedside table.

A place to be seen—because it hadn't been left there.

My voice as I spoke out from beneath my hood was hoarse, chilled by the exercise and cool air outside. "See you soon...Cas."

SIX

That Same Afternoon

As the whiteout cleared, I stared down at the photo I held, sighing at the faces of my mom and dad. They looked so happy, fully geared up to ski like I was right now, the edge of the chairlift drop-off in the background. Together as a couple or as a family? Had I been the one standing behind the lens?

The flashes of memories I had of them were like seeing a slideshow of stills: birthdays, Christmases, vacations, my high school graduation. Nothing came alive in my head, but that's why I was here. That's why I continued to go through the motions. I had a promise to keep…and I couldn't live out the rest of my life without remembering where I came from…and how the most important people in my life had shaped me into the person I was today.

I sighed again as I tucked the photo back into the pile of pamphlets below my winning ticket on the bed in my room. The accommodation was small, but when you made the most of the white dusting outside, you really only needed a place to lay your head and tired bones and muscles after a long day of skiing.

"Love you guys," I said with one last look as I hoisted my ski equipment up.

Through the door, up a set of short stairs, and down a hallway brought me out the back door. The cold hit me first, making my lungs squeeze as it penetrated my snow pants and jacket. One-arming my skis and sticks, I tugged the zip on my jacket up, pulled my beanie down a little further to cover my icy earlobes, and hiked up my scarf to cover my face. I wondered if I'd liked skiing in the past or if I'd been a 'watch from the glass-fronted café' kind of person while others took on the cold and slippery slopes. With my memory still blocking so much of my past, I wasn't getting an answer now. I'd just have to wing it. Try my best. And prove to my parents that whatever came at me in life, I'd jump right in and make the best of it—and the most of it.

"Ready or not…" Dropping my goggles over my eyes, I carted my equipment along the tree-shrouded backtrack, coming over a small ridge to find the slope slowly filling with snow-ready skiers and snowboarders as more flew up overhead on the chairlift. The base to get on wasn't too far away, and with a trudge, sink, and slide, I made it there in one piece.

Clicking my skis on, my nerves shot sky-high as I was boxed-in in line. The point of no return got nearer and nearer as empty chairs circled back around to pick up new passengers. And then I was up.

"Oh, crap." The chair came up too fast, catching my butt and sweeping my heavy boots and skis off the ground. And then I was in the air, going where only birds should go, gliding higher and higher. Oblivious to the chatty couple wearing skis beside me, I tried and failed to control my breathing. And now my goggles were fogging up. How the hell were you meant to get off these things when you got to the top? There was no time to ask, because too soon I was there, gawking as young kids ahead of me easily managed to glide off and sail away, curving around to take on the snow-laden descent.

As my skis hit the raised area something more than fear took over in me. Like I was riding a bike, my knees stayed bent, balancing my weight as I tipped, body leaning to follow the curve. "Oh, thank God."

The way down was suddenly in front of me as skiers and snowboarders passed, zigzagging down the steep incline. My heart skipped with nerves, but as I started to plummet, I didn't lose control. I didn't tumble or land on my backside—or my face. Skis cutting the snow like blades, I started in shallow zigzags, carving my way down. The feel of the icy air on my face, of my muscles working in ways I never knew they could—or had—of my blank mind that thought only of my next move, was freeing. And then instead of feeling my way down, I let everything go.

Thinning the zigzag I raced down the slope, dodging other skiers and bypassing snowboarders with hairpin maneuvers that, rather than terrifying me, thrilled me. I'd done this before. Many times. I still couldn't remember when, but there was no doubt. Snow had been a big part of my life before the 'accident.' A tradition maybe? And one I knew my parents would want me to continue in their memory.

The bottom arrived too soon, and I wasn't ready to quit. I needed to feel that exhilaration again. My memories weren't resurfacing yet, but the thought of freeing my mind of everything that weighed it down for a little while longer was too tempting to ignore.

Coming down the slope the second time was even better. The cold urged me on as did the contracting and releasing of my muscles. When my eyes suddenly warmed halfway down, I slowed, fearing another blackout.

And that's when I saw him.

Still fully conscious, someone appeared beside me without warning. A young boy between eight to ten years old, dressed in ratty snow gear. His smile at me could have lit up the slopes even in the dead of night. "And this is me beating you!" He stuck out his tongue and then he was off, cutting down the track at speed—until he vanished.

I blinked hard and removed my goggles to rub at my eyes. Skiers and snowboarders whizzed by me—because I'd come to a complete stop. I was still conscious, but what I'd seen...a memory? Had I made a childhood friend during a family vacation here? Glancing back up the slope, my jaw dropped and I sucked in a breath. The same chairlift drop-off from the photo of my parents. This *was* the resort they'd taken me to.

And what I'd just seen—that young boy—I had to know if that had once been real. I needed to see more.

I must have done at least another half-dozen runs or more, even taking up other lifts for steeper, longer, and more challenging tracks. None of them returned any more memories...not even a flash of anything that could have been.

I was about to line up again when my stomach clenched, grumbling like it had been for the past hour or so. With the sun falling past the bordering trees, and after the workout I'd done, I was spent, body and mind. Committing to getting back out here tomorrow, I carted my skis back up the hill, dejection weighing me down after failing to remember anything about my parents. Deciding to cart my stuff to the rack outside my hotel—to keep from having to see that photo in my room—I still couldn't stop the loneliness that seeped back into me as my body temp cooled and the icy air crept back in.

When I neared the ridge and began to climb, a figure up ahead through the trees pulled me out of my head. At the sight of the black hood that covered their face, my heart took off like a starting gun had been fired. With combats on their feet and hands deep in their pockets, Hoodie was looking right at me, but then he turned, trekking away.

I cautiously followed as the figment of my nightmares trudged up the path that sided my hotel. When Hoodie picked up the pace, I couldn't stop myself from keeping on after him. I didn't know what I was doing. Why was I following? Everyone around here wore hoods, or beanies, or balaclavas. And yet the prickling of hair over my nape that shot adrenaline through my body refused to let me stop. Real? Imagination? Normal person…*or something else?*

As Hoodie cornered the bend around the back of the hotel I lost sight of him. I raced to catch up, heavy boots sinking and sliding on the squeaking snow. *There.* Up ahead. Laced in dark shadows with minimal light striking through the thick, bordering trees. And entering the back door to my hotel.

Fighting with my ski boots, I dumped my equipment as I passed the equipment rack, tripped over the grates that were meant to clean snow off boots before entering, and slammed right into—

"Jeremy?" I tried to dart back and stumbled again.

Almost tumbling back himself, Jeremy righted my balance as he found his own. "Cassidy, hey! We have to stop meeting like this." His smile was warm as he pushed the hood back from his wavy hair.

I glanced over his shoulder, seeing no one through the glass doors down the hallway. I stepped back and frowned at his black jacket and lack of skis—and saw the ski boots on his feet. No combats. "What are you doing here?"

"Nice to see you too." When I only stared, Jeremy shrugged, not taking offense to the stalker vibe I was throwing out. "Just came from the lobby after a warm drink and some food. My room's just down this hall." He pulled out a key tagged with number thirty and dangled it between us, more of in proof than with any innuendo. Then he pointed to the rack of skis, a brief frown crossing his face at seeing my haphazardly dumped equipment. "Ah, blue ones are mine. I was going to bring them in for the night. I swear my legs are aching already."

"Oh, right. Sorry." That's right, he was staying at the same place. Same competition, same win. And with no one down the hall behind him, the winner was? *Ding-ding-ding. Delusion.* I hoped it was just hunger-induced, though that was wishful thinking. I gulped. "I've been out too. Was heading in for a bite."

"Great, well I'll leave you to it. The food's good, by the way." Jeremy stepped past me, then swiveled back. "Actually, that reminds me. There were other winners. I ran into them after checking in. We arranged to meet up in the morning. Possibly go out skiing as a group. You should come…" He shrugged again. "If you want."

"Uh, yeah. Okay."

His smile returned, the look of confusion at my strange behavior melting away. "We're meeting up in the lobby in the morning at nine-thirty. See you then?"

Unable to shift a growing sensation deep down in my gut—was it to get to know this seemingly nice guy, or to figure out why he felt familiar to me?—my mind was made up. "I guess so."

SEVEN

Eleven Years Ago

Thumping, laughter and loud voices calling out. Study time had ended—for the rest of them. Crouched on the floor in the dark, my nose pressed into a grate on the wall. My thin fingers that were threaded through the patterned metal plate held on tight. The light through the grate wasn't strong. It didn't light up my room. But there was enough of it to see what I wished I could join in on.

The other kids were playing, running and screaming and laughing. A game of tag around two long wooden tables that were messed up with workbooks, crayons, and lead pencils.

Down there with them, C.J. leaped over an upturned chair and spun back as he reached the other end of the hall. Through the window behind him, the lake was bumpy with rain, but the sun shone in, making his blond hair look gold. His happy eyes traveled up to my hiding place. He smiled and looked left to right. Then he nodded and waved at me to come down.

Moving as fast as my legs would go, I ran to the door in the floor and tugged it open. My teddy, Mr. Muddles, was on the ground where the door landed and stopped it from making a loud noise. I kicked the ladder and climbed down. Darkness and shadows were all around me as I reached the next level down.

I stopped and listened.

My neck tingled, but I didn't turn around and go back. I crept on. My bare feet moved quietly along the hallway, missing the toys other kids had dropped. The downstairs noise hid the creaks I made across the wooden floors. Passing closed doors, I stared at the locked one down the end of the hallway as I neared the stairs. The closer I got the faster my heart beeped.

I wasn't meant to be down here.

And that thought scared me.

But I didn't slow or go back. I wanted to be down there. I wanted to be part of the fun. Even for just a few minutes.

I gripped the railing, my foot in the air and ready to take the first step down the stairs. Almost there—

A creak shot my heart up into my throat. Terror made it beep faster and I spun around, racing back down the hall. I reached for the ladder, fingers ready to grab on and pull me up—

A strong hand caught my shoulder before I got there. I jerked back and to the side, crying out as my back hit the knob on a closed door.

"I'm sorry. Father, please—"

His massive hand caught my throat, sliding me up and lifting my feet off the ground. The face that I was lifted to was red with anger. His dark eyes glared into mine, feeling as bad as a hit from his fist. "Where the hell do you think you're going?"

My mouth opened and my throat wheezed as he squeezed harder. But I didn't try to speak. I didn't fight back, either. My arms stayed at my sides. I didn't struggle. I didn't claw at my father's flannel shirt or pound on his chest. I just took the pain and the punishment. When my lungs burned, feeling like a balloon about to pop and my face heated up, I still didn't fight back. A naughty teardrop wetted my cheek, and my eyes rolled like marbles in a game of knockout—

Father released his grip and I fell, ankles and then knees hurting as I hit the ground. But I didn't stay down.

Scrambling up, I tripped on my tingling legs and slammed my hands into the floor. Pain shot up my arm, but I didn't stop. Fighting on, I made it to the ladder, slipped on the rungs, but made it up and through the trapdoor. Spinning and sliding back, I kicked the door shut. My chest felt like it was on fire and my whole body shook.

Loud boots thumped down below as they stomped away, getting quieter and quieter. But I wasn't safe yet.

I clamped my arms around my legs, holding them to my chest. I tried to breathe slower. But then I heard it. His stomping boots came back, getting louder and louder. The noise of them changed— climbing the ladder. I squeezed my legs tighter. My eyes peeled wider.

The trapdoor flung up, then fell to smack on the floor with a loud clap. Mr. Muddles had moved. My father's head popped up and the way he looked at me stopped my heart. "You are alive because I allow it. But you don't exist. You never will." His smile frightened me. "Your punishment will come…soon enough."

He grabbed the rope on the door to pull it up. His eyes moved from my face and down my shaking body, then his face disappeared as he pulled the door shut. There was a clap *then a* tink-tink *of metal and then a* click. *His steps faded.*

He was gone.

With a gulp my throat burned with pain. I knew what my father had done without trying to open the door. Padlocked shut. I was trapped…until he came back.

EIGHT

I awoke with a scream that failed to peel noise from my raw throat. Feeling disoriented and like I'd barely slept, my parents' fiery end flashed with every blink of my eyes. I sat up in bed—*in bed?*—gulping air as my heart belted erratically. Eyes now wide open I remembered my mom's scream and the sight of her burning body. My worst nightmare. Again. Hand over my frantic heart, I looked around.

Safe. I was safe.

I was in my room at the snow resort, my duffel unzipped but still on the bed, and white dust caking up the outside of my small window and blocking part of the slopes off from view. The sun was peeking up over the tree-lined horizon in the distance. People were on the climbing chairlift and skiing down the hill. It was *morning*?

I had no recollection of ever going to bed the night before.

Actually, I couldn't recall anything since my

run-in with Jeremy.

I glanced down at my stomach like it had the answers. It didn't rumble or clench. So I *had* stopped for dinner? What had I done in all those hours? I gulped and pulled the bottle of pills from my backpack beside the bed. So many filled the inside, I wasn't sure if I'd taken one before going to sleep. Which, if I hadn't, would explain a lot. Like the vivid nightmare of my parents burning, and the loss of last night. Unscrewing the bottle cap, I grabbed a glass I didn't recall filling or leaving on the bedside table and downed two pills. I paused right after throwing them back. My contacts' container was on the table too. As I blinked and felt nothing, I knew I'd somehow managed to remove the small green disk the day before—because it wasn't in my eye now.

"How…?"

A chime made me jump, a few drops of water spilling as I saw my phone's screen light up. It wasn't a call. There was no one I had to call. No family. No friends. It was a reminder—I squinted, tabling the glass to tilt the screen my way—to meet the group in twenty minutes.

"Couldn't have given me more time?" I spoke to myself because only *I* could have set that reminder. Now I had to shower and dress *and* look like a normal person in nineteen minutes. "Great!"

I threw off the blanket and stalled in my leap off

the bed. My eye caught sight of the photo of my parents and their smiling faces…and the map that stuck out from a wad of pamphlets. I slid the map free, frowning at the color-printed track. I'd glanced through all the pamphlets I'd been given on arrival yesterday and I didn't recall this one. That's when I noticed the wet patches on the carpet as if someone—could've been me—had walked chunks of snow in.

Feeling a chill, I dropped the map on the bed and quick-stepped to the door, testing the handle. It was locked. A swoop up of my jacket from the stained carpet revealed the key, safe and sound. I shrugged off my unwarranted paranoia. Maybe I'd picked the map up after dinner? Maybe someone had given it to me?

I pressed the button on my phone. *And now I have fifteen minutes.*

With a kiss to my fingers that I pressed to the photo of my parents, I dropped the map on my bed and managed to shower, dress, and even brush my hair and re-insert my contact lens in fourteen minutes. With one minute to go, I collected my jacket and backpack, shoving my pills and phone inside. As I reached the door I paused after twisting the locking nib, then I swiveled back. "No lost opportunities. A full life," I said, darting to grab the photo and zipping it safely into the flat waterproof pocket over my heart. "We'll live it together."

And then I was gone, jumping up two steps at a time, then hightailing it down the hallway, around a bend, and then another, until I reached the lobby.

The entrance was spacious, framed by rock-featured and log walls, and decked out with comfy leather seating, including a central round sofa. The smells of bacon, eggs, sausage and other fried and baked goods wafted from the adjoining lounge that was brimming with noisy people and the clatter of utensils on plates as hot food was devoured. My mouth watered. But before I could contemplate slipping in to bag a muffin or something, movement caught my attention.

By the long front desk, Jeremy's deep-in-thought frown turned upside down at the sight of me. He waved a hand, peering over and around the group dressed for snow in gloves and beanies in front of him. "Cassidy, you made it! Hey, everyone. This is Cassidy."

A sense of being wanted and included lightened my heart as my breath slowed from my rush here. I couldn't remember ever feeling that. At least not with my memory issues. Was this what making friends felt like? I couldn't stop my smile as I came over and the others turned in welcome greeting.

The younger of the two other men stepped forward first, thrusting his hand out to me. "Brad," he said with a wink and a jog of his eyebrows as he eyeballed my rack below my unzipped jacket. "Can I call you Cas?"

"Ah…"

"I'm Jill," a girl who looked my age but with long blond plaits sticking out from her pink beanie butted in, hip-shoving the guy aside. "Stick with me. Born and raised Fernie. I know my way around."

"And I'm Katherine," a middle-aged woman said with a warm smile. The gleam in her brown eyes was full of motherly kindness, and her auburn hair was pulled back into a sensible ponytail.

I caught the older man in the back once-overing me, who straightened as he caught my eye. "Stan Blunt. Retired cop."

I returned their greetings, then stood quietly, listening to their chatter, getting to know who they were in silent watchfulness. Brad was an obvious ladies man, flirting with both the other women as he regaled them with his snowboarding expertize—and shooting me a brilliant white smile as he jogged his brows whenever Jill looked away. Katherine was a spinster, an old social worker who claimed to have no family to call her own. Jill was a waitress, and probably great at getting tips with her cute looks and bubbly personality.

Jeremy let the others talk but neared after a few minutes. He hoisted the strap of his backpack higher on one shoulder. "You looked a bit rushed when you came in." So he was a watcher too. "Have you eaten already? The others came after breakfast."

"So we all ready to head off?" At the sound of the older man's voice—Stan, I think—I looked over at the ex-cop as the others voiced their readiness. Fully dressed like the others, he was clearly ready. I frowned as I noticed a line of red tubular plastic dangling from the pocket of his black jacket. A cord? A cut wire? "Hey, what's this?"

He was suddenly in front of me, his cigarette breath curling up my nose. I stepped back, feeling uncomfortable as he reached for my backpack. He plucked the map—hadn't I left that in my room?— from the transparent plastic pocket and unfolded it to study the trail.

Brad was over the guy's shoulder, excitement dancing in his eyes as he saw the winding track. "I'm so up for that." His enthusiasm turned to goading. "But I bet the girls aren't."

"I'm not a novice," Katherine said, "and I can take it slow if it's hairier than it looks. I don't want to spoil anyone's fun."

"And you, Blondie?" Brad hiked his chin at Jill who folded her arms over her ample chest.

"I'll give you a run for your money."

Jeremy shrugged. "I've done that track before. It's a good distance to get there, but the scenery's worth it."

After skiing yesterday and the feel of letting go of everything bad, a more challenging route was just what I needed to forget my lost time and everything else. And maybe spike a new memory or two. "Sure."

The others started for the tall glass front doors, and I tugged Jeremy back. He'd been right before. "My gear is out back, and…I kinda slept in."

Catching on to what I meant, Jeremy nodded to the buffet room where a procession of food was laid out. "Go fill your pack with pastries or something. I'll lead the others around back. We need to head out that way anyway. See you there?"

Again I smiled. And for the first time, it felt good. "Yeah."

~

Today was nothing like yesterday.

The air was icy, the breeze soft but unrelenting in its chill. The snow was reflective white, the sky powdery blue with white fluffy clouds. But that feeling of freedom and mindlessness was gone. Instead, I felt apprehension. We'd been en route for ages and it had been over thirty minutes since we'd seen anyone outside of our small group. *Where the hell were we going?* "Ah…are you sure this is the right way?"

Jeremy threw a pensive glance over his shoulder. "Yeah, we're almost there." He slowed and frowned. "But I don't like how quiet it is up here."

Right then Brad cut past me on his snowboard so close I almost lost my balance. His quick smile through his skull balaclava creeped me out. "Move it, worry wart. Didn't you hear the man? We're almost there."

We continued on in silence after that. Since the chairlift as high as it would take us, we'd swapped from skiing and snowboarding to trekking through deep snow to bring us closer to our destination. Right now the group chattered, relaying their lives to each other and beginning the process of forging friendships. I couldn't join in. Jeremy had tried to include me while keeping our group's pace steady, but I was good at giving closed-off answers that diverted from further questioning. It wasn't that I didn't want to include myself. I just didn't see the point. Why get to know all these people when I'd never see them again after this getaway? Why put all the effort in when the people I really wanted to be with were dead and buried?

Now as we reached the mouth of the track that from here looked so steep and riddled with snow-covered rocks, sharp turns, and a steep drop-off to one side, everyone slid to a stop and unclipped their skis and snowboard.

"Finally, something worthy of my skill." With his balaclava still in place, Brad jogged his brows at me before turning his charm on Jill who rolled her eyes and went back to tightening the strap on her goggles. "Ready for a show, ladies?"

For some reason, his attention sent a strike through my stomach. Not in a good way at all, but in a dropping, sickening way that made me push against my poles to slide back on my skis and gain a foot of distance.

Katherine frowned down at the obstacle-laden way, looking nervous as she tightened her scarf around her neck.

Stan blew smoke through his nose, ditching the cigarette he'd been puffing on. "If you break something, I'm not carrying your show-off ass back." He tipped his head at the older woman. "I'll hang back at your speed…if you like?"

From the tiny smile and huge relief in Katherine's warm brown eyes, her answer was clear despite her nonchalance. Shrug and inviting head tilt. "Two's company."

"Anyone think they can beat me?" Brad didn't bother to look at Stan, instead focusing his attention on the younger three of us.

Jill shook her head, seeming more concerned with the view through the plummeting hillside of trees than the slope we were about to tackle. "Let's just get down this mother and get back for lunch."

I wasn't the only one to balk at her language. She was so pretty and sweet looking, but right now something was seriously wigging her out.

Jeremy pointed back up at the bend we'd come from to the long track we'd walked, skied, and snowboarded to get here. "It's a harder track with more steep inclines, but we could always go back the way we came?"

"Are you fucking with me?" Brad, just below everyone on the slope, looked livid. "I didn't come all this way and listen to all your boring-ass chit-chat to turn around. Go back if you want, take the oldies with you, but someone is taking this track with me or being thrown down it."

"Now, Bradley—"

"Pull your head in, boy," Stan cut Katherine's motherly voice off before glaring at Brad.

"I didn't say I wasn't going," Jill added quickly before the closing space between the two guys was eaten up by their testosterone. She didn't move, but her words did enough to pull Stan back their way. "I'm..." She shot a glance through the trees again. "I'm just hungry. And I'm not a ski pro. I'll go down at my own pace."

"Soft cocks," Brad muttered, throwing down his board and clipping one boot in. His lips pursed with challenge at Jeremy as he lowered his goggles over his goading eyes. "Guess I'm the only one up here with any balls."

"Any class is more like it."

Through Jeremy's words, something in Brad's expression and what he'd said turned my earlier discomfort into irritation. At the same time, a notion fluttered to mind. If I needed to be alone to free my thoughts and maybe even spur pleasant memories to replace the horror in my mind, there was only one way to get it out here. "You want a real challenge?"

Show-off's surprise was palpable. "From you?"

I pulled my goggles down to cover my eyes. A quick shove and snap clicked my skis back onto my boots. "Ready. Set." I pushed with my poles and turned my skis from sideways to pointing down the descent. And then I was away.

There was a curse from Brad and a click—probably his other boot being shoved into the binding—as he came after me. But I already had the lead and I wasn't giving it up. Not now with their voices and the sight of the others lost behind me. Not with the sweep of cold that battered my nose and lips between my goggles and scarf and freed any thoughts that threatened to prop up. I didn't care where I was or who I was with. What I'd lost and could never get back became a distant memory, one I wanted to hold back for just a little bit longer.

From behind, the cutting of fresh snow sounded as Brad gained on me. I pushed on harder, wanting to keep in front, wanting to keep everything else out. The pain. The horrific memories I couldn't escape. But even as I blinked I saw a flash of red. Flames like a fireball, so vivid and yet gone as my lids reopened. Knees bending further and adjusting my weight, I was ready to plummet so fast it would have been close to free-falling. A beep made me slow.

Where had that come from? Behind me?

Brad was almost around me; the others were up

the hill, making good ground despite their taking-it-easy approach. Though we hadn't gone that far yet.

"Giving up when I'm about to pass you?" Brad whizzed by, cutting so close I pulled up short to keep from being knocked over. "Weak!"

The track had hit a straight path below that fell in a sheer drop-off to one side and had a cluster of trees down by a sharp bend. The other side rose up higher and higher with a jagged cliff face.

As the others neared, panic struck through my adrenaline. There was something about this location. The cliff, the dangerous edge. And it wasn't the fear of someone face-planting rising rock or tumbling off the edge. The show-off sailed up a rise near the cliff on the right and got airborne. "Brad, stop!"

I didn't know why I was calling out. There was no reason to panic. This wasn't that slippery road. The drop-off wasn't about to lay waste to my parents' car and take their lives. And then I saw something. Right by the base of that cluster of trees...*a green light?*

That hooded figure appeared, crouching before the light. Then they were gone.

Brad came down and I saw the angle as he swore. Board hitting on the side rather than flat, his legs twisted. There was a crack and a roar as he hit the ground where the bend hooked left, his shoulder and ribs taking the landing as one leg swung freely.

"I've got him!" Jeremy flew past me, and I

73

reacted, thinking only of getting to Brad as the others followed right behind. He skimmed right past those trees. Past where I thought I'd seen a green light.

Beep-beep-beep-beep-beep-beep!

The sound came from both sides of the track and the fast repetition made me want to vomit. I had no idea what was happening. Was I imagining things again? Jeremy had almost reached Brad who was cursing as the others caught up and we bypassed the trees. "Did anyone else hear—"

BOOM!

Snow and rock exploded from twin sources. The trees were obliterated. The place we'd all just passed, obliterated. That could have been one of us. The others fell as Jill's scream broke through the ringing in my ears. Then I saw Jeremy, skis gone and fighting the soft snow to run my way. He knocked me down and out of the path of a hefty cut of rock that was plummeting straight down at my head.

We landed in a heap, the rock burying on impact in the snow beside my feet. Through our rough breathing, there was a second of false silence.

Jeremy's lips parted like he was going to ask if I was okay, but then the ground vibrated beneath us. "Shit, get up!" He hauled me up.

The others were staggering to get vertical too. Brad was propped up on one elbow and had ripped off his balaclava. His leg was bent at an impossible angle along the shin—broken. I was hauled sideways as everyone rushed. No one was close enough to help Brad who struggled to push up on one leg. His eyes were wide with fear. He fell back down and barked in agony.

"Let me go!" Back against the cliff face, I tried to break away from Jeremy's hold. Something bad was about to happen and Brad was out there and exposed.

And then the rumble delivered. Snow shifted like pure white sheets from further up, one transcending the next and then the next. Gravity took control. And then it snowballed.

Avalanche.

NINE

Chaos.

I gasped for air and scrambled, scraping to get free of the soft snow that threatened to bury me with every move I made. Everything had happened so fast. The avalanche. The screams. Then we along with our cries of terror were all swallowed in the rush. Now I was much lower in altitude. Alone. Further down the slope? Over the edge through the trees? I had no idea. All I saw was white and treetops poking up in random places. Half buried, I was ice cold from the waist down, a Popsicle stick half surrounded. My ears were still ringing.

Where was everyone? Were they alive?

Fear that they weren't swelled nausea through my stomach. My mind whizzed over the events. The strange worry I'd felt. That green light. The *boom* and resulting explosion of snow and wood.

Had that really happened? *A bomb?*

Now I'd been stuck out here for God knows how

long. The sun through the clouds high in the sky shone blinding light down onto all the soft white. Midday…or even later.

"Cassidy. *Cassidy!*"

As if in a sound barrier, I heard my name being screamed from far away. When I tried to turn toward the sound, I sank deeper, the arm I'd levered against the fragile surface vacuuming half my torso down into the freezing ice with it. Ski boots sank in front of me, taking out shins and knees as someone fought to reach me. "Jeremy!" I couldn't believe my eyes as I blinked to adjust my sight. He was okay, a graze on his forehead and one cheek the only sign he'd taken the hard way down with me.

His gloved hands reached out, arms looping under my own to heave me up. "Work with me. Lean sideways. The more horizontal space you take up the less likely you'll sink back down." I did as told and he pulled with all his might, gradually bringing me out of my icy trap. As I stretched out and sucked air, he added, "Either roll or crawl. Don't try to stand."

"Your legs…" I trailed off as Jeremy took his own advice and got horizontal, freeing his shins. When he began to commando crawl I followed, the pack still on my back deciding against the rolling option. Which meant I had my phone and the croissants I'd snatched from the buffet breakfast.

"Where are we going?" I panted after a few minutes, legs still feeling like ice blocks but upper body sweating from exertion.

After a glance back Jeremy nodded up ahead. "Keep going. The others are over there."

"They're okay?"

"Ah...mostly."

The tone of his voice sent a shiver through me. "Mostly?"

Jeremy got onto his hands and knees, testing the solidity of the snow. When he didn't sink he turned and held out a hand. I saw who waited by a tree off to the side where the avalanche seemed to have passed by rather than over as he answered my question. "Brad's not with us."

We'd all been together, all of us except Brad. After breaking his leg, he'd been further down the slope. Right in the path of the avalanche. Right where a mountain of rushing snow had shifted to take him. We'd been swept away too. And he hadn't been that far away.

With Jeremy's help I managed to get vertical. I turned back to where we'd come from, seeing our crawl marks over the fully white covering. "He has to be out there. We have to find him. His leg is already broken. What if something else is? He must be buried."

For some reason I thought of the car accident, of being unable to move while my parents burned, of seeing that hooded face hidden behind a skull-sized boulder. To be trapped under the ice? To freeze or suffocate to death? It was as bad as burning. It was torture.

"Maybe we stumbled onto a track they'd been clearing for some reason?" Katherine was saying with a wide-eyed glance up at the flattened trees behind them. Her arms were squeezed tight around her torso and her scarf was gone.

I trekked after Jeremy who said, "We're still looking for Brad."

I noticed then the binoculars glued to Stan's eyes as he surveyed the landscape with a discouraging expression. "Maybe."

By his side, Jill was shaking and holding her arm as if it was causing her pain. Her blond hair was beanie free and messy, and her face lit up to see me. "You're okay?"

I nodded. "Is your arm—"

"Not broken. Just pulled something."

"Hey!" Stan lowered the binoculars and pointed into the distance. "My sight's not perfect, but I think I see part of a snowboard."

Jeremy took the visual aids and followed Stan's pointed arm. His sudden smile fell. "It's Brad's. At least part of it is."

I snatched the binoculars to see for myself. A hundred yards further down where trees were scarce, I found what he'd seen. It was Brad's board, a sharp cut of it sticking out of the snow with only one binding attached. Because it had been snapped in half, the rounded edge of it buried well below the surface. And in that one bracket—a boot. If those were anything like ski boots, they didn't come off easy. Either Brad was down there. I gulped. Or his leg was. "We…we need to…"

The morbidity on Jeremy's face seemed to match my fears. He stuffed the binoculars into his backpack on the ground. "We need to see if he's all there."

"And if he's alive, it needs to be fast," Katherine added. "Any pocket under the snow won't hold oxygen for long."

"If he's even alive to breathe it."

Stan shook his head at Jill with a frown as Jeremy began in the right direction. We all followed behind, sinking like him with every step. The closer we got, the softer the snow became. Being the biggest and heaviest Stan sank the worst, now having to get all of us to help pull his legs back out for every few feet he managed.

As Jeremy went to continue on I tugged on his arm. "We're faster just the two of us. We can do this."

His lips pursed with a nod, then he called back to the others. "Wait back and keep a lookout in case we sink below. We've got to get to him fast. This is taking too long."

There was no argument and then we were moving as fast as we could, as fast as each sinking step would allow, the snow crunching as it collapsed. Just when we got a few good paces in, the ground would give way and take out our shins. Soon we were up to our thighs with every second step. Then Jeremy suddenly dropped, buried up to his hips. There was shouting from the others, and I waved at them to hold back. "Here, take my arms." With a lot of joint effort Jeremy got free, and then we were crawling again, trying to move fast but having to detour every few yards when our testing hands told us our whole bodies were about to be swallowed.

Finally we reached the piece of Brad's board. The boot stuck in the binding was attached to a leg. Which was either very good news, because we'd found him, or very bad, in the case his leg didn't lead to his body, or even if it did if that body had been fully deprived of oxygen.

Jeremy started digging with his gloved hands straight away. And me? On my knees, I stared blankly and didn't move. The fear of what we'd find was too much. I'd seen too much death already. Lost too much. Yeah Brad was a dick, a womanizer, and a jerk, but that didn't mean he deserved to die. And I wanted to help. But all I could see as I watched Jeremy throw off his gloves to scoop lower was all in my head. A torn stump of a leg with hanging tattered skin around white bone and blood dripping. A blink flicked channels to a blue face, eyes wide and cloudy, mouth open and stuffed with snow that remained frozen from lacking heat.

"Cassidy." Jeremy was puffing for air, wheezing as he kept up the effort. "Help me. Please. I need you."

Those few desperate words snapped me out of my head and I scrambled to the other side of the hole he'd dug out. Throwing my hands in I scooped and shoved the snow up and back, getting deeper and keeping what we took out from falling back in. On my knees, my shins were below the surface, the cold eating through my ski pants like dry ice. But I didn't care. I barely even noticed. Because that leg continued on to a thigh and hip, and as we moved sideways, bypassing what would have been Brad's body rolled on its side, we rushed to clear the cover from his face…and found more black material. An arm, held up and bent, sheltering a head of dark brown hair.

"Brad!" Jeremy called out.

There was a second of silence as we slowed, the fear that we were too late swiftly setting in. Then there was a shift, ever so slight. The head below that sheltering arm had moved. "Am I…dead?"

"No," I breathed, total surprise at his survival surging through me like a heat wave.

Brad began to grunt and struggle. He swore in pain as his body twisted to face up and his leg didn't follow. "Get me out. Get me out!"

He began to panic, and we worked faster,

digging out around his body before he could lose it and snap his leg clean off…or cause a collapse that swallowed us all.

After minutes that felt like hours, Jeremy hauled the guy free and they both fell down onto their backs, gasping for air. Brad's leg was not in a good way. His blue pants were stained red and through a tear in the material I could see a glint of bloody white bone.

Every part of me shook with strain and my face heated at the sight of his injury, but I managed to perch on my knees and wave to the others. "Got him!" Then I looked around at the unfamiliar landscape, taking a few deep breaths to still the swimming in my head. Partway down a slope, I couldn't see chairlifts in the distance or any of the hotel rooftops. Glancing down at Jeremy, our location expert and, from what he'd displayed, group leader, I had to ask. "Where do you think we are?"

His blue eyes diverted from the white-dotted blue sky, nothing in them reassuring after a studious look around. "I have no idea."

~

Brad grunted and cursed. "Since we're lost out here and virtually screwed, anyone want to touch on the elephant in the wilderness no one seems to want to bring up?"

Stan and Jeremy each had their arms strung around Brad's torso, helping to drag his broken leg that had been splinted with his snapped board and Jeremy's T-shirt. Neither slowed their pace behind us as we continued through the snow. They made no effort to answer Brad's question either, Stan glaring sidelong at the guy and Jeremy sharing a fleeting look at me before gazing back up the powdery descent we'd navigated down over the past hours.

The avalanche, if our bearings were right, seemed to have cut us off from the resort. Jill's phone and my own had no reception. Not when we'd started walking and not any of the times we'd checked since. SOS calls returned that annoying beeping sound too. If the avalanche had taken out the cell tower, who knows how long it would take to get reception to dial 911. And now the sun was falling, dipping dangerously close to the snow-topped horizon of trees. A hazy chill grew all around us.

Despite the quiet within the whipping icy wind, we all knew what Brad was hinting at, and to my surprise, Jill beside me sniped over her shoulder at him. "You mean the fact that you triggered an avalanche that could have killed us all while being the show-off dick you are?"

"That wasn't my fault, or are you as dumb as you are blond—"

"Knock it off, Brad." Jeremy looked like he was ready to drop his hold on the guy. Like he blamed him too. "If you'd stopped when Cassidy called out we wouldn't be in this mess."

"Cassidy called out what?" Katherine looked from the three guys to me, her cheeks and nose red from the cold like the rest of us.

Before I could reply, Stan filled the void. "Yeah, that's right. You told show-off with a death wish here to stop." His annoyance at Brad turned to suspicion as he leveled his dark eyes at me. "Why?"

Now everyone did stop, all eyes on me in wait. And what was I supposed to say? That I'd had a bad feeling? That even though I'd never been on that track—as far as I knew from my memory lapses before the 'accident'—I had felt some…I don't know—*something?* That I thought I saw a green light that could very well have been the thing that detonated with an explosion? That my hooded nemesis had been there—in my mind?

That'd go down well.

I was days out of hospital. My mind was a mess. Clearly. I was lost and I had no one in this world. No Friends. No Family. Getting into my psyche and suicide attempt and imaginings and everything else to suspect someone was targeting me wasn't just something I wasn't about to air. It was insane. Impossible. So I lied. "I…I knew you were going to take that jump," I said to Brad, faking condescension. "You'd taken all the others on our way there. And this one was the biggest, and right near a drop-off. I thought you were going to go over the edge. Not break your leg."

"Who cares about his broken leg?" Jill pulled her hood back over her head as snow began to spear down again. "What about the explosion? We all could have been blown to pieces."

I shuddered and clutched my jacket tighter around my neck, remembering the sight as those trees were obliterated.

"If Brad hadn't been showing off," Katherine said with a shake of her head, "that could have been him."

"Anyway…" Stan jerked Brad on, forcing Jeremy to help them onward as the rest of us kept on through the thickening snowfall. "There used to be blasts like that to clear old snow from high up. It was a safety precaution to prevent avalanches being triggered accidentally and swallowing people."

As we climbed up a hill, I went over the day's events, starting with my morning of waking with lost time. When I got to the part where I met everyone in the lobby, I remembered the wire I'd seen hanging from Stan's pocket. It could have been an earphone wire or a charger cable. But it had a blunt end, not a plug. I spun back around. "How do you know all this?"

Stan shrugged one shoulder, unconcerned at my questioning voice or stare. "I was stationed in Fernie a long time ago. We'd hear the blasts sometimes. See the snow tumbling down the mountains from a distance."

"Dammit!" Jill cursing a few feet ahead stole my focus as she turned to face all of us. The plastic pocket in her hand protecting her phone from the elements dangled from above her head. "There's still no cell reception."

"Just keep trying at every peak." Jeremy's expression was hopeful and encouraging, but for some reason I felt like it was fake. Like I'd seen it before. He scanned the darkening horizon with a deepening frown. Then he sighed with a shake of his head and nodded us on. "We need to keep moving. We don't want to brave the elements once it gets dark. We need to find shelter."

Already the cold was plummeting. I could feel it seeping through my ski gear more and more with every passing minute. My toes and fingers had already been numb for hours, and the chill was spreading fast. With chapped lips and windburned cheeks, the effects would only get worse. Out here we could freeze to death if we didn't find somewhere to shelter us from the elements. A lonely howl echoed in the distance. Or we could get eaten…if a wandering cougar or lynx stumbled upon us and we were too slow and frozen to look like anything but prey and to fight back.

With everyone sensing the urgency of getting to somewhere, we all kept on, over the ridge and down another valley. For every step I felt we were getting further and further away from where we needed to be, heading away from the lodge instead of closer to it. But with the sinking snow blocking our way, we didn't really have an option.

When the sun had sunken well below the trees, not only were my toes and fingers frozen numb, my hands, feet, and face were too. I lost my footing following the others up a hill and fell. The snow kept my landing soft as Jeremy called out to see if I was okay. "Yep!" I called ahead, my head lifting as I tried to wave to them.

Katherine took Jeremy's place at Brad's side, and he came over and tugged me up, keeping his arm around me. The others took a breather as Jeremy led me up the hill. When he looked at me, his brows were drawn together.

Before I could question the worry that froze his features, my breath hitched. Not out of exertion or pain, but out of shock at the view over the ridge. "Oh my God," I uttered. My head snapped sideways as I shouted down to the others. "Quick! Get up here. You all have to see this!"

Like I'd just screamed, "Bear behind you, run!" Jill, Katherine, and Stan gained a boost of energy, the older two rushing Brad up the hill right behind Jill to meet us. Silence stretched out for the longest moment as everyone stared. Jeremy, still with his arm around me hadn't moved or said a word. Down below the steep hill was a clearing of white. Beyond that…a chalet, big with a wooden exterior and free of any movement or vehicles.

"Un-fucking-believable," Brad said.

Jeremy released me suddenly and scrubbed a hand over his mouth and chin. "It'll do for the night."

"No…" Jill had her goggles off and looked white as a ghost. "Anywhere but there…"

TEN

"What do you mean *there?*" I looked down at the large rundown dwelling, my lungs feeling unexplainably tighter. When I panned back across the others, I saw mirroring staid expressions across their faces before setting my frown on Jill. "You know this place?"

Jill shook her head, blond strands of hair that had escaped her plaits now dusted with frost. "No. Of course not. It's just the…the place looks creepy. Haunted even."

"There are no such things as ghosts," Katherine said with a shake of her head, patting Jill's shoulder while still holding on to Brad's other side.

Brad, unlike the others, appeared relieved at the find. "Despite the look of it, I'd rather wait out indoors than out here in the fucking elements. I need to get off this damn leg too."

Stan's unfocused eyes shot from the white expanse below and up at Brad's words. "Might even have power and food. It's worth a look." He began slowly down the hill with Katherine's help to drag Brad along. He called back over his shoulder at us. "Take the long way around, unless you feel like a dip in that iced-over lake."

My mouth gaped as I studied the wide expanse separating us from our surprise shelter. If Stan hadn't said anything I'd never have known. "How do you know there's a lake?"

Instead of answering, Stan let out a grunt as Brad swore and Katherine squeaked. Not even fifteen yards diagonally down the hill, they'd hit a soft patch.

"The whole way around is going to be a snow trap," Jeremy called out as the others clambered out of the snow. "We're going to have to cross the lake." His gaze narrowed at a shivering Jill then at me. His lips twitched as he nodded up at the horizon where only an orange hue glowed with failing strength between the treetops and the blackening sky. He shrugged his shoulders with a deep sigh. "We don't have a choice. We can't stay out here."

When he began after the others, Jill took off to keep up as if being alone out here with the fall of darkness and the rising chill, compared to where we were headed, was suddenly too much to take on.

I hesitated, watching after the five of them as they fought the soft snow and whipping wind to reach the concealed lake. I couldn't put my finger on it, but I couldn't shake the shiver up my spine. Something felt wrong. But what were my options? Stay outside and freeze to death, or seek refuge until we could send out for help or chance our luck over the fallen snow to get back to the resort?

"Wait up!" I followed them down the hill, gaining on Jeremy and Jill who still clutched her arm. The snow below us seemed to thin out as I kept my focus on the growing facade of weathered wood on the two-story-plus-attic chalet. There was at least one chimney I could see. "Maybe there's a wood stack inside. We could build a fire..." I shuddered at the flash of spitting flames and remembered shrieks as my mom burned. I struggled to keep my breath normal as I gasped. "Ah...except I don't have a lighter or matches."

Jeremy faced me while continuing to walk backward. "Lucky for us I packed matches." He patted his backpack. "They're in a watertight—"

"Ahh!" Jill's cry cut Jeremy off but didn't drown out a loud crack. And then she was gone. Swallowed by the ground.

"What the hell?" The snow had thinned and even hardened. We were on a buried build-up of ice.

I went to rush forward without thinking, but Jeremy caught my arm and yanked me back a few steps. "Cassidy, no!" he rushed as more cracks rang out. I felt one beneath my feet as I stared at the place Jill had disappeared from. "She fell through the ice."

Through the falling specks of white, I saw it. A jagged cut with thick edges marked a hole in the snow, white specks disturbing the surface that looked like a rippling mirror. "We have to help her!"

"I know. We will."

More cracks sounded and Katherine cried out as Stan tugged Brad and her back. "If we come back we'll all sink."

"Cowards," I muttered, pulling free of Jeremy's grip. A gurgled shriek cut the icy air as a hand bobbed out from the hole. My eyes were pleading. "What do we do?"

Jeremy lowered his backpack gently and I copied, cringing as more cracks forked out like hairline fractures along the ice we'd cleared in our retreat. "Follow my lead. It's just like the soft snow. Larger surface area."

We both got down on all fours, then our bellies, using our hands and feet to propel us slowly forward. With each foot closer that hand bobbed up again. Only one…because she couldn't use the injured one? Was she getting paler? It was hard to tell in the fading light. Her cries as her head broke the surface were getting shorter, quieter. But we were almost there. One more foot…

A louder crack made us freeze. I'd felt the vibration, close but not beneath me. "Jeremy…"

"I can't go any further. But you're almost there."

I was in this alone. Jill's life was in my hands.

Her fingertips were on the jagged hole's edge, her head was just above the water. "Help me, please. I can't die here. I escaped. I got out. Don't let me—"

Her head dipped below the water as her fingertips slipped from the edge. I scampered forward, heart pounding and fear peaking as cracks threatened to swallow me too. Biting off one glove I plunged my hand into the water and felt—nothing. My hand pulled from the freezing cold. There was nothing to see but black ripples as bubbles floated up. "Jill!"

I went to plunge my whole arm down into the depths and froze like a statue. A hand had broken the surface. Large, masculine, and blue. It wasn't Jill's. I gasped. "What the hell…"

"Grab her!" Jeremy called out as the hand sank back down.

But I couldn't move as my skin crawled like it was alive with flesh-eating bugs. I couldn't comprehend what I'd just seen.

Sudden movement revealed Jeremy scrambling despite the fresh cracks, but he was too late. And yet he didn't stop, shoving me back as he dove head first into the hole. And then he was gone too, a splash left in his wake.

Shock, confusion, and everything else abandoned, I dared to meet the edge, hearing the frantic voices from the rest of our group carried on the wind as I stared. I had to do something. I had to—

Jeremy's head broke the surface with a gasp. His lips were already blue. "I can't find her. I'm going back—"

The edge he gripped snapped off and he plummeted down below the surface.

"Jeremy!"

My soaked and freezing arm plunged back down, the cold like being stabbed with a million needles. But he wasn't there as I flailed my arm around like a lifeline. There was nothing to grip onto. My arm came free, eyes searching the disturbed black pool when I heard a dim thudding.

Instincts drove my actions, and I followed the sound on all fours until I felt the vibration—right beneath me. I shoved the snow back from the icy surface. Jeremy was below, hair gravity free and lips pinned as his face squeezed with lacking oxygen. Panic had a tight hold of me, but then I saw something…another face. A boy's with light blond hair and scared features. Suddenly not below the water but in my mind and above the surface, he pulled the hand of another kid from the water. "I won't let you go," the boy promised as he hauled with all his might.

Vanishing without explanation, Jeremy's face now all I saw, I felt the fear I'd seen on that boy's face deep in my gut. I had to save him. I couldn't let him go. I had…there had to be something. I glanced around frantically. The others were too far away, still screaming words at me I couldn't make sense of with the thumping in my ears. Then I saw something closer. Our backpacks. I slid a few feet across the ice to them, but as I tore through the main zippers and rummaged, spilling clothing and croissants, I found nothing hard or big enough to work as a hammer to break the ice.

Mind racing as I scampered back, I felt a twinge of relief to see his face where I'd left him. Jeremy was still alive, but I could see the twitching across his face. In seconds his body would force him to breathe. To take in a lungful of water. And I couldn't let that happen. I needed… I patted down my body knowing I had nothing…until I got to my boots. Heavy and with square edges across the front made to clip into skis.

I tore the clips open, cutting my frozen fingers on the latches. Then I tugged one boot free. "Watch out!" I screamed, hoping he could hear my warning as I held the boot high above my head. Then I drove it down. Once. Twice. Third time—*crack!* I hit four more times, ignoring the forking cracks beneath me as I widened the hole. "Jeremy!" I cried out when I was done.

But I couldn't see him.

My hand delved in deep, all the way to my armpit, and I blindly searched the—

Someone snatched hold of my wrist, and I jerked

up at the shock. Then I saw his face. "Jeremy!" Tipping back on my butt, I used all my strength to pull him up and out, sweating and cursing until he came free with a grunt of power to land on top of me. He rolled straight off, landing on his side, spluttering water and gasping for air.

After a few long minutes he rolled onto his back, still struggling for breath as I sat beside him and stared at the death I'd just pulled him from. The others were still calling out, but I didn't have the energy to respond. Didn't have the brainpower to care what they knew at this point. Because the outcome was clear in who was sitting next to me and who wasn't. "She's gone, isn't she? Jill's…gone."

Jeremy levered up beside me, water squeezing from his clothes as the front compressed. His cheeks were red, but his lips were still a horrible shade of blue. "I…I saw her. I tried to grab her but she was too low. Sinking. She wasn't moving…"

ELEVEN

Ten Years Ago

My chest hurt from laughing as I ran and my ski boots sank a bit with each step into the soft white snow. My skis, as I dragged them, left wavy tracks behind me with each step. "I'll catch you, C.J.!" I called, my warm breath coming out in white puffs.

After a stolen hour on the private slope that was outside the resort's boundary, I was full of energy. My legs would hurt tomorrow from the exercise—I didn't get out much—but for now… "You can't beat me forever!"

C.J. stopped suddenly as I got closer. His skis fell from his shoulder. With his hood already pushed back from our race against the freezing wind, I saw his face become the color of snow. Instead of looking like he'd seen a ghost, the look on his face got harder as his cool blue eyes glared.

I became a mind reader as he looked at me with terror. Run! *But it was too late.*

The crunch of boots through snow ripped my eyes from C.J.. Already past the corner of the tall log walls and the attic window I'd escaped from, my father was out the front doors and stomping my way. Even with the many windows he had to pass to get to me, and the wild look in his eyes that promised pain, I didn't turn and run. It wouldn't help me if I did. My nine-year-old legs couldn't outrun him. I'd learned that already. The hard way. His way. Trying to get away always made him madder.

So I waited, frozen in terror of what my punishment would be.

There was always a punishment. Even when I wasn't bad. But this time I had been. Sneaking out was naughty.

Father looked even bigger in his thick overcoat, towering as he stopped right in front of me. His tight, angry lips separated, curving with a terrible smile. "You broke out, you little bastard. Naughty. Naughty. You never learn." He grabbed my neck and squeezed.

"Let go!" C.J. ran and jumped up to catch my father's arm. Hanging in the air he tugged, but he was my size. An irritation. "Stop it. Let—"

My father let me go, and I choked out, "Run, C.J.!" too late.

Father caught my friend's arm and tore him off his shoulder and threw him down. C.J. scurried back, tripping as he tried to get up like he'd hurt his leg. I didn't call out to him again. He was safe now as all that rage came back to me. Father snarled like the animals he hunted as he snatched my arm and marched me away. I tried not to trip in the softer snow, but I couldn't keep up. A teeth-flashing roar from my father made my heart beat so fast it hurt.

And then we were at the lake.

Fully frozen, I could see patches of blue sky between fluffy clouds on the icy top. He was going to make me cross the thin surface? Was he going to order me to stay out here all night with the animals that howled and hunted?

His hand smacked my face.

I cried out before I could stop myself and fell to my knees. He reached for me, and my arms shot up to cover my head from another hit. Instead, he yanked the skis from my shoulder and held them in front of him with both hands. He spat down at me, "I won't stop teaching you. You will learn your place or break being taught. The choice is yours."

He stepped onto the ice and smashed the skis down like a giant hammer over and over again.

I saw C.J. back by the long house. He was crouched on his feet like he was about to run out and save me. I shook my head. "No. Stay," I said without making a sound. Saying anything out loud would only make things worse; another try at rescuing me would only hurt C.J. too.

Near where C.J. crouched, I saw another kid

standing at the open door. Jill. Her hands covered her mouth as she watched. And when she saw me looking at her, the scared look on her face changed. Her eyes dropped. Her hands lowered to clutch each other. She told on us for breaking out.

More bashing on the lake made me look away from her. A hole had opened the frozen top above the black murky water. The hole was small enough to fall through—if you were small. "Time for a reality check." I didn't move as Father's cold hard hand grabbed my throat and lifted me high. I knew what my punishment was, his idea of a cold shower. Hanging above the hole, my ski boots were so heavy. His smile showed his yellow teeth. "One, two…"

He dropped me on three and I fell. The splash of water was so cold it felt like I'd been stabbed by his 'toys.' My knee smacked the edge and my elbows did too. My head going under cut off my cry.

I ached all over and my boots dragged me down. But I knew I had to fight for the surface before I lost where it was. Before it started to frost over. Before all the air in me was gone and I ate the water. I tried to swim up but the more I fought, the faster my thoughts got. And then I stopped fighting to swim so hard. I wondered if it would be so bad to stay here. Maybe death would hurt less than being alive.

My chest got tight. I needed air but there wasn't any down here in the black. The hole up high was shrinking. I didn't want to go back. Not really. But then I thought of C.J.. If I didn't take the anger, my father would give my punishments to my only friend. The only person I cared about and who cared about me. The only person that made my life okay sometimes. The only person that made me happy and could make me laugh.

I couldn't leave C.J.. I wouldn't. Not ever.

Feeling like my boots were heavy rocks, I kicked as hard as I could. I clawed at the water above me, trying to get higher. Everything hurt: where he'd squeezed my throat, where I'd hurt myself from falling. My skin burned in the freezing cold, and my insides tightened as I pressed my lips shut. Don't breathe yet. Don't breathe. Up, up...up... The hole grew and grew. I kicked harder. And then I couldn't hold it anymore. I sucked in the icy black—and then my face found air.

Catching the edge with frozen fingers, I coughed. Water sprayed from my mouth. My body felt like it was being squished as I breathed and coughed some more. Blinking my stinging eyes, I saw Father standing above me. He smiled when my fingers slipped off the edge. I dipped under the water again and kicked to bob back up. "Help me." I reached with one hand and my other grabbed the edge again. I couldn't hold on and then I was sinking. "Help—" I sucked water in and coughed as I kicked up again. I kicked harder. My boots were so heavy. This time my grip on the icy edge held on.

"Please. Father." I reached for him, trying to get higher. When his smile grew wider I caught his bootlace with one finger.

"Think about leaving down there?" He chuckled and shook his head. "Then by all means…"

"Father, no!" I cried as he turned and walked away, his bootlace sliding through my numb fingers. "No. I'm sorry! Help me—"

The loss of his bootlace threw me back. I lost my hold on the edge. The water swallowed me all the way and I thrashed. My lips and nose broke the surface once, twice—I saw the roof of the attic come and then fall—but I couldn't get higher. Soaking wet in my ski clothes, my legs became numb. They wouldn't kick no matter how hard I tried to make them. I couldn't get back up. And now I was sinking. My reaching arm disappeared in the dark as the hole above shrank.

He wasn't coming back. My father. The man who'd always hated me had left. He wanted me dead.

And his decision was final—

A kid-sized hand appeared from nowhere. The grip as it caught my wrist was warm and so tight. I wasn't sinking anymore. The hole above grew slowly as I got pulled up. I worried I'd start sinking again, but the hand didn't let go. It was cold now too. As cold as me. I couldn't feel it. But I could see it, and I kept my eyes on that hand as I got higher and higher.

I gasped as my lips broke through the water. The sound was wheezy and it felt like fire burning in my chest. For a few seconds I just sucked air in and forced it out. My eyes lost the fuzzies and I saw C.J. looking down at me. He was pale like before. The front of his jacket and arm was dripping wet. His breathing was rough too, and his wide eyes were wet from crying.

"It's okay. I won't let you go."

I knew he wouldn't. He'd do anything; even risk his life to save me. This wasn't the first accident *I'd had.*

Eyes searching, I looked at the house my father had come from. He wasn't there. Jill was gone too. My father had left. He wasn't watching from one of the windows on the first or second levels. He'd left without knowing if C.J. had gotten to me in time. Without knowing if C.J. had saved me.

As C.J. lifted me out of the water, I didn't feel sad that my father didn't care if I lived or died. I'd known that deep down for probably forever now. Nothing I ever did or tried to do fixed how he felt about me. And I didn't know why. But right now that didn't matter.

Finally out of the icy black, we fell down, faces to the sky as we gasped for air. I looked at my best friend, my only friend, and smiled. "Thank you for saving me. Again. I almost died."

C.J. grabbed my icy hand and didn't let go. "I'll

never let that happen. I'll never leave you."

TWELVE

Jeremy shivered as he tested the front door. Then he hesitated, frowning before shoving the unlocked door in. A gasp of stale air wafted out of the log-built double-story. He spoke for the first time since the others' questioning had died down, his eyes flicking back to me out in the snow for only a brief second like he couldn't bear to hold my gaze, before returning to the others. "Let's g-get inside before we freeze."

Stan and Katherine, each with their arm around the surviving loudmouth, shuffled forward without a word. Brad's broken leg caught on the soft snow as they dragged him inside, and his stony expression pinched. His cocky attitude had long dissipated, the enormity of one of our group dying so soon after the avalanche and Brad's brush with death had shaken us all to the core.

I didn't follow them inside. Instead, I faced away, staring at the lake and the freezing-over holes

I could no longer see from this distance. In the almost darkness, I swear I could hear Jill's pleas for help on the breeze that batted my face. When I blinked, I saw her terrified face. Another blink. That blue hand. And another blink. That boy's face under the ice. The same one I'd imagined while skiing yesterday?

Oh, God. What was wrong with me? What did it all mean?

When something icy touched my equally freezing hand, I jerked. At my side, Jeremy shivered in his saturated ski gear. I was shaking too, from the cold and so much more. I'd been lost in thought staring at the lake, at the peaceful quiet that would in any other situation have been so picturesque. Now that beauty was a nightmare in the flesh, a horrible dream I couldn't wake up from.

Jill was dead.

A girl I hardly knew, but who I unexplainably felt responsible for—because I'd let a delusion shock me. I'd stalled from grabbing her reaching hand. Jeremy had almost died because of my mistake too.

"You need to come inside." His voice was warm and gentle as it puffed out in white mist, filled with concern that felt somehow expected. "We n-need to get warm before hypothermia s-sets in." That icy touch returned again, his digits sliding across my palm slowly to curl around my hand. I was so cold the cuts on my fingers didn't even sting as he tugged. "Come on."

With my wet pants brittle as the water started to freeze and my bones unreactive and feeling like cold metal poles, another little tug had me stumbling.

Jeremy caught me before I could fall, his arm around me hauling me close and keeping me upright. Chest to chest, my face was so close to his, my mouth inches away. My breath caught as our eyes met and I told myself it was from the cold and surprise of being caught. My blush told a different story, one that was unacceptable with all we'd been through and the fact that I didn't know this guy.

I pushed away. "Ah...s-sorry," I stuttered, my teeth chattering. I glared down at my legs, forcing them to respond to basic motor functions. "You're right. We n-need to heat up."

Without looking back at him, I scuffed my way inside, feeling no warmer than I had been outside. Beyond a dusty foyer that was dark with wooden walls, and led back to an even darker hallway, we found Brad and Katherine in what looked to be a communal area. I looked around rather than at Jeremy.

Katherine peered out a doorway across the room where only another door beyond what looked like a hallway was visible. Her arms crossed over her chest kept her gloved hands rubbing up and down to gain warmth. "Stan should be back soon. He went to have a look around."

Perched on the arm of a sofa with his pant leg hiked up, Brad looked over the makeshift bandage Jeremy had made with his T-Shirt. It was no longer white but stained with patchy red. He said nothing.

I checked my phone—the only phone our group now had access to—then shoved it into my backpack. "No reception."

In the ominous silence that followed, I scanned the room. The moon was rising beyond one of the three fifteen-paned windows, adding a bluish glow to the dark space. A total of six stained sofas in varying patterns and colors semicircled the sizable space, some with tears and foam visible. Stag antlers hung skewed from one wall, and a moose head hung proudly on the adjacent wall. The standout between the two widened my eyes. A massive brick fireplace blackened by past fires and choked with clumps of ash. For a second I forgot everything, the sight of neatly stacked piles of firewood on either side blanking my thoughts.

Exactly what we needed, but—I frowned.

Unlike the dust and grime that covered everything and made me want to cough as I breathed in the thickened air, those two stacks were not just neat, but pristine. They looked like they'd just been stacked there.

"Someone lives here," I spoke what I was thinking.

"Doubtful." Now as I looked at Jeremy, I saw he

was staring at the stacked wood too, his expression puzzled. "Too m-much snow to drive a vehicle through. Even for a four-wheel drive. And I d-didn't see any snowmobile tracks."

"Jeremy's right," Stan said as he entered from the doorway across the room. His face was grim as he sighed. "No one's here. There's a kitchen back there filled will dusty old cans. Pipes are frozen solid. And there's no power."

Katherine eased back against the wall, staring off into space. "Was there at least a can opener? You must all be starving by now."

Stan shook his head and Brad let out a morbid laugh, releasing the torn material he'd been peering beneath that wrapped his broken leg. Some of that old cockiness returned to his handsome face as he looked up. "And here I thought I'd gotten a break from my custodian duties and shit of a life for once. Trip of a lifetime my ass."

The exact phrase the winning flyer had declared.

A shiver crawled up my spine as I remembered the flyer being slipped under my door. I'd seen someone outside my dorm, but then they'd disappeared. Like a ghost had been tasked to leave the prize and vanished when its job was complete. And now we were here, trapped by snow in this abandoned creepy place with nothing but a potential fire—if the wood was dry enough and Jeremy's matches had survived our ordeal.

110

My much-needed escape from my all but abandoned university, Christmas at home, and my first birthday entirely alone, had backfired. Because even as I stared back at the fireplace, the thought of lighting that wood and creating flames to heat us brought back their fiery end and my mother's screams.

I winced and looked away, pausing when I glimpsed Stan and the contemplative look on his face. "What's wrong now?"

Even though I didn't say his name, he responded, shaking his head as if he had been miles away. "When I received the vacation win in my mailbox, I thought it was a prank. When it pulled through as legit, I didn't say anything."

Jeremy spun upward from the pile, arms full of firewood. "Anything about w-what?"

Stan's eyes narrowed, his brow creasing. "I never entered to win this trip. Did the rest of you?"

My heart stopped before starting back up, thumping against my ribs with a vengeance. The response of the others confirming they had entered was like white noise in my ears. My mind was racing, back, back. To when I could have received the flyer…the weeks before my release while I was 'away,' stuck in a place that was so stringent and restrictive on outside influence.

"Cassidy? D-did you enter the competition?"

I jerked back to see Jeremy staring at me, the

look on his face the same as when I'd woken on the bus after my nightmare of—

Oh God, I couldn't linger on that. Not now.

I tried to breathe normally, fighting the urge to hyperventilate. I needed to get a grip on myself. The others watching me with confusion, suspicion, and pity was already too much. Telling them the truth was not an option. Too many questions would be asked. Questions I didn't want to or couldn't answer. "I..." My voice caught in my throat as my brain scrambled to make the words come out. It wasn't impossible that I'd received the flyer at CWC and entered the competition, but it was highly unlikely. And more than that, I had no memory of ever entering. Receiving the win had been a total shock. "Y-yeah," I finally said. "I...I entered b-back at school before w-winter break."

That contemplative look melted from Jeremy's face and he nodded to the others and hoisted his one arm of firewood higher. "I'm g-gonna get the fire started here so Cassidy and I c-can dry off." He glanced around then through the middle frosted window where the last of the sun's light was lost beyond the horizon's treetops to strengthening moonlight. "Why don't you s-see if there's any gas lamps or candles anywhere? That moonlight won't c-cut it if more clouds blow in."

"There weren't any lamps in the kitchen," Stan said. "But this place is huge. So many rooms not just on this level but up above. There'll be something somewhere."

Stan had time to search the upper level too? I hadn't thought it had taken me that long to get inside after my morbid daydreaming beyond the door with Jeremy. But maybe it had. Or maybe he was just guessing how many rooms a big abandoned chalet like this would have.

Katherine made her way to Brad and waved Stan over. "Let's get Bradley in a bed before we start searching. I saw one in a room right off the foyer."

"Screw sleep! What about my leg?" Brad barked out as the others went to help him up. "This wrap is doing shit all and I need a better splint. Pain killers and antibiotics would be awesome too."

Katherine knelt and hiked up his pant leg, making him hiss through clenched teeth. She whistled out her breath. "You're out of luck on the meds I suspect. But a lamp pole or something could work as a good splint. More material will hold it in place." She nodded up at the older man. "Give me a hand to move him? Bradley, it's probably best for you to stretch out and get some rest in too once I fix you up."

"You know h-how to do that stuff?" The question from my mouth surprised me, not because it was intrusive or anything, but because I hadn't meant to ask it out loud. In the situation we were in things needed to be done. Staying alive for one.

113

Backstory wasn't important right now.

Katherine's smile was warm and kind, but there was a hint of sadness lurking behind it. "I've done a number of first aid courses. A line of work I tried out when I, ah…quit being a social worker."

When she didn't elaborate, I didn't ask. But I wanted to. Something in her expression said the reason she quit her job ran much deeper than trying out a new line of work. Still, it wasn't my business. With all my secrets I appreciated my privacy; others deserved theirs too.

Returning her attention to Brad, Stan stepped in and helped the guy up from the sofa. "I'll find a can opener too and a pot to heat something on the fire with," he directed back at Jeremy. "You got a light? Mine died on our trek here."

Already back at the fireplace, Jeremy placed the last log on the peaked stack he'd been building. "Got matches in my pack," he called back, dumping his backpack on the dirty ground beside him.

And then we were alone, the footsteps and sound of Brad's dragging foot fading by the second.

I ventured over to a tall decrepit cabinet back by the opening to the foyer, the movement helping ward off the shivers, but doing nothing to deter my train of thought. With shuffling as Jeremy weeded through his pack and scrunching as some paper was wadded into kindling balls, I was still stuck on what Stan had revealed. He'd never entered the competition.

As I pulled one of the tall doors open, I didn't see with my eyes what lay inside. Instead, my sight became internal, staring off into space as I tried to remember. Nothing new or relevant came to mind. Then the crackling of starting flames derailed my brain as that horrible fiery end rushed back. I squeezed my eyes shut so tight I saw starbursts. My whole body warmed and perspired as if I was back there beside the wreck and feeling the flames that burned my parents alive. But then it all vanished, the sounds, the smell of smoke rising around me, the past, the present.

Eyes still shut tight I saw a computer screen before me. The Internet banking I was logged in to said 'Welcome Cassidy' and showed a single bank balance of seven hundred and fifty-two thousand dollars and a few cents. My parents' entire life savings. The money I'd inherited after their deaths, with not a single family member to share it or the loss of them with.

As the memory I'd forgotten until now made me want to see more, there was a shift. Now I was in a lecture room at school, people moving around as they descended the stairs siding the rows of chairs to exit out the door up front. I was still seated, able to see the blackboard with *Psychoanalysis – Freud Vs. Skinner* written in white chalk. Psych class.

A flutter over my shoulder had me jerking as a stack of flyers landed on my desk. *Entry forms for the snow trip.*

"Hand them out and you're a shoo-in," a raspy yet indiscernible voice promised.

I twisted in my seat to find the rows behind me empty. Movement had me twisting back to see a guy taking the stairs down two at a time. Seeing them from the back in a black hoodie, only their fingers were visible as their arm came up and waved.

"Hey, you found blankets."

Snapped out of my reverie, I spun to find Jeremy right behind me. "Oh, it's y-you." I was breathing hard from the shock and couldn't hide it.

Jeremy frowned. "I didn't mean to startle you. I called before I came over, but you didn't answer. You okay?"

I laughed, but it sounded off as I tried to catch my breath and control my chattering teeth. "Uh huh." Unable to stand the way his eyes searched mine, I turned back to the cabinet. I sucked in my breath and unzipped my jacket, my body suddenly too hot beneath the wet material. What I saw surprised me. Jeremy had been right. The shelves were lined with blankets, all folded neatly like they were waiting for visitors. I picked one up and sniffed. It was dusty, but not too bad. A hint of detergent still clung to the woven fibers.

"You didn't enter the competition, d-did you?"

Thoughts instantly diverted, I spun with a blanket clutched in my hands. "How did you…I m-

116

mean, why would you th-think that?"

Jeremy stepped back like he could sense I needed the space. "Come, sit by the fire. You n-need to warm up."

Moving first he gave me the distance to follow and I laid the blanket out over the dusty floor. Then he removed his boots, shoving them right up near the fire, and sat back on the rug. My soggy jacket—wet from plunging my arm into the lake and from Jeremy falling on me—was laid out beside me to soak up the fire's warmth. Leaving my damp thermal top on, I sat quickly, a good foot away from him—and well out of the fire's reach. Forcing my lungs to breathe normally, I tugged my boots off, minding my sore fingers before wrapping my arms around my propped knees. If I didn't say anything maybe he'd just drop the subject.

He didn't. "I s-saw your reaction to what Stan s-said. It was all over your face."

Lie! my mind screamed at me. But my lips didn't play along. Something about the guy beside me made me want to spill my secrets, or at least one of them. "Someone in psych class was handing flyers out. I d-don't remember if I entered or not." Or if I'd done as they'd asked and handed them around to other students.

"You don't remember?"

The way his eyes narrowed with concern made my honesty streak turn the breaks on. I'd said too much and now I needed to say something to shut this down. "I've had a pretty shitty few months. My m-memory hasn't been the best. I've had other things on my mind. And no, I don't want to talk about it."

That perplexed look returned to Jeremy's face, closing off the concern he'd expressed moments ago. "You're the boss."

As the words left his mouth, he frowned deep and looked away, staring into the fire. My eyes had widened, my expression dropping. It was like I had heard those exact words before—from him.

But that was impossible. We'd never met before. Or had we?

THIRTEEN

When the silence had stretched beyond an hour, Jeremy and I continued to sit quietly. He'd shifted closer to the fire a while ago, bringing his wet clothes nearer to the drying flames. Finally, he got to his feet with a clearing of his throat. "I'm gonna go see what the others are up to."

The closed-off look across his face kept me from jumping up to tag along. For one, my clothes were still wet, drying slowly with my distance from the fire. And two? I still couldn't get past our interaction, the feeling of familiarity I'd felt and the way he'd said those few simple words: *You're the boss.* Still, I had no memory of him, and I wasn't about to get into any line of questioning that could backfire to turn the tables back onto me.

Now as he seemed to wait for a response from me, I stalled in making one. A strange sensation was coming over me, one that made my body flare with heat and lightened my head. Oh, no. Not now. Not with him here. A blackout was coming on, and as I blinked my lids fast like butterfly wings, I knew I couldn't hold it back. I couldn't let him see me like this. He had to go.

Levering one arm back on the blanket, I forced my lungs to behave normally and faked a smile. The cuts on my bare fingers hurt as they pressed into the blanket. "I'll—" I cleared my throat, feeling like it was stuffed with cotton wool. The smoky scent in the air tickled as I gulped. "I'll keep the fire going."

His frown from me to the blazing flames said the thing was lit pretty good and well without the need of intervention. But he didn't say what we both knew or question my blinking eyes and slow but obviously deep, rising and falling chest. Instead, he shrugged and turned, exiting through the doorway to the other hallway.

The second he was out of sight, I lost control of my supporting arm and slid down. My palm left the blanket, fingers skimming the rough floor that drove tiny splinters into the cuts. I barely felt it as I used the last of my bodily control not to smack my head. Lying so still I may as well have been paralyzed, all I could see was the licking of those burnt orange flames; all I could smell was rustic smoke and faint detergent from the blanket.

Until my eyelids crept shut.

I came alive like I'd been resurrected out of thin air. Running, I was running, legs pumping and bare feet slapping linoleum down a bright corridor. The doors I bypassed were shut tight, all the same, each with a keyhole and a small square window to peer into. But I didn't stop.

With air sawing in and out of my lungs, I felt like I was running for my life.

The one thing I was focused on was the wide glass doors up ahead. They were closed beneath a small black box with a blinking red light. Thick red letters were painted across the glass barrier: Restricted Access. The reflection in the glass kept me from wondering what kind of facility I was pelting through. Black pants and a dark hoodie. The person I'd dreamed of only nights ago that'd bludgeoned me to death and dismembered my body.

Before I could wonder if I was just losing my mind, or somehow seeing a supernatural warning of something horrible to come, I slowed abruptly when there were no more doors to pass. The remaining left side of the wall was hip-to-ceiling-high glass. Inside was a watch station set up with TV screens and behind the desk a guard sat in his dark blue uniform, earphones covering his ears as he read a car magazine. There were two doors out of the station. The one I was crouched against, and one in the corridor that bisected this one beyond the glass doors. I jammed what was balled up in my fist into the crack between the steel and the jamb.

My gaze slid up as a buzzing sounded. The

camera mounted to this side of the wall pivoted my way. From where I stood, it looked like the only place to escape its view was if you stood right underneath it, crouched below the sight of the guard.

But I didn't even attempt to hide.

Instead, I stepped out from the wall enough to be seen. I heard the guard curse, and the stomp and slap of his shoes and tabled magazine, as he got vertical. Then I stepped forward and faced the glass barrier, arms crossed over my chest as if taunting the guy inside.

He paused when he seemed to recognize who stood outside the glassed-off room. Annoyance marred his features. "That's every night this week. I told you last time it was the last time. This time you're going to solitary."

I felt a smile pull at my lips. I held up my hands and watched without worry as the guard snatched up a long-handled stun gun, and jangled a ring of keys to unlock the door to get to me. I heard the bolt slide and click, then the door swung open—and the two pieces of wired plastic I'd jammed there with backing tape to keep them in place separated.

A boom erupted out of sight, shaking the doors down the corridor and vibrating the glass wall and doors.

With the guard distracted by the blast and resulting screams of people that couldn't be seen, I snatched the keys and smashed one into his eye. A scream peeled from his throat, cut off as a fire alarm blasted from the megaphone opposite the camera. And then the stun gun was mine and jammed into his throat. And held there. "Let's see how you like playing the cow for once," the voice from my mouth was a snarl that promised this was just the beginning.

The guard's body turned rigid and the lack of relief from the electric contact brought him to the ground in a fit of shakes. When his eyes rolled the stun gun was finally removed, and his body was dragged into the glass room. Without closing the door, I yanked off the guard's shirt and pulled it over my hoodie.

Just in time as three other guards raced down the corridor outside the restricted area.

Moving too fast and clearly distracted by the screams they were rushing toward, one yelled out, "Fire! Release the doors!"

"Just what I had planned," I murmured, facing the desk of TVs and switches. A peeling label marked 'Door master control' sat above a keyhole, and I rummaged through the key ring, trying one after the other. On number eight, a nondescript key slid home and turned without protest. I hit the large buzzer-like red button below—

And the glass sliding doors slid all the way open.

So did all the doors to the rooms down this corridor and the adjoining ones. I was out there in a few easy strides after stepping over the unconscious guard. The distant screams continued as I walked, patients—some in gowns and others in pajamas—broke out through the doors. They took no notice of me, scurrying like rats around and past me at the sight of their freedom that was up for grabs.

Now with a hint of smoke in the air, I strolled down the center, a focused direction as chaos moved around me. With a bend to the left, then right, and left again, the corridors gave way to a tiled foyer area. The guards were on the ground. Dead or unconscious, I didn't stop to find out. The other prisoners had taken them down. And beyond the glass? A gravel driveway that led onto rolling green grass and perfectly positioned mature trees that made where I'd just come from seem misplaced.

I was out. The hooded person I'd conjured in my head, or someone more sinister? Someone real? My answer came as if the escapee had heard my thoughts.

Looking down, I saw a photo of myself, a close-up of my face when I'd been full of life and free of the horrors that had turned my world upside down. *How the hell did this psycho get a photo of me?* The voice from their lips was almost guttural; a rasp that felt like nails down a chalkboard. "I'm coming for you…Cassidy Lockheart."

~

I came out of the blackout with a gasp, ratcheting upright and eyes flinging open. Heart thumping in my chest like a mallet, my quick breaths made me dizzy. Fear had me cowering and blinking to regain my sight. Fire, dust, those black marble eyes on the moose—

And Jeremy kneeling right beside me, openly watching me with a stumped and suspicious look. His hands were up in the air in surrender like he'd been trying to rouse me until my shock awakening. He quickly stood and paced back a few steps, his hands lowering in more of a placating way as if he expected me to jump up and run...*or attack.* "What happened?"

I'd seen variations of the looks he gave me countless times over the past month during my hospitalization, especially after my initial and subsequent retelling of the 'accident.' I couldn't stop the shudder that rocked me. Hoodie was back, and in my dreams, he was coming for me...after escaping the same hospital I'd just been released from.

Either my mind was fucking with me. Which was totally plausible and a great thing to convince myself of—even if it did make me a little nuts. Or...the alternative was so much worse. To believe that there was someone after me, targeting me for their own purpose, would mean that the 'accident' had never been an accident at all. I couldn't accept that. And I couldn't tell anyone what plagued my mind, especially not this boy-next-door looking guy who seemed a little too interested in me and what I was about. I wouldn't be locked up again, and I didn't need to confirm his weird factor with facts—true *or* in my head.

"Cassidy?"

And now I'd been sitting here like a weirdo, staring into space after he showed normal and expected concern for me and my erratic actions.

I shook my head. "It was nothing." I stood and paced from the rug to the dusty floorboards. Then I suddenly stopped, seeing the concern deepen across his face. I slid my thermal sleeves up to my elbows and crossed my arms over my chest. Now I was displaying defiant behavior? I dropped my arms. "I guess I dozed off. I had a bad dream." More like a nightmare.

"More like a nightmare," Jeremy repeated word-for-word the sentence I'd just completed in my head. "But…are you sure you're okay?"

"You've never had a nightmare before?" As I stared him down, feeling like everything inside of me was at risk of being uncovered, something occurred to me. I was alone with a guy I hardly knew, a guy who'd left to round everyone up and get intel on our situation. Something in my gut tightened as if in warning and I optically searched the space. There was still plenty of wood by the fire—possible weapon—but he was closer. Back in-between the sofas and draped in shadow, I noticed an odd toy here or there. A doll. A plane. A block. *Weird.*

"Where are the others?"

"I never found them."

My heart leaped up my throat like it wanted out. I took a step back, absently rubbing my hands up and down my bare forearms—until I felt tiny pricks from the splinters in my sore fingers. "What does that mean?"

"I never looked." He spoke faster as I took another step back, his expression dropping as he picked up my panic. "I heard a thump as I was heading down the hallway. I came straight back to find you lying on the floor." He frowned, brows pinching together with unmasked concern. "You wouldn't wake up." He edged closer one slow step at a time. "After coming to my rescue, you could have a concussion." Glancing from my face down, his gaze stopped on my arms and the way my hands had stalled in their rubbing. "What *happened* to you?"

Fear forgotten I looked down with a start. I already knew he wasn't talking about the small cuts and grazes on my palms and fingers that gripped my arms. Frown back in full swing, he was staring at the many cuts and scars along both my forearms. The ones I'd sustained after tumbling down that embankment and being thrown from my parents' car. Some were already faded to white; others were still pink. Cuts mostly, but a few larger and odd-shaped scars mottled the fleshy proof of the hell I'd survived when *they* hadn't.

Even though I knew it was too late, I pulled my sleeves back down. Covering my face with my hands, I slumped onto a sofa, dust puffing up and tightening my lungs more than the memories already had. In spite of everything, the words from my mouth were honest. "I was in a car accident not too long ago. No seat belt. My parents..." My mom's screams pierced through my eardrums as if I was hearing them here and now. I squeezed my eyes shut for a moment then forced them open. "They—they didn't make it. I did. Just over a month ago."

"Oh, shit. Cas, I'm sorry."

A nickname only my parents had used that I'd kept reserved for their memory since their death. It was my instinct to tell him not to call me that, but the true sympathy in his eyes and the hint of familiarity I couldn't explain kept me from telling him not to.

When I said nothing in return, he turned to the fireplace leaving his back to me. Bending down, he grabbed a cut of wood and stoked the fire with it, his back rising and falling with slow breath that seemed labored. When he stood again, he didn't face me at first. His voice was low as he spoke. "I know it's not the same, but I lost my parents too. I was really young so I can't remember them too much." Now as he faced me, his downcast blue eyes lifted with unmaskable grief...*or maybe it was guilt?* "I ended up being adopted by this amazing couple. I had a

128

really, really good life with them."

He turned his attention back to the fire and I stood, almost dry socks adding new prints to my retreating ones from before. For some reason, I felt like his sorrow was connected to the life he'd had after his parents' deaths rather than at losing them. As a child, had he felt he didn't deserve to be happy when the people who'd created him were no more?

Jeremy shrugging out of his partially dry jacket kept me from asking as he dumped the thing over his backpack—a backpack that had a badge with the University of Calgary emblem across the back. "You go to Calgary University?"

Despite my surprise it would explain a lot. Like how I felt I recognized him. Why he'd been boarding the bus from Calgary Airport. It could also explain a lot of his strange watchfulness if he knew me or of me when I'd been acting like a total stranger.

"Uh, yeah. " Jeremy glanced down at his pack before lifting his eyes up to mine. "It's my second year. I'm a psych major with a secondary in criminal law. I want to become a hostage negotiator." His gaze fell, something dark passing over his handsome, prominent features just before his blond hair fell forward over his troubled eyes. He sighed slow and deep, then looked up at me. "Why do you ask?"

So he didn't know me, or at least he hadn't consciously placed where he'd obviously seen me before. And in a big school like that and being a year apart, I guess it made sense. "I'm a first year at CU. Psych major too."

FOURTEEN

Jeremy's surprise was obvious in the widening of his eyes that soon narrowed into sharp speculation again. "I can't believe I've never seen you around." He half smiled then shrugged one shoulder. "I know I'd have remembered your face if I had."

And yet it was so clear to me that he recognized me on some conscious level in the way that I recognized him. Maybe we had never met, but I was becoming more and more sure that I'd seen him before this trip.

I cleared my throat when neither of us had said anything else. The fire was burning bright and my thermal top was almost completely dry. My legs were only half frozen with my thermal pants below the ski material still damp. I hugged my arms around myself, glancing at the doorway. "I uh, guess we should find the others."

Jeremy nodded, lips pursing. "If that hall's any indication," he said, glancing to the doorway, "and after what Stan said, it might take a while." He bent and pulled his jacket back on then glanced to my own dust-caked and still-wet one laid out on the dirty ground. Rummaging through his backpack, he pulled out a dark blue hoodie. "Here. To keep you warm."

I froze as he held it out to me. My rational mind said, *everyone wears hoodies, especially in winter.* But my irrational mind just kept replaying the glimpses of my hooded attacker that was supposed to be a figment of my imagination.

Jeremy threw his arm out suddenly, grasping my elbow. Not in any malevolent way, I realized as I began to fall. I'd stepped back at his kind gesture and tripped on my own pack edging the blanket. Now face to face, I froze, his breath warm on my face. An eternal second passed, then he released his hold that scalded me with sensation as he stepped back. "Sorry, I only…" He jogged the hoodie he still held. "I'm sure you have one already. I didn't mean to…"

"It's fine." His genuine concern at my unexpected reaction had me grasping the hoodie that he let slide through his fingertips. "I…I don't have one. Thank you."

He said nothing as I tugged it on; the smell of the fibers part detergent and what must have been his own clean scent. He didn't move as I bent down to my backpack and pulled out my phone. There was still no reception. Dialing out 911 only returned those same annoying beeps. And yeah, this place was big, but I hadn't even heard a noise since they'd left.

I shoved my phone back into my pack and stood. "Let's find the others."

Leading the way, I followed Jeremy from the room, leaving the dancing flames on the walls between shadows behind. From a long, thin table out in the hallway, I picked up a candle. It was old with dried spilled wax down the side. "Have you got those matches?"

Jeremy turned back to me, pulling the small cardboard box from his pocket. When the wick was lit we continued on.

Out here was just as dusty and bare of anything much, a long hall that diverted up a wooden staircase and further down to a few open doors. Jeremy mounted the first steps, the decrepit wood creaking under his sock-covered feet. The thought of following him up there made my breath come faster and made my chest feel like it was about to explode. "Ah…" Noticing a small teddy bear the color of rich, dirty caramel further down the hallway made me pause. It was propped on the ground against the wall below the stairs, and from here something stood out. A square shadow line. A door below the staircase? "Hey, check this out."

Not waiting, I bypassed the carved banister that

was full of scratches and indents where someone had written illegible words. Being a few feet closer made me pause. I'd been blinking as dust stirred up—and the matted teddy bear had vanished. My eyes were playing tricks on me again, but as I crept closer, I saw that the door was real. There was no handle or hole to pull the door out, and without suggestion, I pressed a palm into the middle edge on the right. There was a click and the rectangular barrier popped open an inch. Jeremy was right behind me as I opened the door fully and stepped inside, the candle in my hand bringing orange warmth to the cramped space.

"It's a storage space," Jeremy breathed, seeing as I did the boxed-up possessions that were stacked around the edges.

I frowned at what I saw first. Some boxes had old toy parts hanging out. Abandoned chalet—or something else entirely? Other boxes had blankets that must have been the main contributor of the mothball smell. A few had broken ornaments and lamps stuffed inside and all of them were open, their cardboard flaps sticking up like they were displaying the objects inside.

All except for one.

It was a smaller box and cleanly taped shut. Its position in the center of the small space drew my eyes straight to it and wouldn't let them leave. Those broken toys became a distant second thought.

"This stuff is seriously old." Jeremy had started rummaging through the displayed objects, but something in me screamed to know what hid inside this one closed box.

Dropping to my knees, dust puffed up as I lowered the candle beside me. I slid my hand over the closed flaps, surprised at the lack of dust that layered the top. There was no label either, nothing to hint at what lay inside these sturdy cardboard edges. Fingers twitching to uncover the contents, I yanked at and pulled the tape from one side back, peeling a layer of the box away at the same time. I repeated the action with the crossed-over tape and then lifted one flap at a time.

My heart hammered as I retrieved the candle and peered inside, plucking one of the thin square items free. Covered in dust as if this box had been exposed for a long time before being taped shut, I brushed over the cover of a book—no—a photo album, I realized as I cracked the red plastic-coated cover. Inside was a large photo that took up the whole page, followed by many more in the same layout. Two lines of kids, smaller ones up front and taller ones in the back. To one side stood a man, his expression set with harsh lines and eyes that would make any child cower. To the other side was a woman, unsmiling and well covered in a fully buttoned blouse and floor-length skirt. Each photo was the same, except for the kids, new ones appearing as previous ones disappeared each subsequent year.

This place was a school?

I frowned down at a photo from ten years ago. A few boys were messing around, their faces blurry. But they weren't what held my gaze. A young girl did. Small and skinny with straight blond hair. It couldn't be...*Jill?*

The central kids held a board with dates ranging from seven to over twenty years ago—except the one for eight years ago was missing. Before I could wonder why, I read the white letters on one of the photo's plaques. *Fernie Orphanage.*

This place had been an orphanage—not a school.

"Hey, what's that?" Jeremy peered over my shoulder, reaching out to take the album. He sucked in a breath as I released my hold, his stare intense on the photo that was open.

"What's wro—" The sheet that slid from the back cover cut my question off as I caught it. What I saw kept me from questioning his reaction to the album. It was a deed to this place left to a guy named Kasey Whitmore. The same name I'd seen in the fogged-up bus window.

Jeremy came closer. "Cassidy, I..."

A hooded shadow passed the door and then I heard footsteps beyond the storage space rushing down the hallway.

Adrenaline already sky-high, I jumped up and dropped the candle. The flame doused and wax sprayed out through the dust. My paranoia was on high alert. After my dreams and every other strange thing that had happened, I reacted without thinking and dodged around Jeremy out into the dark hall. Another ruffling sound turned me back toward the communal area we'd originally come from.

A shadow surrounded by orange flame light shrank across the floor through the doorway.

"Stop!" I raced after them, stumbling on my pack that I swear was closer to the entry as I flew into the room. Scrambling up I was alone, but then I saw something that hadn't been there before. Folded neatly in half on the middle sofa Brad had been on earlier was a newspaper. The date was from almost two months ago and the headline made my heart stop.

MENTAL HOSPITAL EXPLOSION SEES DANGEROUS PATIENT ESCAPE.

I remembered the flash of torn newspaper I'd glimpsed yesterday before boarding the bus. But then something else took over.

"Code 10—Kasey Whitmore. Bring Backup." I heard the speaker announcement in my head and felt like I'd been transported back to the hospital. But it couldn't be real. I hadn't been stuck in that place back then...or had I? I thought of the way Doc Bethany had said, *"I hope I don't see you again."* Was that suicide attempt not my first? Did this escapee know me?

137

"Cassidy, what's wrong?" Jeremy entered from behind, his running steps audible as I spun to face him. "Are you okay?"

"I—I heard…" I sucked air, my lungs feeling like overinflated balloons. My lips refused to cooperate with my uneven breathing so I spun back to snatch up—

The middle sofa was still dirty with dust and stains, but that was all. The newspaper was gone. Vanished. Another figment of my imagination? *No.* I'd been so sure. And my nightmare, plus that remembered speaker announcement…

But I couldn't ignore the facts. The entry from the foyer was yards away and Jeremy had entered before I'd turned to face him. No one could have snuck in without him seeing. My horrible nightmares were taking conscious form? Why? The answer came to me quick as a flash with the clenching of my stomach. I hadn't taken my meds with lunch— because there'd been no lunch. After the avalanche and Jill—

I stopped that train of thought. I couldn't go over that horrible event yet.

I shook my head, unable to look up at the guy who was probably staring at me as if I was batshit crazy. "I thought I heard someone. One of the others. I saw…"

His socks made barely a sound as he stepped closer. Holding my elbows in his hands, his voice was gentle. "It's been a shitty day. Really shit. What happened—none of it was your fault. Not any of ours. But I think you're in shock, your brain is processing everything as a threat."

As I looked up the understanding on his face seemed to acknowledge that he'd noticed me reacting to him as a threat too. Not that my reactions and weird behavior hadn't made that abundantly clear. "Why are you being so nice to me?"

His brow pinched and he half smiled. "You remind me of someone I used to know a very long time ago. Someone I wished I'd been there to help when they needed me."

FIFTEEN

Caught off guard, I retrieved my medication and shoved the bottle into my pocket while I gained my thoughts. As my mouth parted and I looked up at Jeremy, he seemed to close off right before me.

Footsteps and quiet chatter sounded out down the hallway then, stalling the questions I'd been ready to fire at him about this person he'd let down. For some reason, the pain in his eyes affected me, touching me in a way I couldn't understand. Maybe it was simply the recognition of guilt. God knew I had buckets of the stuff since causing my parents' deaths. More than that, I felt the need to confide in him, to ask if he'd heard someone beyond this dusty room like I had before running back here. For the first time, I didn't completely fear the strange look I'd normally receive from such a question, and I wanted to understand why.

But my time right now was up, and none of those questions were passing my lips with our incoming audience.

Only two of the three who'd left on a seek-and-find mission reentered the communal space. Katherine looked less shaken than before, her cheeks rosy and nose not anymore after escaping the cold and horror we'd left outside in that lake. Yet her mouth was a straight line before she spoke, still showing that, like me, she hadn't forgotten the horrible accident that had taken Jill's life. "Brad's recouping out in that room." She motioned beyond the door that led to the entryway.

"This place used to be an orphanage," Stan filled in without explanation. He shared a quick tight-lipped look with Katherine, but said no more, shoulders shrugging like it was common knowledge.

"We know," Jeremy said, crossing his arms over his chest as he perched back on a side sofa's arm below the wall-mounted antlers. "We found photos under the stairs."

His stance and the look on his face screamed of that suspicious curiosity, almost like he was trying to figure something out as he watched the older man. It was a look I fully understood as I turned my frown at Stan. With how we'd found that box under the stairs, it was clear the guy hadn't found out this place was an orphanage that way.

In any normal situation, I'd have let any questions go. But today and this whole trip were becoming more and more strange. Was it all a bad coincidence, or were we all being set up? Glancing to and from where I'd seen the vanishing newspaper, I looked Stan in the eye. "What makes you think this place was an orphanage?"

Stan shrugged again, but Katherine spoke before a word left his lips, her voice shaky as if what she had to say somehow affected her. "Communal bedrooms with multiple, single beds. More toys too. Some dolls, wooden trains, the odd kids' book." She stared blankly up at the moose head with its black marble eyes as if lost in thought. With a shiver she shook herself and refocused. "There's not much, but by the state of everything, those items passed through many small hands."

"Now the good news. Well, sort of…. No can opener, but—"

"Oh, here." Remembering the croissants, I dug into my backpack and handed three out. "And the good news?"

Stan rubbed his hands, which I only now noticed were stained by black smears, and then snatched the last croissant. "There's a landline but it's newer and needs a power source. We also found a generator down past the kitchen in a storage room."

I wasn't an electrician, but I couldn't see the problem. A phone line meant we'd have the ability to call emergency services even if the line wasn't connected. "Doesn't having a generator fix the phone problem?"

142

Jeremy sighed and I bent down to my backpack, taking the opportunity to covertly down a pill from my pocket while retrieving my phone. I straightened and bit into my own croissant.

"There's no fuel, right?" Jeremy guessed. "The generator's empty."

Stan's lips thinned into a grim line and he nodded. "Yeah. So I reckon we split into two groups and start looking. There has to be something here, either inside or out."

My body tightened at the mere thought of having to venture back out there. Out into the freezing cold that was now draped with black night. Out to Jill's final resting place, her wet and icy grave that she would never escape from. "O-out…" My voice quaked and I spat crumbs. "Out…*there?*"

Jeremy stood up, his look of sympathy at me short-lived. "I'll take outside. Katherine?"

The middle-aged woman nodded, shoving the rest of her croissant into her mouth as she zipped her jacket from her chest all the way up her neck. "Sure. Fine. There could be an old snowmobile or metal drums around the house or buried…" She paused and shook her head. "Anyway, we'll find out."

"Then Cassidy will come with me." Stan's smile was as warm as the fire, its flames dancing in his eyes. "We'll take the rest."

I looked fleetingly at Jeremy as he tugged the zipper up on his own jacket that couldn't possibly have been one hundred percent dry yet. For some reason, and in spite of my paranoia, I felt safe around him, but I couldn't bring myself to go out there. Plus with only so much firewood, getting the power going could mean keeping us alive and getting us out of here if we ended up stranded for days. "Okay then."

Less than a few minutes later, Jeremy and Katherine were braving the cold outside, the snow blowing into the foyer cutting off as the door pulled shut. I tugged my boots back on and followed Stan out into the hallway. In my hand I carried the relit candle Jeremy had retrieved, holding it with both hands. The thought had occurred to me to use the flashlight on my phone, but conserving battery, which was already low, seemed more important for now. Stan headed further down the hall, and I went to follow—

A sound stopped me dead still. It had been quiet, but I couldn't confuse it. A clamber of feet—and not feet that thundered in ski boots. The noise had come from upstairs. "Uh…Stan?" He turned back, one brow hitched in question. "Did you already search all of upstairs?"

He shook his head. "About half of it." He glanced up through the railing. "You want to start up there?"

Not at all. Not after what I'd just heard. But the patter of little feet? My mind was playing tricks on me again, and although my body wanted me to flee, I

144

knew I had to pick the other option. Fight. In psychobabble terms, I had to face my fears, quash the imaginary and replace it with reality. My meds would kick in soon—I hoped—but until then…
"Yeah. You mind?"

Stan answered by stomping in his ski boots back my way and taking the lead up the wooden staircase. Each step creaked under our heavy boots and Stan's shadow thrown up onto the peeling wall was huge and ominous. My unease grew with each step, that chill returning to my bones without the fire's warmth to chase it away. "So, Stan…" I grappled for normal conversation. "Ah, you come to the snow often? Are you from around here?"

Stan threw a quick narrowed look over his shoulder, continuing to walk on. "I don't vacation much. No family to go with. I still live down in Fernie."

Like Jill had. "Oh…" I felt bad for asking. No family. Guess I knew how that felt now. Being a local, maybe that's how he'd known this place was once an orphanage. Something made me wonder if he'd ever had family and lost them, but my tongue and lips wouldn't cooperate to ask.

Clearing the stairs, Stan hooked left, trailing past the weathered banister as I followed behind. "I've already checked the rooms down the other way."

I glanced back down the dark hallway, seeing messy boot prints in the dust that disappeared into

145

each room. But none of the open doors siding the hallway held my attention. The door ending the hallway did. Staring, I couldn't look away. There was nothing unusual about the door, except that there were no prints to indicate Stan or Katherine had checked it out like the other doors down that way. "You didn't check that last—"

I tripped on my feet and smacked into Stan. He turned to catch me, hard hands on my shoulders stabilizing me before brushing slowly down my arms to let go. I stepped back fast as he hiked his chin in that direction. "Only door with a keyhole. I guess it's locked."

He continued on his way with a frown, checking the doors on either side of the hallway as I lit the way. Still unable to shake my discomfort that had now risen, I fired off another question. "So, you're a retired cop? You don't seem old enough to be retired."

As Stan opened the way into a room stuffed with metal-framed beds, his eyes slid to and from me again. He was at least a few years older than Katherine, but late forties to early fifties wasn't retirement age these days. "I voluntarily retired seven years ago, almost to the day."

Moving from this room down to the next, almost the same layout was found. But where I noticed an action figure and airplane in the last room, this one had a few stuffed pink and purple toys. "You see some horrific things in that line of work," Stan added as he closed the door and faced me, eyes gliding from my chest and up to my lips. "It changes you…or so my wife told me when she left."

He reached up and stepped forward, and I sidestepped to get out of the way, wax spilling from the candle and over my hand. I clenched my teeth at the burn, but Stan hadn't been reaching for me, he'd been reaching past me to the last door.

With candlelight swaying from my cradled hands, Stan frowned at me before pushing his way into the last room.

Dirty and cracked tiles stretched out before us, leading to a wall of four showerheads at the back, two toilet cubicles, which only one of had a door, and a stained basin. A communal bathroom. Without shower screens or curtains, without privacy. Had the children at least had separate times to bathe for girls and boys?

My skin crawled at the thought of what things could have gone on in a place with so many unwanted or orphaned kids, and I rushed back out of the room to clear my head. Grappling to rid the racing sensations from my body at the possibilities my plagued mind suddenly conjured up, I focused on the candle flame, the way it flickered and danced.

Stan joined me out in the hallway. "Guess we should help search down—"

"Wait." A gentle creaking had penetrated the

sound of my heart beating in my ears. It was a back and forth *crik, crik,* and it was coming from… "Up there."

Looking straight above my head, I saw a rope hanging from the ceiling with a knot tied at the end. In the dull light, I almost missed the large square cutout that framed the rope.

"A trapdoor." Reaching up, I wasn't tall enough to grasp the rope. "Can you?"

When I looked at Stan, his face had turned to stone. Still he reached up, threading the knot between his fingers and tugging down. The cover popped open. "Look out." With one arm he swept me aside, catching a suddenly descending ladder with his other as each panel extended into place. "It's an attic."

He'd already been up there? I dismissed my internal question straight away. There'd been no footprints down this way before we arrived together. So how had he—

"After you?" He stood aside, sweeping one arm out toward the ladder.

I frowned, but took hold of the rough wooden railing, minding my splintered palm as I climbed one-handed and held the lit candle, trying not to spill more wax as I went. When I reached the top, I saw the trapdoor over my head was fitted with a latch that had an unbolted padlock hanging from a metal loop. "Can you hold this?"

Handing the candle down, I was surprised to find Stan had started climbing up right behind me. Looking down at him, even though I felt rigidly uncomfortable to have him so close, I didn't immediately move away. I couldn't. Something struck me as I peered down at him. Like I was seeing his face not as a stranger I'd never met beyond this horrible trip, but as someone I'd come across once before. My mind refused to place him though, and as his hand on the ladder slid higher, closer to my thigh, I snapped out of it.

"Ah…" Getting higher and twisting so my backside wasn't right up in his face, I unhooked the lock and pulled the latch open. Then I pushed up, surprised at how heavy the door was to lever open. Clambering up into the space, the dank smell of mold and mildew filled my sinuses, but I couldn't see much in the dark.

Stan made it up a moment later, the candle highlighting so much of the long rectangular room with sloped ceilings on either side and a single window that had one of its nine connected panes cracked. A small, darkened patch sat below the moonlit window, where snow and rain had seeped inside.

Feeling an instant shiver from the cold that blew in through the broken glass, my mouth gaped at the few things that decorated the space. A lumpy mattress was wedged up the end in the corner on the ground, the sheets various shades of brown, and not because that was their pattern. A dirty bucket sat to the side, and I shuddered to think what it had been used for in this locked space. A dirty teddy bear—was it the same as the one I'd imagined downstairs?—lay haphazardly on the scratched and discolored wooden floors, legs and arms askew and head spitting fluff from its neck.

My mouth gaped, but then something else stole my attention.

The left wall was plastered with crayon drawings, and the details got clearer and clearer as I edged closer. Some showed rough sketches of two kids playing under a smiling yellow sun or happy raining clouds or sharing a cupcake or a book.

Others made me gulp.

Stick figures with bulbous heads and angry eyes. A small stick figure crying fat tears under a black scribbled sky. Pictures of this room and a larger-than-life monster standing over something scratched out in thick black with red patches seeping out.

As I turned, I saw more dark and creepy drawings plastered across the wall behind the trapdoor opening. Someone had lived up here. One child, or many? Had the 'naughty' kids been banished here for discipline? Either way, I knew one thing for sure.

This dirty horrible space had been, at the very least, someone's personal prison.

SIXTEEN

Nine Years Ago

Lying stomach-down on the floor, I stared through the grate on the wall. My stomach ached. So hungry. *The bite I had taken from the hard and green, furry roll had made it worse. But I didn't look back at the bucket next to my bed. Even though my tummy squeezed, I made myself stay. Made myself watch. When I didn't get to play with C.J., this was the best part of my day.*

Through the flower-shaped metal, the mess hall wasn't loud with laughter and running. The other kids weren't playing tag or food wars right now. Lunch was still an hour away, a meal all of them got every day. But not me. After my last punishment, food had only come two times this week when Mother sneaked me up an old leftover roll.

I was still in trouble. I didn't know why this time. But I knew it was my fault. It was always my fault. Ever since my sneak out way over a year ago, I was always in trouble. I was still locked in the attic. But at least I could be me up here…so long as he *didn't visit.*

The room was long and big. The roof was only tall enough in the middle for adults to stand up fully. I had a bed on the floor. The springs stuck out a bit, but it was okay. Better than the cold floor. The covers were dirty. They were always dirty. Mother wasn't allowed to wash them when I was in trouble.

Which was all the time, even when I hadn't been naughty.

I stared down at the other kids around the two long mess hall tables with their eyes all facing forward. My heart hurt a little. It wasn't just because I was left out like always, locked away while they ate, played, slept, and learned. It was because of the man standing up the front. Below his tidy brown hair, his green eyes were kind behind his glasses as he spoke to all the kids, looking at them as if every one of them mattered to him. As if teaching them English, math, geography, and history made him happy.

His name was Tom Stewart.

I clung tighter to my diary and the almost empty pen I'd been using to scribble down everything he taught the other kids. Aside from Mr. Muddles, my diary was the most special thing I had.

I'd never met the teacher, but something deep inside me wished I could. He never yelled. He never got angry. He was always kind and gentle. Nothing like my father. And a million times more than what my mother was in the small things she did when Father wasn't around to stop her.

Like he had done twice already this week, Mr. Stewart turned his head to glance up the tall ceiling at the grate I watched through. Like he could see me. Like he knew I was there. Like he wanted to meet me too.

I felt whole for three long seconds, my heart heating up and going as fast as running bunny legs at the same time.

But then she wrecked my daydream and my hopes.

Walking fast into the room, my mother looked back at the hallway door she'd come through.

Mr. Stewart called out to all the kids, "Chat over the places in the world you've heard of that you'd like to visit. Brainstorm with each other."

When Mother reached Mr. Stewart, she glanced back at the door one more time. "You can't do that." Her hissed words were quiet, but the tone echoing off the high ceiling let me hear them above the chatter. "He'll see you."

Mr. Stewart looked toward the door too, then curled his fingers around her arms to pull her closer. "I don't care. Let him see. I can't forget what you told me. All these years..." Unlike all the other times I'd watched him, something other than kindness flashed across his face. The chatter of the kids got louder and I struggled to hear, missing every few words. "Better...tell him. My...does not belong...and neither...you. Run...with me. Leave... Please."

My mother pulled away, tears falling from her eyes and down her cheeks. They dripped onto her cream blouse when they got to her chin. "I can't...that. You know...can't. He'll never let...leave—"

"...don't ask. Don't tell... Just leave, ...both of you. We...be a fam—"

"Is there a problem?" My father looked scary as he stomped into the room. The door slamming behind him shut all the kids up quick and made me jump. I hadn't seen him; my face had been scrunched into the grate to hear the words they'd been getting so upset about. Father's face was red and his eyes bulged in that awful angry way. He'd heard what they'd been saying.

My mother had already scampered back and wiped her face dry. Her shoulders were hunched and her head was down, eyes staring at her shiny black shoes.

She stayed silent as Father came right up to Mr. Stewart and glared down at the teacher. Spit sprayed from his mouth as he said, "I asked you a question, teacher."

Mr. Stewart looked to my mother then back at my father. He didn't step back even though my father was so close he was breathing on him. Unlike me, Teacher was a fast learner. Cowering only made him madder. When he spoke, a little fear poked through. "They're coming with me. We're leaving."

"Him!" Fire could have shot from my father's eyes as he yelled at my mother. She hunched in further, backing up until a dry-erase board on wheels stopped her. With his nostrils wide like an angry animal's and teeth flashing, my father screamed, "Everyone out!"

Chairs scraped and tumbled over as the kids jumped up and raced for the door. Some of them fell as others pushed to get out first. They'd seen the result of my punishments sometimes. Even though he'd never used his anger on them, they knew he was dangerous.

Mother went to race after them but Father caught her arm and yanked her back. His large hand went around the back of her neck and her eyes widened as he shoved her forward.

"Let her g—"

"You're fired! You no longer work here."

Mr. Stewart grabbed my father's arm but he didn't say anything else. He couldn't. My father had him by the throat too, his fingers squeezing.

"You—with your green fucking eyes—will leave now and never come back. If I see you again..." He smiled at my mother, but it was the scariest thing I had ever seen.

When his eyes flicked up to the grate, I jerked back like he'd hit me. My cheeks burned as if they were remembering the last time he had. Everything looked blurry now, but I couldn't make my shaking arms and legs work to move back to see better. But I didn't have to, my father's voice was loud enough to hear clearly.

"If I ever *see you again, you fucking piece of shit, I will kill them. Both of them. And then I'll hunt you down and cut out your fucking heart. Don't think I haven't had plenty of practice."*

Even with everything blurry, I knew as his face turned that he was looking at the stag head on the wall above the blackboard. He'd killed it himself. Hog-tied out on the snow where he'd shot it, he'd dragged me out there and made me watch as he cut out its heart. It had still been beating as he held it up in his bloody hand.

I couldn't breathe as I remembered what he'd said back then, with his reddened knife pointed at me as I stared. "One day, your time will come. I promise you."

Shoved back, Mr. Stewart fell and rushed to get back up. Something more than fear was across his face, but he didn't say anything as he backed up to the door and escaped through it.

My father whispered in my mother's ear, his eyes lifting back up at me with a terrifying smile. I didn't need to hear what he told her. I could guess what was coming from just that look and all the other times I'd seen it before.

I was going to pay.

SEVENTEEN

Staring at the desolate and isolated location that looked like it had been at least one child's personal hell, I was so stuck in my head that everything else was forgotten. What I'd been through. The events that had brought me here. Jill's death. I couldn't look away from those child-drawn pictures. Some even had messy words scratched in black and red: bad, nauty (misspelled), truble (also misspelled), punish, pain...*alone*. My heart broke a little, those words resonating deep down inside of me. "Those poor children. Do you think they—"

Stan's broad hands landed on my shoulders, heavy and clinging. The breath he sucked in sounded like he was *smelling me?*

My eyes widened and, as I got past the initial shock, I sucked air and spun. "What are you—"

Stan caught me by the arm to keep me from backing up. Even in shadow, his smile was warm like before, his eyes hooded like he was imagining something other than this slice of hell we were standing in or the fact that we were strangers to each other. The candle was no longer in his hands. Now it sat back by the cutout in the floor, creating his shadow that swallowed me whole. "I saw the way you looked at me on the stairs."

"I…I…" Words refused to form, my lips gaping but failing to say anything more. His grip and the way he looked at me, eyes flicking from my eyes down to my lips then to my chest, made my heart leap. Made my breath come faster. And not because I was into what he clearly had in mind. Was this middle-aged guy seriously coming on to me in this horrible place we were trapped in after all that had happened today? He couldn't be. Not here. Not now. Not with me. We didn't know each other. I wasn't interested, not in him. Not in anyone.

And yet I couldn't move.

This situation, being alone with a man in seclusion, felt like an evil dose of déjà vu. Because I'd been in an abusive relationship before? I couldn't remember any more than I did now, and despite my wide-eyed frozen stance, Stan stepped closer, removing the small space between our bodies.

I shook my head, some motor function response finally getting through. "No. I…"

"Shhhh." His hand came up and he pressed a thick finger to my lips. When he spoke, his cigarette breath batted my face with each word. "No one will know. I promise. I can keep a secret. A new one to forget the old."

"The old?" When I stepped back, his grip tightened. Something other than lust gleamed in his dark eyes. Something deeper. Desperation. I shoved against him to free my arm. "I said no—"

Stan's other hand came up, gripping my jaw and pulling it close. Then his mouth came down on mine, slanted, slightly parted, wet tongue searching.

Adrenaline lit like fire inside of me, setting my insides alight. I'd said no. I'd pushed him away. And now, I was fucking pissed.

Palms shooting up I shoved into his chest, breaking his hold on me. My hands cranked into fists and I swung, belting right into his nose. There was a horrible crack and blood spurted out, speckling my face and Jeremy's hoodie and pouring down Stan's face.

Stan stumbled back, that desirous look replaced with malice. "You psycho! Lead me on and then *this?*" He shook his head as he backed up. "The hell with the lot of you. I'm getting out of this shithole. I never signed up for any of this shit."

Spinning away, he stomped back to the trapdoor. The candle fluttered in reaction, casting his ominous form across the picture-plastered walls then back at me. And then he was gone, disappearing back down the ladder without a glance or another word.

The fire that had so quickly ignited in me

vanished as the candle's dancing flame regained its calm and steady burn. A chill took over as I smeared his blood across my face. Had that been my fault? I'd tried to say no, but I'd been so taken off guard that I'd stood there saying nothing. And I *had* been looking at him on the ladder, though not for the reason he assumed.

Releasing my fists, my bones ached in the hand I'd hit him with, the pain worsening as I flexed my fingers. I sighed hard, absently meandering further into the attic and over to the window that glowed with white-blue light. Beyond the icy glass, with the full moon's light up in the night sky, I could see the disturbed snow over the lake's surface—our tracks to get here. I could just make out the two holes in the thin top layer that were darker but unmoving like they had already frozen over.

Today had been the day from hell, and that was from me, one of the uninjured survivors. *Poor Jill.* And now Stan was furious.

I peered straight down, wondering if I'd see him storm from the building at any second. He couldn't possibly be serious about leaving, not now in the freezing cold of night.

With the cool wind blowing through the cracked pane, my breath came out in white puffs. I leaned my forehead into the glass, enjoying the way the chilled surface cooled my hot cheeks. Maybe I was cursed since my parents' deaths. Though, considering my memory lapses from before the accident, maybe I had always been cursed.

Lifting my head back up, I froze and stared. The large steam round from my breath that had reached out to the frosted edges shrank on the glass, getting smaller and smaller. I blinked hard—but what I saw didn't vanish.

Finger-written words tainted the shrinking steam. Two words that sent a shiver down my spine and made my heart seize.

One down.

As the steam faded to nothing, disappearing the words, I stared in shock. But after that newspaper, I had to know if what I'd seen was real or not. Another delusion?

Leaning closer, I breathed out in short bursts to fog up the pane again. Each breath was like a stab to my heart as each of those letters returned. *One down.* Someone had written this, this cryptic and telling message…because they'd seen Jill die?

As the steam shrank again, the words fading, I remembered those footsteps. Light from the candle sent a shadow of my face onto the clear glass pane as I stepped back. Or not. The outline wasn't mine. The face…wasn't mine. It was sheltered by a hood.

I spun to face them head-on—

Pain exploded across my skull. My legs turned to jelly and my eyes rolled. As I hit the ground, I felt every place my body impacted. And with my last blink, I saw that same dark hooded figure standing over me.

EIGHTEEN

KASEY

Leaving the unconscious woman on the ground of the attic, I pulled on the edges of my hood to make sure I was concealed. Then I moved down the steep ladder as silently as a ghost. With keen eyes scoping out what was visible of the upper level and hearing no close-by sounds, the coast was clear.

One down? Not for long.

Knowing this place better than I even knew myself, and with my adrenaline pumping after witnessing the interaction between that young woman and that older, disgusting excuse for a man, the actions to come were a plan to play out.

Boots moving quickly and quietly along the hallway, and then faster down the creaky steps, the aggravated muttering and shifting from the communal lounge had my smile widening beneath my hood. "Like a mouse in a maze."

Cutting across the landing at the bottom of the

stairs, I planted my back against the wall and stood statue still at the side of the opening.

The same older man was in the room and alone, his angered face highlighted by those licking and hissing flames as he tore two croissants from the young woman's backpack and shoved them into his pockets. "Phone. Phone," he muttered. "She took the bloody thing with her."

I held back the rough sigh I wanted to let out. Dragging him from here would take more effort than I wanted to expel. I needed to conserve my energy...for later.

Darting past the stairs, I hooked a left into the narrower hall entry in two seconds. On the third second, I jutted my elbow into the wall. The sound was loud enough and echoed back the way I'd come from.

"Hello?" The older man had heard. Just as planned. "You guys out there?"

Easing further back around the bend into total darkness, I listened, hearing the man's stomping feet coming after me. Walking backward, I hooked left and then left again, not needing light to navigate my way.

"Jeremy? Katherine?"

The man's following steps slowed and I jutted my elbow into a door I passed.

"Hey, you got a light?"

He continued after me, and then I eased around

the last bend. My back met the solid barrier of a dead-end wall. At least it looked like a wall, the wood panels matching the rest of the walls and acting to hide the door that led to…well, we'd get to that soon. Because right now the heavy footfalls of that man were nearing. And with what I held tight in my hand—a rusted memento that I'd experienced time and time again—I was rearing to go.

"Can you hear me? Did you find fuel?"

When he was almost at the intersection, I stepped free of the shadows, my hood concealing as ever. "I've been waiting."

The man paused briefly, then squinted, eyes searching the darkness my hood created. "Is that—"

I lunged forward and thrust the knife right into his gut. My other hand caught his arm and yanked him closer as he gasped, seeing close-up exactly who I was. "Yeah. It's me." The man went to shove me back, and I retracted the knife and swung. Driving the hilt into his broken nose released a geyser of fresh blood. He fell like the bag of shit he was. "Lights out."

Murmured voices reached me then. They were coming from the other end of this dead-end hall where the other exit to the communal room was. Where the fire was burning bright and warm. But they were moving, growing closer.

Good thing I did this here.

Turning back to the dead end, a slight shove in

the right place popped the entry open. Musky, earthy air ballooned out, the smell bringing nausea to my stomach that I refused to let deter me. Grabbing the man's ankles I tugged, sliding him out of eyesight and into total darkness. The voices grew louder. "Stan? Cassidy?" I resealed the padded door behind us just in time, cutting off the calls.

With a sigh, I breathed in the smells that raised my pulse, not trying to fight the old panic that resurfaced. Fighting that feeling only made it worse. Years of experience had taught me that...among other things.

Gathering up the man's feet, I hauled him down the dark tunnel, letting the descending curve of the ground direct me rather than my eyes. There'd be plenty to see soon enough.

By the time I'd cleared a few gentle left and right curves and continued straight for a stretch, I finally reached a rickety wooden door. One boot kicked it in. I dropped the man's ankles.

The light from a small, dirty window that framed snowy trees added enough visibility to see what lay inside. The nausea that gripped my insides turned to fire at what was still set out—exactly the way it had been all those years ago. What had once been a normal old table stood erect in the center of the small hut, an almost vertical platform that was on a gradual lean. The metal brackets at the top and bottom left and right were still there, and just as *thick as I remembered. The large trolley to the side had the top and lower shelf stocked full of instruments, most metal and all varying in shapes and sizes...depending on the intended torture to be handed out. Each was rusted and marred with a dark substance.*

Blood.

I got to work, knowing my visitor wouldn't stay unconscious for much longer. Rope from the trolley was tied to both his wrists and then his ankles, and then each end was strung through the metal brackets; brackets that would never break no matter how hard you thrashed to get free. His feet were restricted first. That was the easy part. Gathering snow from the window I unlocked, I drizzled the cold flakes over his face. When nothing happened, I laughed at my gentle approach and slapped him.

The man started to stir, twitching on the ground as his consciousness returned. I moved to stand behind the vertical platform, watching from around the edge. At first he groaned, looking confused as his feet refused to shift, then he rolled and planted his hands on the dirt and he pushed up, getting to his feet that were stuck wide apart. He faced the exit, oblivious to what loomed behind him. "What the fuck?"

With a blink he saw the rope on his wrists at the exact moment I yanked the two ends from behind the platform. Off balance with his feet so far apart, he fell back against the solid wood, his hands flying up as I wound the ropes around an anchor on the back and tied them in place.

The man tugged and tried to kick. "What's going on? Where am I?" And then he saw the trolley. "Fuck. Shit. Who's there? Show yourself, dammit. What are you going to do to me? Where the fuck am I?"

After long minutes of grunts and curses, all of which would never be heard all the way out here and with the padding that lined the long stretch to get here, his thrashing started to ease.

I stepped out quietly from behind the platform, fingers trailing over the instruments of pain. "My personal hell. Or should I say yours."

"What the fuck. You? You b—"

Before he could finish I swung a rubber mallet at his jaw. He howled as spittle and blood flew and tugged harder on his arms, trying to get them free.

"You may call me Kasey, Stan. And only Kasey."

"You psycho!" He screamed, but with his jaw off kilter it sounded more like 'o-syo'. He thrashed harder and then stopped just as suddenly, seeing the grubby window and the white landscape outside. Grimacing, he screamed with slurred speech. "Help! Help me! I'm in here. Fucking help me!"

In the midst of his cries, I tugged the cigarette packet from his pocket and lit one with my Zippo.

After a puff, puff sent smoke tendrils up into the air I pressed the end to his suspended wrist. The stink of his burning flesh saturated the chilled air before he reacted to the pain.

"What the hell? Hey, stop. Seriously!" He writhed, tears welling up his eyes as I re-lit and butted the end out again. As I re-lit a third time, the smell of acrid smoke now masking the dirty smells in the hut, his voice turned from shocked and demanding to desperate. "Please. I'm sorry. I—"

His lips pinned shut as I put the cig out on his inner elbow. Tears rolled down his dirty cheeks, creating clean, wet tracks. "It's a bit late for that. The damage has already been done."

"Damage? What damage? I didn't do anything. Please." His eyes darted to the trolley, seeing the array of deadly instruments that cluttered up the shelves. He gulped and shook his head. "You don't want to do this. Kasey? Kasey, please. Let me go and we can forget this ever happened. I'll leave. I'll walk out and never come back."

"Like you did last time." Confusion stole the fear from his face and I ran a finger along the dirty hilt of a curved blade that almost looked like a crescent moon. I began to hike up my hoodie to expose my stomach.

"What do you mean, last time—" Stan stopped talking mid-sentence. He gasped at the sight, at the countless burn marks and long and short scars that

were as individual as they were straight and gnarled. "What happened to you?"

Now holding the curved blade by the hilt I came closer, gripping the man's chin as I raised the weapon. "Before you first came here, and every day after that…Father's discipline. But unlike me, you'll be the lucky one. You won't have to live through it again and again. My gift to you." He started to squirm, so I pressed the blade to his neck. Crimson leaked out and I smiled as he went still. "A one-session pass."

"No. You've got the wrong guy. I don't know what you're on about" He shook his head quick and short, more red leaking out around the rusty blade.

Releasing his chin, I pulled the neck of my hoodie aside to reveal a small scarred starburst. A bullet hole—well it had been…back then.

Sudden realization etched its way through the fear straining Stan's face. "Kasey… Kasey? You're… It can't be." But the widening of his eyes as he studied my features said he knew differently. "No." As my blade lowered, he shook his head faster, fighting with renewed intensity to free his hands from the restraints. "No!" The material of his snow gear cut open easily. A few nicks leaked red as I hacked both sides of the fabric away. "Stop! No! I didn't know!"

In his screams, I swooped up pliers from the trolley and caught his tongue between the ends. His *eyes popped as the blade sliced in one swift motion. Red sprayed as the pliers came away, landing on the dirt with half his tongue. Blood streamed from his mouth and over his chin, waterfalling down to his chest.*

I held the business edge of the blade to his throat and ended his bloody shrieks. "You didn't want to know."

NINETEEN

Nine Years Ago

Father's strong voice woke me from sleep. I sat straight up in bed and knocked Mr. Muddles off the edge. I snatched him up quick, but Father wasn't climbing up into the attic. The door on the ground was shut. My heart got quick anyway, and I tried to breathe slower as I slid my legs over the edge of the mattress. My feet were bare and my thin clothes with holes didn't make up for not having shoes or socks. Winter was almost here, and this was just the beginning.

"As you can see…" Father's voice traveled through the grate and up into the attic. "Everything here is above board, officer."

Dropping Mr. Muddles, I rushed to the grate and peered down into the mess hall. Standing beside my father at the door was a tall man dressed in police uniform. His belt was even equipped with a gun. A sudden sense of hope made me breathe in

174

deep. Could this man save me?

"Call me Stan," the officer replied with a nod. "Though with more than one report of child neglect and misconduct, I am sure you understand that I must perform a thorough inspection."

"But of course. As I said before, I am more than happy to oblige." Father's tone was light, but the clenching of his jaw was a clue. He was like a pot of soup about to boil over.

At my father's lifting hand, the officer moved through the room, shifting things on the long tables and flicking through the other kids' tests and artworks.

My mother appeared at the door from the kitchen then, and my father's eyes became angry slits as he slid them her way. She didn't come inside and she kept quiet as she looked up at the grate I watched from. Her eyes were sad, but she shook her head at me and then pressed a finger to her lips.

My hope died and I started shivering from the cold. Even with help right here she wanted to keep me hidden. Keep me a secret. Why? Life couldn't be worse if this cop helped us get away from here. It just couldn't.

"If you don't mind me asking…" Father's voice again, but this time there was sharpness to it. "Where did these reports come from?"

The officer paused, dropping a stack of paintings on the table he stood at. His lips became a straight line and he turned to my father—right as a kid's head poked up over the window ledge from outside. C.J.. Oh no. My gaze shot to my father as the officer said, "Given the nature of the reports, I am not at liberty—"

"A child, maybe?" My father was glaring at the window C.J. had just been peeking through. He'd seen him. "And, if I had to bet on it, I'd say the teacher, no?" My father smiled a little too widely when the officer didn't answer. He leaned back into the end of the desk my mother now taught all the other kids from. "Children like to create drama for sport. You are more than welcome to question each and every one if you like. Though I have to add, someone with a grudge for being let go for questionable behavior with those exact children is hardly a trustworthy source."

"Are you saying the teacher was inappropriate with one or more of the children?"

My mother's face had turned white as the snow outside. Her mouth hung open but she said nothing as her eyes became wet. Instead, she left quietly through the hallway door.

Father shrugged. "As soon as I heard I let him go. I told him never to return but didn't file a report with authorities. You see, other than what I've been told, I have no proof."

"Well, I can see where this accusation may have arisen from..."

As the officer kept talking, my thoughts were going too fast. The teacher had been told on for something he had never done. Something he would never ever do. Mother was pretending nothing was wrong—like always. And after C.J. also telling on my father I knew I'd be punished no matter what this visitor did.

So I made a choice.

I stomped my bare feet and rushed to the grate, twining my fingers through the black metal.

Father's head whipped upward faster than the officer's, and even though I'd made the choice, I scrambled back and out of sight.

"Who's up there? I thought all the children were playing outside."

Talking as normally as possible through clenched teeth, my father said, "Rats probably. They like to get into old boxes and junk. I really need to get onto the wife about spring cleaning early. The cold seems to bring them in."

"Uh huh." The officer sounded unsure, and I heard footsteps. "I think I'd like to tour the upstairs too. That is where the bedrooms are?"

"For the younger kids and early teens. Though as I said, Stan, all the children are out—"

"Yes, outside. I know. But just so I can close this report fully, I'd like to have a look...if you don't mind."

There was quiet and then Father spoke, "Of

course. Be my guest." Footsteps sounded again and I rushed to the grate to see them leave the room.

I didn't wait and listen. Instead, I grabbed a red crayon and began to scribble on the wall in long messy strokes. There was creaking as they came up the stairs. I kept scribbling. The second my father climbed up here, I wouldn't be able to say a word. Fear would catch my tongue. I needed to leave a message. They were still talking, but I couldn't make out the words anymore. There were squeaks and creaks as doors opened and shut and I scribbled faster. Through the attic floor, I knew what room they were going in and out of. There were four sets of bedrooms upstairs, two for the younger and older girls, and two for the boys. Even though it was still freezing cold, I had stopped shivering. Sweat made me wet and stuck my T-shirt to my body. They'd finished in the boys' rooms first and were leaving the first girls' room for the second one. Then they were back in the hall and my message was done. My hands shook, fingers curling around the red crayon stump as I waited.

"I appreciate your cooperation, Mr. Whitmore." Two lots of steps began to walk back toward the stairs.

"Not a problem, officer."

They were leaving. The cop was leaving.

I wanted to make a noise, but fear stopped me. Father would know I'd made the sound. All the other *kids were outside. But...*

I had an idea and slid down onto the floor. My knees burned from the holes in my jeans but I didn't stop. Finding my secret spot, I pulled out my tattered diary—the last birthday present Mom had given me years ago—and a pencil. Flipping past the filled pages to the back, I scribbled 'Help Me' *and then ripped the section out. Folding it in half, I rushed to the door in the ground and slipped the page through the crack on one side as they passed right below. My face was hot and wet and my heart stopped as I became like a statue.*

"What is this?" The officer's muffled voice reached me through the floor. Had he seen the note? "Is that a door up there?" I heard a creak and then the ladder slid down. All my hope rushed back, but fear made me feel like I was choking. There was quiet for a bit and then a clunk, clunk *as the lock on the other side of the door was fiddled with. "Why is this locked?"*

"As I said, good for nothing rats. I've laid baits up there and we're waiting for them all to die off. Probably smells like rot by now. Should be a few dead already. I could dig around for the key, or—"

"Mr. Whitmore, I am sure you do no expect me to buy what you're selling. Rats are not so loud—I know, we've got an infestation at the station. Those little buggers love the donuts. And this..." After a short gap, the cop started talking again. "Rats don't

have opposable thumbs to write with. Now, as I see it, you only have one choice. Unlock the door, or I'll break it open."

Instead of Father talking, I heard noises. Clattering. Then the padlock clanged open. But the door stayed closed. "Now, I don't know if you have children, but if you do you'll understand. A strong hand is needed at times, you know? To teach them respect and obedience."

The trapdoor opened then and I crawled backward on the floor having already re-hidden my diary. His face was blank, but his eyes burned me like those horrible things he smoked. "This is my child Kasey. After causing problems with the orphans, and..." He turned as the cop followed him up and saw my scribbled message in large red letters on the back wall. Help. His teeth clenched. "As you can see this defiance is in need of repercussions."

I didn't know if the cop knew what repercussions meant. I didn't, but I was smart enough to know he was talking about my punishments.

The cop frowned at the big red letters. Then he looked at me and beyond me to the dirty bed. "How long have you been locked up here?"

"Only a few hours," Father said before I could answer. "Since just after breakfast. I was set to unlock the door after you left so lunch wouldn't be missed out on."

"Is that true?"

The cop saw the new bruise on my arm, but he didn't see the rest. My clothes hid them. And I wanted to show him the rest. I wanted to say I'd been up here for years...not hours. But my lips wouldn't move. Father was watching me and his tight fists promised pain if I breathed a word against him. I nodded without meaning to.

"Are you certain?"

The creak as my father stepped closer had me nodding faster. "Yes. Certain." Whatever that meant.

Now the cop looked at my father. "This is still not okay. The locked door. The state of this attic."

"Look, Stan. *I understand your position. I really do. My life is helping kids. So, so many kids." Father's hands were open at his sides now. "But if this little bit of discipline is made into something bigger than it is, the press will have a field day, and then all the kids we feed, house,* and *protect will be turned out. This place could be shut down because of your opinion on how I discipline my own child."*

"Now, Mr. Whitmore, this is a little more serious and not so cut and dry as—"

"Please, if you will. Perhaps we should continue this discussion downstairs?"

The officer looked at me again, then sighed. With a stiff nod, he followed my father back down through the trapdoor that was pulled shut behind them. Even though I couldn't see him anymore, I

181

couldn't move.

The next thing my father said made my heart sink. "I could make a generous donation to your department to cover your wasted time here. Maybe I could even send a cash reimbursement straight to you instead, if you see your way to understanding my position. This discipline is as much to teach as it is to protect my child. The orphans get jealous and act up at times."

I didn't know what my father was doing was called, but I understood it. He was offering the cop money to go away. To leave and not report what he'd seen in the attic. I held my breath as I waited for the officer's answer. He couldn't take the offer. It was wrong. He couldn't believe all the lies.

"What do you say, dear? A nice reward for following up false leads? For being thorough in his job."

"Yes, of course." Mother's voice was soft but loud enough for me to hear. She was there. She'd heard everything. "I uh, was just coming to unlock the door so Kasey could help me prepare lunch. I do hope you don't judge us too harshly for our parenting. This is not something that happens often, but sometimes it is a requirement to keep the peace."

"I see..."

Again there was quiet, and after what seemed like forever I heard a slap. "It was nice to meet you, Mr. Whitmore. Keep your nose out of trouble and take care."

"You too, Stan. Would you please show Officer Blunt out, dear? I'd like to chat to Kasey before lunch."

The stairs creaked and I crawled backward across the floor, cringing at every noise I made. Then I heard it. Climbing up the ladder. The sweat on my skin felt suddenly cold like ice. The door swung open and was laid quietly on the floor as Father appeared. The look on his face made me wish I was already dead.

What was to come would be so much worse than dying.

So, so much worse.

Father came up through the hole in the floor and stalked toward me. His boots slapped the ground half as fast as my drumming heart. Both sounds echoed through my ears. A look of murder made his eyes crazier, and even though I knew better I scurried back. The raggedy jeans I'd worn and slept in for the past week caught on a lifted nail. I heard a tear but kept scrambling back, staring in horror as his expression became more deadly for every extra step he had to take after me. And then there was nowhere else to go. My back hit the wall.

Spinning around, I shoved with all my strength to lift the window. It scraped open an inch as my toes slid out from below me, and fresh cold air swept inside. Scrambling up, I bashed my shoulder and then my elbow into the gap, cracking one of the window's glass squares. Another inch. Not enough. My head wouldn't even fit through.

There was no escape and then his thick fingers snatched my tangled hair and tugged. I bit back a cry when chunks were ripped straight from my scalp. And then we were moving, Father hauling me along as my bent legs fought to crawl backward at his stomping speed. Finally, I got onto my feet and his hold on my hair let go—so he could catch my hips and throw me over his shoulder.

I should have fought. I should have begged for him to let me go—but I didn't.

As he climbed down the ladder, I stayed hanging over his shoulder. A dead weight. My breaths were too fast, and instead of speaking, I worked on making them slow down. The darkened upper-level hallway passed too quickly, and then so did the break for the stairs. We didn't go down them. He continued down the hallway.

I gulped, my throat feeling like something big as a fist was jammed in there.

Today I would not be used to teach the other kids what happened to naughty children. Today my punishment would be something to add to my nightmares. Horror come to life.

My body trembled as heat raced through my insides. I felt like something inside me was going to break free at any second—to save itself from what *would come next. Teeth chattering I managed a whisper, "I'm sorry, Father. Please. I'm really sorry."*

His hurting grip on my dangling legs squeezed tighter, and I felt like something beneath my skin was about to split apart.

When we got to the end of the hall, I stopped breathing, waiting for his reply...or worse.

"Yet you let the teacher know of your existence. Did you leave him a note too?"

I didn't answer and he didn't ask again. Telling him I hadn't told the teacher would make him even angrier. Telling him I had, even if I hadn't, wouldn't change what was going to happen next either.

When father shifted his weight, my eyes slid shut. I heard the sound of metal touching metal, and then a click. The door he stood at opened, and then closed behind us, locking us inside. My heart got faster as he kept walking, and then it raced when I began bouncing on his shoulder. We were going down steps—his secret back stairs. It smelled like dirt as we got lower, and then we were on the ground. Eyes still squeezed shut I knew the sounds I heard, the jangle, creak, and whoof, were him picking up the kerosene lantern and lighting it with one hand. As he moved now, I saw the swaying glow behind my closed eyes.

And then we stopped.

Shoved off his shoulder, I fell to the ground. My

185

bones exploded with pain as they smacked the dirt, but I sat up as quick as I could and opened my eyes. Playing dead or pleading would make it hurt more. I kept my mouth shut.

With the kerosene lamp on the trolley, everything on top was neat and lined up. Like always. Most of the items were still dirty from my last visit. From all my visits. He never cleaned them.

When he came at me, I held my hands up so he could grab my wrists to pull me up. I glanced from the open door to the tunnel before my eyes shot back to the trolley and a long thin knife. My legs throbbed as I remembered the time I tried to escape. I wouldn't run this time.

"I see you are capable of learning."

I forced myself not to shrink at his voice. The anger in it was still there, but that wasn't all.

"Take your place." I didn't move, my body was frozen. It knew what was coming. "NOW!"

Catching my arm, he thrust me at the flat table he'd fixed so that it stood up like a slanted wall. My back hit the rough wood, but I kept from making any sound or even scrunching up my face. My eyes closed again as the ropes were fastened, first around my wrists, up high and out to each side. And then my ankles, tugged out to the table's bottom edges. The ropes burned and cut my skin as each one was tightened. I forced my breathing to stay normal even though my heart wanted it to race too.

There was a scraping sound and then a sort of click, and my eyes cracked open. His special square black lighter. I almost sighed as stinky gray smoke filled the air. Father puffed on a cigarette to my right, standing between me and the trolley. His narrowed eyes watched me, and his lips on the cigarette were tight with each pull. Smoke curled from his nose. When he ashed the tip, I didn't move anywhere that he could see. Still, every part of me got tight in readiness.

The hot end of the cigarette landed on my arm near my tied-up wrist. I mashed my teeth and pressed my lips together. I wanted to scream.

"You should know better than to interfere like that." Father lit the tip again and puffed it until the end was red and sizzling. "And telling your little friend to make complaints..." He pressed the glowing cigarette to my inner elbow.

I screamed in the back of my throat and tears spilled down my face as sweat attacked my forehead.

His hand covered my mouth and he pressed his heavy body into mine. "Did you think you would get to leave your home, you good-for-nothing little bastard?" When I remained quiet, his empty hand caught my neck and he squeezed. "I asked you a question, bastard."

My chest got tight and I couldn't suck air, but I managed to rasp, "No."

Father let go of my neck and I sucked air

quickly, just in case. But he didn't strangle me again. Instead, his fingers grazed over the shiny and dull items on the table. "D-don't you want another smoke, Father?"

I'd felt the pain of every weapon on that table. Some scraped, some burned, and others cut. The burning was better than the rest...most of the time. Anything that could cut could also stab. And if he spent enough anger burning me, maybe I'd get away with just that this time.

When he lit up again, I remained still, staring to my left at the little window outside. I blinked. Tiny white flakes were falling, sprinkling so gently down. The first snow of winter. A change that happened every year out there, while nothing ever changed inside these walls. Now as the burn landed on my shoulder, I imagined I was out there among the dancing trees where birds fluttered and flew about. That like them, I was free. When the re-lit end touched the base of my neck, I didn't react. I didn't even blow the dripping sweat from my lip. Right now, my body was in this hidden hut, but my mind was out there with the birds. Away from this. More burning spots came, to my neck, my other arm, my legs...my chest.

I noticed then that my T-shirt had been torn partway down the front. The burning had stopped too. My eyes left their daydream outside quick, expecting to see a dirty knife pointed at my ribs or my stomach. There wasn't one. Well, not in those places. This time his long and rusty blade pressed into my neck, right under my jaw.

The other look I'd seen before had taken most the anger from his face. The way he stared at me made me feel like something he'd stepped in. Like I was disgusting.

My mouth opened. I wanted to say, please don't. *But nothing came out. Nothing I said now would stop this. I'd tried them all.* Stop. No. Please don't. Sorry. I didn't mean it. It won't happen again. I'm sorry. I'm sorry. I'm sorry! *Nothing had worked.*

"You don't want another smoke?" His answer was a cruel smile, and I wanted to die.

His large body towered before me, his top lip curling and breath hot and sickening as he breathed over me. "You have his fucking eyes." And then he whipped the blade downward.

Heat and stinging burned from my neck down my chest, but my cry escaped only as he swung back, smashing the handle's end into my eye. Red exploded and the whole side of my face throbbed as hot blood leaked out. I couldn't see out both my eyes, but I still saw him and his smile.

"You're as worthless as your lying whore of a mother."

TWENTY

"Cassidy!"

I groaned and shifted. My head pulsed in agony and wet warmth coated my face. With the rapid blinking of my lids, I saw erratic flashes of light. The power was on?

Hands caught my arm and I recoiled, my last memory rushing back: the hooded person behind me and that exploding hit to my temple. The gash across my forehead throbbed as more warmth trickled from it. "Leave me alone. *Please.*"

"Cassidy, it's me."

Hands came at me again and I scampered back, wiping frantically at my eyes to clear blood from my face. "I'm warning you, I'll…" What? I was alone and weak. Practically blinded. What the hell was this person doing here? What did they want with me?

"Cas, it's okay. It's Jeremy."

I froze as his gentle voice registered. Blinking my sight clear I gazed up. A concern-riddled face looked down at me, backlit by the single flickering light bulb in the stained ceiling. *"Jeremy?"* I was up in a flash and in his arms, frantic eyes darting in the erratic light from shadow to shadow for a threat. "Oh, God. Did you see him?"

"See who?" He held me back at arm's length with a frown, scouring my face and then further down. His brow creased. "What happened to you? And don't even try to tell me you fell asleep again."

Now was not the time to come clean about my blackouts. That wasn't what had happened anyway.

I stepped back from him and meandered around, trying to piece together what I thought had happened. Pacing back to the window, I breathed on the glass, creating a large round of steam. I choked back my gasp. The message I'd seen was gone.

Peering over my shoulder everything else up here was the same. The dirty bed. The bare space. Those haunting drawings. I turned back around and almost stumbled, stubbing my boot on a raised nail. I frowned down at it, feeling some kind of panic stir deep within. Could that hooded guy really have been here? And if he had been, why had he knocked me out and left? Maybe it was just another nightmare. Maybe I'd blacked out and hit my head. I reached up to touch the stinging gash on my forehead with soft fingers, hissing through clenched teeth as I saw the sharp edge of the window ledge. Maybe…probably.

I scanned past Jeremy, looking for any clue that

someone else had been here. There was blood on my hands from wiping my face. A little more stained Jeremy's hoodie I wore but was hard to see on the dark fibers, and there were a few specks on my dirty, white pants too.

"What's going on, Cas? Where's Stan?"

My shoulders tensed as I recalled that look in Stan's eyes. I turned away and glanced out the window again. Snow was falling steadily, blanketing the trees and whitening out the lake and those holes in the ice so much that if you didn't know what had happened down there, you'd never find out. I let my leveling-out breaths fan across the glass. Still no message. Not even a smear to suggest it had been wiped away.

"I…I…" My suspicions would make him think I was nuts. Telling him about the message that was now non-existent would do the same. Had that along with glimpsing that hooded person all been part of a nightmare? Had Stan's come-on been made up in my subconscious mind too? Not knowing struck fear through me. And there was no way I was going to bring up more of my patchy past to this guy I hardly knew. "I…" Stalling for the right lie to come to me, I let my eyes travel from Jeremy's boots and up. "You, uh…got the generator working?"

Jeremy's boots and the lower leg of his ski pants looked a little dirty, which in this dusty place wasn't unusual. And his pants were black, which showed up almost everything. "Uh, yeah," he answered, while my gaze continued to travel over him. "Found a drum of fuel out back. There wasn't much in it. It might last the night. But the phone…the lines have been cut."

His jacket was lighter, a background of white with a gray-and-black repeating pattern over the top. Then what he'd said registered and I did a double take. *"Cut?"* Vandals or something worse? I hurriedly checked my cell to find no service. A quick dial still wouldn't connect me to 911. If that avalanche had taken out the tower, it clearly wasn't fixed yet. "Phone's use, ah…less." I frowned as I pocketed my phone, eyes narrowing at Jeremy's jacket. Gray and black weren't the only other colors that mixed with the white. "What's that on your jacket?"

When Jeremy's hand came up my heart leaped beneath my ribs. Red. His palm was *red.* "It's blood."

Already at the window, there was nowhere to back up to. Being knocked out. Jeremy. The pieces made a terrifying puzzle. "It was *you?*"

Jeremy walked closer. "What was me?" He looked confused, which only increased as I went to dart sideways to skirt past him. But the ceiling dipped, and as I crouched, he struck out and caught my arm. "Cas, wait."

"Let me go!" I tugged and tugged, and then I

fell. He'd done as I'd asked and was now standing over me with a perplexed look.

Jeremy knelt down to my level, the wooden boards below him creaking. "Did something happen to Stan? Is that why you're so freaked out?"

"Stan? What do you mean *happen to him?*" I heard his nose cracking in my mind as if I'd gone back in time and swung my fist again. Some of the blood on me was his. I'd broken his nose. "Oh, I…" I was letting my mind run crazy. My delusions, conscious or not, were not coming true. They weren't real. Trapped out here with no way through the snow, there was no one coming and no one going. I had to have blacked out. It was the only rational explanation. But that still didn't explain the amount of blood—still somewhat glossy and wet— on Jeremy's hand that hung over his propped knee. Stan's injury must have been worse than it had looked. Jeremy had helped stem the bleeding? "Is that Stan's blood?"

Jeremy's expression darkened. His lips thinned into a grim line. "I think it could be."

I looked to the open trapdoor, not hearing a sound, then back at him. "What do you mean *think? Where is everyone?*"

Jeremy shook his head. "The others are downstairs. I've been searching."

My heartbeat pounded in my ears. "For what?"

"Stan's missing."

~

I shadowed Jeremy down the attic ladder, keeping close but not too close. Something was bothering me even more than my scary delusions and my run-in with Stan. On one hand, being near Jeremy made me feel safe and like I wasn't alone. The tense smile he sent over his shoulder as he reached the ground still managed to relax me.

He held his hand out to help me off the lowest rung that was higher than expected from the scuffed floorboards. I hesitated, staring at the drying blood across his palm.

On the other hand, his appearance in the attic after I'd blacked out—*been knocked out*—as well as being a student from my own school and even being on the same transport to get to the lodge just seemed too convenient.

What if he wasn't who he said he was?

"Ah, here…" He swiped his hand across his pants, making the mostly dried blood smear and flake away. The lights down here were on, flashing so fast they were almost solid. He held out his hand again. "We really should find Stan."

I took his hand, watching his face for any change as I reached the ground. Then I pulled free and glanced around. "Where's Katherine?"

Jeremy seemed to notice my stance and frowned. "With Brad in that downstairs bedroom. I left her with him to get some rest so I could come to find you both." He looked over his shoulder at the lit hallway and toward the stairs. "So far I've only found you. And since you fell up there…" His blue eyes traveled up the ladder. "I am assuming the blood puddle downstairs isn't yours?"

Puddle? I gulped with a shake of my head and began walking. The way Stan had looked at me and grabbed me vaulted through my body as the memory flashed like lightning in my mind. "No. It's…it's not mine—"

Jeremy hooked my arm and I jerked back to a standstill, my heart drumming and eyes wide. The look on his face was concerned, not wanting. "Cas, what happened up there?"

His eyes searched my face as if wanting an answer he already expected. But he couldn't know what Stan had done, or that I had overreacted and broken the guy's nose for coming on to me. *Could that puddle Jeremy had found been from that?* Neither answer would alleviate the panic that was fast rising inside of me. What if the puddle was larger than a broken nose could explain? I needed to see the evidence to calm my thoughts that were beginning to race with nightmarish possibility. And after that, we needed to find the guy…if he was still here.

"It doesn't matter." I tugged my arm free of Jeremy's hold. "We just need to find Stan. Where did you say you found the puddle?"

Jeremy's eyes narrowed but he tipped his head. "Follow me."

Back down the creaking stairs, we didn't continue toward the front room where the fire continued to crackle or to the mess hall that was adjacent from this wide hallway. Instead, we turned the other way, bypassing the storage area below the stairs and continuing further back. Light became scarce as we rounded a corner to the left and even more so as we swung right and then right again. The majority of light bulbs down here were burnt out. A few were smashed—like someone had taken to them with a bat. The few that did work flashed like they were on a strobe sensor, illuminating an old toy here or there—train, rag doll—and all the dirty scrapes along the cobweb-laced walls. We passed a few closed doors along the way and opened them to peek inside. Each housed areas that were blanketed in more dust and cobwebs. Furniture was covered by pale sheets. The undisturbed dust build-up across the floors proved no one was inside any of them.

Stan wasn't inside any of them, and he never had been.

Finally we reached another bend. One way led to a dead end, and the other down another hallway. In the darkness, where only faint light grew around the bend up ahead, I saw the dark patch even before Jeremy pointed. "There," he said.

My stomach dropped as I inched closer and

closer. When I knelt down, my hand came up to cover my mouth. The blood puddle had clearly been disturbed. Jeremy's smearing hand was an obvious culprit, but that didn't seem to be all. There was a smear to the other side. *As if a body had been dragged.*

I shuddered then shook off the image that branded across my mind. We weren't in my nightmares; we were awake. I recalled what Doc Bethany had said. *"The things you dream are not real, they are only figments of your traumatized mind trying to process the tragedy of your parents' deaths."* Even discounting my overactive imagination, I couldn't ignore the reality. The puddle was a decent size. It spanned longer than my hand and outstretched fingers. "Can a bloody nose—"

A loud creak brought my head up lightning fast. The sound had come from further down the hall we hadn't checked yet.

"It might be Stan. C'mon."

"Jeremy, wait…" He was already moving, and I got up quick to jog after him. I didn't want to be left behind in the flickering, creepy dark, and I didn't want Jeremy off on his own either. Despite my confusion, I suddenly felt an unexpected need to protect him. "Wait up!"

Around another bend, Jeremy pulled up short and I bumped into him as I failed to stop in time. I was about to ask why he'd stopped so suddenly, but as frigid air swept past me, I didn't need to. The view as I stepped beside him revealed the rest.

The front door—the same one we entered this unnerving place through as a group—was wide open. A mess of white powdery snow littered the floorboards. Beyond the door, holes were visible in the snow, each one oblong in shape and deep.

"Footprints," Jeremy said on an exhale.

Together we walked closer until we were only a step away from outside. Icy snow blew in, hitting our faces. But I took no notice of the cold that was swiftly returning to my warmed body. Because outside…drops of blood marked a path away from the house alongside the footprints.

"Why the hell would he go outside?"

I knew the answer as Stan's angered words spat in my subconscious. *The hell with the lot of you. I'm getting out of this shithole. I never signed up for any of this shit.*

I turned away, leaning my back into the open door. The blood had to be from my assault. Now that the scene set the story, there was no other rational explanation. "It's my fault." I blinked and almost felt Stan's mouth come down on mine again, slanted, parted. My insides clenched and I swallowed, remembering the ashtray taste of his mouth. "I…he…."

Now looking intently at me, Jeremy reached out to touch my elbow. "He what? Cas, what happened?"

I shook the images and Stan's voice away. If the guy died out there, I knew it would be my fault. Like Jill's death had been. I hadn't been wrong to reject him, but had I needed to do it so aggressively? "I…I hit Stan. I'm pretty sure I busted his nose."

"So that's where the blood came from." Jeremy's eyes glazed as if he were piecing things together. Then his brows drew inward and he looked up. "What did he do to you?"

Surprised that he wasn't judging me for my attack, I took a moment to answer. "Ah, he…" I glanced down and to the side. "I overreacted. I said no, but he didn't listen. I should have said it again. Louder. I should—"

Chilled fingers grazed my jaw, tilting my head up. "Cas, you can tell me. *What did he do?*"

I gulped, imagining it all again, feeling his warm and rough lips on mine as he clutched my jaw. "He grabbed me and kissed me. And I hit him. Stan stormed off. He said he was leaving." Harder snow fell outside and I shuddered to think of Stan out there braving the downpour. "I guess he did."

TWENTY-ONE

A male's sudden scream cut the air. Jeremy and I spun away from the arctic chill blowing through the door. Tensed to run, expecting to find Stan, I stalled as Jeremy's warm hand settled over my arm.

"It's not Stan."

Before I could question how he knew that, Katherine's head poked out through the last door we'd rushed by to reach the front entry. A tense smiled pulled at one side of her mouth. "Brad's not doing great. I need alcohol. That bone's punctured the skin quite badly along his shin. Since we could be stuck here a while, I'm going to need help straightening it, but first it needs cleaning."

"You know how to straighten it?" My stomach clenched at the thought of watching or even helping. To hear the cracking as the bone was forced back into its correct place...

"I studied to become a nurse after, well..." She sighed with a shake of her head, leaving me to wonder why she was hesitant to mention her social working days. "Anyway, the sooner this is done, the better it'll be for him."

"Yeah right!" Brad's deep voice called with mock strength, the strain visible in his shaky tone. "You just wanna torture me some more. Isn't it bad enough I'm stuck—"

Katherine stepped into the hallway and shut the door, cutting off Brad's rant.

Jeremy nodded toward the opening to the communal area. "I saw some old gin bottles in the back of the kitchen when I went to fill the generator. There were some dish towels too." When his head swung back, his mouth opened, but Katherine spoke first.

"Why's the door wide open? Do you want us all to catch our deaths?"

She looked at me as if I had to have been the stupid one to let the accumulating fire warmth get swept away. In retrospect, the fresh chill in the air had been a chain reaction that linked all the way back to my actions. My assault on Stan. My tongue stumbled for words, "I didn't. I…it was…"

"Stan took off," Jeremy clarified as a fresh burst of frigid air blew icy snow across our backs. His look my way as he released my arm with a squeeze was a promise that he wasn't about to reveal everything that had gone down or my involvement. "But I'm going to see if I can bring him back. He won't have gotten far—"

"You can't go out there," I cut him off as I gripped his arms. After my latest blackout, that ominous blood puddle, not to mention the creepy and disappearing message I'd imagined—*or not*—my paranoia was skyrocketing. On top of all of that, Jeremy had already risked his life to try to save Jill. He'd almost drowned. The sudden thought of him out there alone terrified me. If anything happened to him; if he didn't come back… "What if you get lost? What if you fall through the ice? Or get buried? Or—"

"I'll be fine. *I promise*." His smile lit warmth inside of me like a gentle flame burning brighter and brighter. My panic was quashed by a subtle calm. "I won't go far. And I won't be long. If he's long gone, I'll come back. I'm not leaving you…" He blinked and shook his head, then looked back up the hall—to Katherine. "I'm not leaving either of you. I'll be back soon."

As he zipped his jacket higher and donned his hood, I hugged my arms around myself. In those few moments, I'd forgotten we weren't the only two people here. I forced myself to glance away as he stepped outside, the falling blanket of white almost obscuring him beyond sight. "Ah, I'll go find the alcohol." I didn't want to be around Katherine or Brad right now. Feeling confusion at my interaction and the sensations I'd just felt with Jeremy, I needed some time alone.

"Head past the fire and through the mess hall beyond the other hallway," Katherine said with a nod and a kind smile. "The kitchen is right past that room."

I turned away as Katherine returned to the room, and blankly walked into the communal area. Warmth grew around me as shadows danced across the floor and walls from the fire. Maybe I did know Jeremy. Again I wondered if he'd somehow been part of my life before the *accident*. My heart heaved, but I kept my focus from thinking of the family I'd lost. According to him, we went to the same school. Maybe we'd been friends. Maybe... I gulped. Maybe we'd dated?

I shook my head as I passed through the other hallway with the stairs, heading for the mess hall Katherine had directed me to.

No. We couldn't have dated. Memory problems or not, I'd remember that. If he'd been part of my life, I'd remember *him*. With his personality, charisma, and good looks, there's no way I wouldn't—

I jerked to a sudden stop, my gaze turning from dazed to razor sharp.

I wasn't alone.

I was halfway across the mess hall, passing behind two long tables with miss-matched seats. The mirror on the wall beside the door I was heading for reflected the door I'd just come through. The open door behind me that wasn't empty. A shadow was backlit by the flickering light out in the hallway. The form was clear. In raggedy jeans with holes in the knees and a torn sweater, and with roughly chopped, short dark hair was…a child. A girl?

"Hey!" I spun toward them as the kid took off through the door. "Hey, stop!" My boots slapped the floorboards as I took chase.

My mind raced. *Real? Unreal?* How could a kid be in this desolate place?

I cut left as I burst from the mess hall. Between sparks of erratic light, I saw the child's bare feet and dirty jeans clear the top steps as I ran up after them. How had she moved so fast? "Wait. I won't hurt you. I just want to talk to you!"

When I reached the top, the upper level was deathly quiet, aside from my panting and the buzz of faulty lights. No pattering of small bare feet. No slammed doors or even slowly closing and creaking ones. But I knew where the child had gone. Still down from my exploration up there, the ladder from the attic was extended.

She was up there. I was sure of it.

Moving with quiet steps, I mounted the lower rungs and began to climb, barely feeling the wounds and splinters in my hands and fingers anymore. With fear and curiosity peaking, the run had jacked my heart rate sky high, and the higher I got the louder it thumped. I could hear the thump in my ears and feel the heavy thuds in my chest as my heart bashed against my ribs.

I was following a kid. Just a kid.

But the higher I got, the more I started to lose it. My palms were sweating, threatening to lose their hold on each rung as I climbed higher and higher. I was scared…like I had been as I stared up at that hooded face over me after the car crash.

I shook my head to throw off the sensation that shot through my veins like caustic acid. I felt like I was about to break. Because of a kid? A little girl?

Or because I suspected what I'd seen wasn't real?

If I was imagining things, imagining more than the hooded nemesis from my nightmares, was I finally going off the deep end? Was I at the point of no return?

There was only one way to find out.

Forcing my hands to shift as they trembled, I lay my fingertips on the opening and stepped up. Higher, higher.

The flickering light above me blacked out. Eerie moonlight replaced the yellow flashes.

I scanned the attic as I slowly crept through the trapdoor. Same empty space, same dirty bed…same chilling pictures. And same window to glimpse down to the frozen lake. But not everything was the same. I felt it as a gentle sweep of air fanned the sweat covering my face. The window was…wide open.

Real. *Not crazy.*

Without forethought, I ran, one boot smacking the floor after the other. Getting closer. Closer—

The tip of my boot hit something—that damn nail—and I went sprawling, sharp pain returning to my hands as I broke my fall to save my face.

A loud bang wrenched my head up before I could scurry upright. The window was shut, slammed closed. I jumped to my feet as fast as I could, my palms and one knee aching from hitting the ground as I ran. And then I was there, a cut along my finger bursting open with a flood of red as I tugged on the window. It wouldn't budge. "What the—"

The lights returned without warning, blinking like never-ending flash photography. The reflection of something bright and messy behind me made my heart skip a beat. But it wasn't a person. Not this time.

I spun around and stared, seeing it every time that one light bulb illuminated, unaware that I was stepping slowly closer and closer. My knees gave out, and I fell to them, head still raised and eyes refusing to look away. Across the back wall where all those drawings no longer were was a message— smeared in fresh blood.

Help.

I froze as one of my senses heightened. The hair on the back of my neck prickled. Inside my open hand that was damp with warm, wet blood I felt something...a smaller hand clasping my own.

My jaw fell open; no sound came out. I wanted to move, to scream, but I was frozen stiff. Oh no. Not now. My head heated up as that small hand gripped tighter. My eyes began to roll back in their sockets.

A gentle voice whispered in my ear, young and determined. "Sleep now, Cassidy. I will protect you from the horror. At least for as long as I can."

TWENTY-TWO

KASEY

Standing beneath the light bulb I'd untwisted to dull its erratic light, I watched from the shadows. Two down already, I was itching to add number three to my list. Or should I say, to strike it—them—from my list. Knowing my next target made my anticipation grow. This one deserved everything I was about to dish out. In all the years that had passed, who they were hadn't changed.

That woman, Katherine, stepped out of the room near the front entry. She looked calm and on task, though something behind her eyes hinted at deeper thoughts. "When I find the others, I'll get that gin and come back."

"Bring the whole bottle back!" that mouthy guy demanded through the door. "And hurry up. My leg aches like a bitch!"

Katherine's expression turned from

contemplative to a scowl. She didn't respond as she strode toward the front door and opened it to peer outside. But she wouldn't see Jeremy. She couldn't. With a sigh, she closed the cold air back out and continued on her way through the room with the crackling fire.

I removed myself from the shadows while Bradley's voice and the words he'd used grated on me to the point that I felt like punching the wall. I didn't though. I kept my anger inside as my memories of that day so long ago resurfaced. She'd been helpless. And he'd been an animal. Something that was in need of being put down. Back then I'd been weak. A child. But not anymore.

Peering in, I saw the room draped in off-white sheets that covered dark wooden furniture. An exposed chaise was positioned off to the side against a wall of peeling wallpaper. The master suite. A room I'd never stepped foot inside…until now. I walked into the room, not bothering to sneak in, one arm folded behind my back.

"That was quick—" Brad's words cut off as his head came up, seeing me from the large central bed he laid back in. "Oh, it's you. Did you…?"

He trailed off as I held my finger up to my lips. "Shhh." I watched him as he looked around and past me like he expected someone else to arrive. Then he frowned at me, probably seeing the glint in my eyes or my smile as I shut the door behind me. My smile *pulled wider as I reached the foot of the bed, my boots nudging the decaying rug below.*

"What's going on?" Brad demanded and went to shift, sitting up with a grunt to throw his good leg over the edge as if he sensed he needed to get away. The other was well and truly broken, I saw as the blanket over the damage shifted. There was a glint of bone through all the messy red and pale, jagged skin. "What are you—"

I swung my arm out from behind my back and Brad flinched. My insides jumped with glee at his shock.

He registered what I held and his rising worry fled. "'Bout fucking time." He reached for the almost full bottle of gin I gripped the neck to. "Hand it—"

I swung, smashing the bottle into his temple. It exploded in a rain of clear liquid and shards of glass. Brad fell back on the bed, dazed but not quite out of it. My adrenaline skyrocketed with anticipation and I jumped on top of him. I snatched the pillow out from under his head and planted it over his face, pressing down with force.

Brad reacted then, arms flailing, fingers scratching, and legs shifting—even the broken one— trying to kick me off.

I wasn't going anywhere. I'd waited all these years for this. I'd planned. I'd stalked.

This was my time.

When his muscle function lagged from lack of oxygen minutes later, I spoke into the pillow as I held it down. "Payback's a bitch, but you sooo deserve it. And I'm going to make every second count."

His arms batted with barely any oomph, missing me completely now, tipped with blood from the scratches he'd scored early on. I removed the pillow as those once strong and restraining hands fell off the side of the bed. But the fun wasn't over with yet. Not by a long shot.

"Wakey, wakey, bitch." I backhanded his face.

Brad's eyes flung open, the whites marked with red veins. Fear encompassed his face as he gasped for breath. "Why? Why are you doing this?" He shook his head, but I didn't miss the way his hands clenched into fists.

I tisked my tongue. "Not yet."

The pillow came down as his fist cranked up. He'd hope for more than he had as he hit nothing but air, the lack of oxygen in his body failing his bicep. Like it had when she'd been stuck on that bed, not frozen in horror alone, but in the torture of being air deprived. His legs trembled now as I held the pillow in place, his hands barely batted my arms before falling limp.

I removed the air block again and smiled down at him. "What's the matter, Connor? Don't like being on the receiving end of your fun games?"

His lids blinked rapidly, then spread wide. "Who the hell are you? How do you know my—"

"Uh, uh, uh." The pillow came down again as I added, "That would be cheating." He wasn't fighting back anymore, he couldn't. Like she couldn't. I breathed in deep, imagining what his lungs felt like, imagining the burn he must be experiencing. I let him get a bit more air. "Guess who I am and...I'll let you go. Say my name, bitch.*"*

Brad's eyes widened, showing off the reddening of his whites. "No." His head shook frantically. His hands trembled, fingers clutching the dusty sheet beneath him. "It can't be."

"Oh, can't it?"

I covered his face again and drilled my boot down into his bloody shin. He screamed, the sound swallowed by musky filling as warmth penetrated the barrier. I shifted on top of him and unbuckled his pants. Brad, Connor—it didn't matter—thrashed with renewed force, knowing, or at least suspecting, what was to come. Something worse than being unconscious.

A twinge hit my stomach at what I had planned for him—but then I saw a flash of how she'd looked on that messed-up bed with him between her legs. Bare butt and barely consciousness as he went to trust forward.

Brad's thrashing died suddenly. He'd blacked out. Like she never had that day.

I threw the pillow aside and laid into the guy with my fists, bashing into his face over and over. Crimson sprayed up but his blood-red eyes only flared open as I tunneled a thumb into the tear in his leg, making him suddenly gasp for air.

I cold clocked him.

A crunch rang out as his cheek cracked beneath my fist that burned with heat at the connection. Worth it.

He teetered between here and out of it. So I worked fast, whipping a knife from my waistband. I kept my eyes on his face, on his slowly rising and falling lids as I nicked various—vital—spots along his body, cutting his long-sleeved top and pants as I went. In his almost unconscious state, he barely jerked at the cuts as his vibrant blood flowed out. The blood loss would kill him eventually, but not before…

I tugged his pants and boxer briefs down and took hold of his manhood without looking down.

Brad's head shot up at the sensation of my strong grip, and horror stripped the haze from his eyes. He saw the knife I held in one hand, and his flaccid dick that I gripped in the other. He knew what was coming. "No," he croaked. He tried to move, and gulped when he couldn't, seeing the blood leaking from his shoulders and upper thighs—where I'd cut the nerves to take his mobility. "No, please. God no. I'm sorry. I'm sorry. I'm—"

His mouth gaped as I cut into the base of his dick, but no scream came out. He was hanging between awake and out cold, lids heavy and head lolling side to side. The blood loss was creeping in fast. A quick shift back and forth, back and forth, and the appendage came away. I crawled up his body and shoved it into his mouth, making his eyes widen as a muffled cry finally escaped.

Then his eyes froze open, the whites blood red. The tension throughout his body vanished.

I climbed off of him and felt nothing. No remorse. No delight. Just nothing.

In a dead voice I said quietly, "You didn't say my name."

~

Almost Nine Years Ago

I backed away from the square window in my room as I watched Father trek footprints away from the house across the snow. With his shotgun swinging in his hand, I knew where he was going. And how long he'd be gone. Buck hunting with the sun low in the blue sky and heading down to the snowy trees. If I was lucky, I would have an hour or even more out of the attic to play before he came back. An hour to be just one of the other kids.

Moving faster now, I reached the trapdoor and heard a click and then the sound of sliding metal.

215

The padlock was removed. Heaving the door up, I saw the top of her head with her curly black hair as she disappeared back down the stairs. Since I'd been good lately, Mother had been letting me have little outings when Father was away. After explaining my sometimes freedom—her special gift to me—she hadn't spoken about it again. Her last words had been, "If you push this too far it won't be me who takes the blame."

I never wanted her to get in trouble, so I nodded to show I understood—and even got a quick hug with her that first time. My first hug from her in so long. The last one had been on my tenth birthday, over a year ago. Remembering the way she'd held me this time for those few seconds made my arms and chest feel warm now.

Hitting the ground, I ran down the hallway, heading for the second boys' bedroom. The one C.J. slept in. I hoped he was there now. It was better if he was. Other sounds drifted up from downstairs of kids laughing and moving around, playing. I didn't want to have to go and find him down there. None of those kids liked me. They always looked at me like they knew I didn't belong. Like I was different. An outcast.

Grabbing the doorjamb, I swung into the room but stopped just as fast. The room was empty, only metal-framed beds and messed-up blankets along with a few toys: a truck, a ball, and other boy things.

I sighed and turned to leave. Now I'd have to go down—

"This is boys' territory," Connor said as I bumped into him. His hazel eyes glaring down at me through dark brown hair sent panic through me. I stepped back, but he followed after me. "You don't belong here. You don't belong anywhere."

"I know. I..." I met the railing of a bed—his bed—and my bottom hit the mattress. My head shook quickly. "I was just looking for C.J." I tried to get up but Connor pushed me back down. "I was leaving."

"Not anymore." One corner of his mouth lifted into a smile and I shivered, feeling a sudden prickly chill. "You're not going anywhere."

Knowing I needed to get out, knowing what he planned to do—because I wasn't a little kid anymore, and because this wasn't the first time—I leaped up, bare feet smacking the ground as I darted around him. Connor caught my arm, his strong hand hurting me as he tugged me back. I pulled and pulled but he was stronger than me. He was older, by at least a year or two. He was a teenager now. "Connor, please. Don't. Please. Let me go!"

"I will." His smile stretched wider as a few other boys came into the room. Standing inside, they watched and folded their arms over their chests. No one moved to help, and I didn't beg them to. One boy stood watch just outside the room—ready to call out if my mom came upstairs. Connor's eyes shifted from

217

my eyes to my mouth, then down to my chest. Being eleven years old there was nothing really to see, but his eyes got brighter anyway. "I will let you go...when I'm done with you."

He shoved me back on the bed and I cried out. Connor muffled the scream, covering my mouth with his sweaty hand. And then he was on top of me. His other hand grabbed my throat. "Is this how your daddy does it? Huh?" He shoved his hips between my legs and pushed up. I could feel hardness—his penis—pressed into my ratty jeans. "Well, is it?"

His choking hand let go, and as I sucked air, he yanked down my top to touch what my father had called 'little buds'. "Mom! C.J. hel—"

Heat exploded across my face with a shock of pain. Connor had slapped me. "Shut up, little slut. Take it like you always—"

"Help me!" I screamed, my jaw hot with pain. "Hel—" A pillow landed over my face and pressed down tight. I thrashed on the bed, head shaking side to side as I screamed to get air. But I could barely move.

I went still below Connor as he kept on touching my chest. My T-shirt ripped with how rough he was, but I didn't fight back. I'd been here like this—with him—before. And I'd lived through it. Concentrating on sucking air through the thick pillow that stunk of dirty hair, I tried to turn off what I felt. Tried not to feel Connor's wet mouth slobber over my neck, and lower, my— Don't think it. Don't feel it, *I told myself, but it didn't help. Every wet and rough touch was too real. The rubbing, the licking, the sucking.*

My head became light then and my grip on the pillow's edges came loose. My hands fell to the bed.

"Oh no, you don't." The pillow lifted long enough for me to see Connor's smiling mouth and wet chin. "You're going to enjoy this as much as you do with your daddy. Say my name, little bitch."

"I hate you." I meant to spit the words at him, but without enough air and with my lungs burning, the words were soft and raspy. "I'm going to—"

The pillow came down again, and I sucked in as much air as I could before there was no more. My need to get free came back suddenly, and I kicked and scratched. Connor cursed. I'd gotten his arm, and knowing I'd made him hurt made me fight even more.

His body pressed down harder into mine, squashing me. Something, maybe his arm, came over the pillow and pressed it down hard. There was no air anymore, only oily yuck. I couldn't breathe.

But I could still feel.

His hand shoved between our bodies, moving, pulling. My jeans were undone and tugged over and over until cool air hit my bottom. My pants were down now, all the way to my ankles. So were my panties. Connor was back between my legs. His body and my jeans shoved my trapped feet back towards my bottom as he pressed closer to me.

Even though I couldn't breathe, I fought harder. My body shook, I felt funny, stars bursting behind my closed eyes. His skin—his penis—touched me, hard and jabbing. I bucked harder, but then I couldn't anymore as his hand touched me down there. Stabbing fingers poked inside. My body went stiff then let go as my head spun. The stars faded to endless black.

Connor spoke. The words were muffled but sounded like, "Good little slut."

His hips wriggled in-between my legs again and I felt something bigger rub on me as his fingers came away. Now I prayed to pass out. I didn't want to feel this. To remember this. He'd never gone this far before. But he wasn't stopping now. And I was still awake. I wanted to die.

I felt horror as sharp pain ripped into me. It swarmed out from between my legs. I bit my lip, feeling like I was being torn in half, feeling like—

A moving ruckus sounded and Connor was ripped off of me. The pillow came free as I curled to the side, gasping for air. Light from the ceiling flooded in and attacked my eyes, making everything look watery as I blinked my tears away.

"You rotten pig. How dare you." The look in C.J.'s bright blue eyes was scary as he punched Connor in the gut.

Connor folded over, coughing for air. The other

boys were already gone, even the one out in the hall.

"You're gonna pay for that." Connor spat as he went to stand straight, but C.J. grabbed his head and smashed his knee up into the boy's angry face. Connor stumbled but caught onto a bed frame. He spat blood, the look across his face pure hatred. "Fine. Have your go with her. She likes it, you know. She—"

Connor's words cut off as C.J. stomped forward. Connor's hands came up quick and he sidestepped to the door, giving me one last horrible grin before running away down the hallway.

C.J. breathed in slowly, closing his eyes as he breathed out. Without looking at my naked legs and bottom half, he turned to me and came over. Picking up a blanket from the floor, he slid it over me and helped me to sit up, wrapping the cover all the way around me. He pulled me close and I laid my head on his chest. "Are you okay, Kasey? I mean, I know you're not. I—I'm sorry I wasn't here to stop him. I should have…"

"I don't want to talk about it." I felt the warmth of fresh tears behind my eyes, but no more came out. Locking what had just happened away with all my punishments from Father, a numbness let me breathe and not feel the throbbing or stinging below as much. "I'm okay. I am."

C.J. nodded. "You're the boss."

After that, we just sat there, quiet, with C.J.'s

arm around me. I didn't shake or cry anymore. This was different compared to the other times, even with my father. It felt like I could pretend that what had happened hadn't really been me. Like it was just a bad movie, something nightmares were made of. Like one day, I might just wake up and this would all have been a horrible dream. I held on to that idea, to that ... hope.

What other choice did I have?

TWENTY-THREE

Footsteps brought me out of a blissful haze of pure nothingness. No nightmares, no lingering flashes of disturbing images. I blinked lazily, but then the shrinking darkness brought back the faulty jarring light. I lurched upright fast, searching the intermittent shadows as my mind reconciled the direction of the sound. But everything was quiet. No footsteps. No…

My head snapped up with a sudden rush of memory and I staggered to my feet. The creepy pictures, the ones that had disappeared to reveal that bloody cry for help, were back in place. I took a step closer, then another. The trapdoor was shut—I hadn't closed it—but that wasn't what I couldn't look away from. Up where all the black and red strokes of crayon that covered the angry eyes, stick figures crying fat tears, and hulking monsters, something was visible between the close-placed sheets.

Red.

I tore one picture down, then another and another. The red grew and grew with each removed layer until the patchy message, scrubbed away but not completely gone, was unmistakable amongst the remaining drawings. *Help.* I frowned as I touched the mold-stained wall. The message hadn't been written in blood. It had been scribbled in red crayon.

I thought of the little girl again with her hacked hair and bright eyes. She'd left this message and led me here.

Sudden footsteps jolted me back. They were down below, and they were heading this way, moving at speed. *Oh, shit!* The steps faltered, then the tone changed. Someone was coming up the ladder, creeping slowly.

The girl's voice I'd heard whispered through my mind. *Sleep now, Cassidy. I will protect you from the horror. At least for as long as I can.* Real? Unreal? Was something coming for me now? Something bad? Something to fear?

I turned and ran for the window. An indescribable fear had its hooks in me. I had to get out. I'd break the window if I had to.

A crack burst up and ricocheted off the trapping walls and I fell. I caught myself before I face-planted, wrists crying out as I broke my fall. The floorboard beneath me had split in two, and my boot was stuck. Shifting to my backside, the sounds of climbing were now gone as I tugged. There was a creak as I heaved and then wood sprayed up and I fell back.

Breathing hard, I listened for someone's incoming. When I heard nothing, I frowned at the damage—at the small secret space my boot had unearthed beneath the floorboards. A place to hide something you didn't want to be found.

Scrambling forward I reached in and pulled it out. A book that was old and worn with dog-eared edges and dirty pages. The front cover was blank, but the inside wasn't. In messy handwriting was a name. *Kasey Whitmore.*

This was a diary. In the name of the person who owned this place. The same name I thought I'd seen on the bus window and had heard in my head as a speaker announcement when I imagined that newspaper.

A creak brought my head up. Someone was out there waiting on the ladder. They'd been listening? Pulling my knees to my chest, I was about to—I don't know what. Scream. Run. My first attempt had gone so well.

A knock-knock came and I froze. Then the trapdoor flung open with a reverberating clap as it hit the floorboards.

I clutched the diary to my chest and threw a hand out to jump up.

But then someone's head poked up through the

opening. Panic receded from me in a wave and I exhaled. "Jeremy."

"Here you are." He climbed all the way up, lips pursed and eyes troubled. "I was calling. Didn't you hear me?"

"Ah…." All I'd heard were those footsteps. I pushed upright, my grip on the diary tight. "I ah…what's wrong?"

Jeremy shook his head as he came closer. "Stan must be long gone. I couldn't even find tracks further out. The snow's covered them, I guess. I told Katherine on my way in. She's sourcing food for everyone." He frowned, noticing the torn-down pictures that littered the stained floor and the remnants of the crayon message, which was illegible—I now realized—if you hadn't seen what I'd seen. When he looked back at me with a sigh, his gaze dropped, noticing the broken floorboard and then what I clutched in one hand. "What is that?"

Glad he wasn't questioning why I'd ripped those drawings down—how could I explain that?—I dropped back onto the dirty bed. Puffs of dust billowed up around me, making my throat scratchy. I coughed. "A diary. I think it's from the g…ah, kid who used to live up here."

I shivered at the memory of that voice and the glimpse of her I'd seen in that mirror before chasing her up the stairs. Stealing a glance at the long-gone creepy message begging for help gave my shiver a longer life to attack my spine. Looking away and to the side, there were no small handprints on the windowsill that had been opened and was now shut. Had anything I'd seen and heard been real? Was I seeing a ghost…or just a figment of my damaged imagination? Was I making more out of those red remnants on the wall? The more I stole glances at them now, the less clear it was that they'd ever spelled out that visual plea for help.

"I haven't read it yet," I added as an afterthought.

Jeremy looked troubled as he eyed the old book with its cracked and curling front cover. "Maybe we should just go and get some food with Katherine."

I didn't ask what was behind his expression. I didn't get up to leave either. A sensation inside of me was compelling me to crack the cover again, to read what was scrawled inside. I needed to understand what all of this meant, and what—if anything—it had to do with me. "Then I'll come soon." I folded the cover back and turned over the page with Kasey Whitmore written in fat, messy letters.

Jeremy didn't shift away from me, instead, he sighed again as he settled down beside me on the bed.

The writing started out bad, hard to read. Obviously from a child's hand, I made out what I could, piecing together the tale of someone that may never have been heard before. This child was scared and alone. Between entries that seemed to be messy English notes and math equations, she wrote about being bad, of doing things normal kids did, and then being in trouble for them. Her mother sent a smile or even allowed a hug every now and then, but for the most part, she was uninvolved. This kid yearned for comfort, and to feel like she belonged, but with each page her emotions grew more pained. Almost every entry, even from the start, ended with *Why does my father hate me?* He never spent time with her, aside from what she called *'my time to learn a lesson.'* He called her names and scolded her. He made her a prisoner up here for being bad. Each day she watched from the window and...

I glanced around to find a grate in one place where the wall met the ground.

"She watched them all. Never able to join in." Jeremy's words brought my head around. He was staring down at the page I'd been reading. Sadness encompassed his expression. "She was alone."

Something inside me made me want to comfort him, and before I could think about it, I shifted my free hand and covered his. When his hand upturned and he laced his fingers through mine, I didn't ask what he'd experienced in life that made him relate to this kid. Instead, I gave his hand a squeeze and turned the page. "She had a friend. A boy." I read about their time together, how he'd helped her sneak out, and how he was always there to back her up. To protect her. *"Even just a short while with C.J. made me forget how scared I was for Father's next lesson. He made me happy. He made me feel normal. With him I could smile for just a little while."* Tears stung my eyes as I read those few lines out loud.

"And the boy tried to help her." Jeremy's grip on my hand tightened, but he didn't look up at me as he spoke. He flipped the page, reading as I studied his pained expression. "Every time someone came that should have helped her, they turned a blind eye."

I blinked, surprised at the sadness in his voice and the speed that he'd read that new page. As I looked, it was all there in black and white. A social worker. A policeman. A teacher. No one stood up for her. They all left her there. One of the kids, a girl, had gotten her in trouble time and time again. And a boy named Connor, one of the orphans, did horrible things to her. Targeted her. Bullied her.

Jeremy turned another page, bringing my attention back to what was written. He sighed deeply. "And then her only friend left too. He left her alone."

I frowned down at the page, reading the despair and anger of the child who'd lost the only person that made them feel okay. The only person, a kid like her that she named C.J., who'd treated her with kindness and love.

Heat swamped my face as a tear fell. I turned

another page, needing to know what happened next. Needing to get a clue as to how this poor child died here. How she'd become the ghost I was seeing. It was the only explanation—even though it seemed completely crazy—that made any sense.

Sticking out of the spine were jagged paper edges. Someone had ripped a page or two out. I wondered why as the words beyond those lost pages blurred before my eyes. But the visual loss wasn't only because I was crying silent tears. "Oh no." *Not now. Not again.*

"Cassidy, what's—shit!"

Jeremy's panicked voice vanished as I toppled forward, face heading for the ground. My sight vanished before I hit—

And then I was somewhere else, somewhere dark and rank. Strapped to an erect board, my wrists and ankles were tied with rope. Despite the snow falling down outside a small dirty window, I was wearing a sundress. I tugged, but the bindings wouldn't give. Dreaming?

Horror seared through me as an older man stepped from a tunnel into this small shed-like space. Even though shadows concealed his features, the look on his face was full of disgust as his eyes raked over me. "You're never getting out of here, you little bastard. No one is left to save you now." He stalked toward me.

"Who are you? What do you—" I cried out as he

gripped my hair and pulled, wrenching my head up and making pain shoot through my neck. Then his mouth was on my own, hot and wet. It moved to my cheek, my neck… "No! Stop!" I squirmed as his body pressed into mine. *Wake up dammit! Wake up!* This was a dream—a nightmare. It wasn't real.

His hand speared between my thighs and traveled up, lifting my dress. Everything was too real, too realistic.

No longer sure I was dreaming, I bucked, tugging over and over at my restraints. "Get off me!"

He tore my panties, the material scraping my skin as it snapped. There was a sound of a buckle, and then his pants fell. "You're mine. I own you."

Not real? Real?

"Stop! No!" I thrashed, lost to anything but the fear that coiled through me. "No, no, no, no—" I screamed as he shoved himself into me. Heat seared where skin tore. Tears streamed down my face as he retracted them shoved in quick, repeating the thrust over and over and over…

As numbness overcame me, and my tears continued to fall, I felt an emptiness take over that allowed me to think, to distance myself from what was being done to me. This couldn't be real. There was no way. I'd been awake with Jeremy in the attic—reading that poor child's diary. Now I was here. *Being taught a lesson.* The thought was like a whisper in my mind as the pieces fell into place. Is this what the little girl had lived through? Had this been her life...before she died?

The jabbing penetrations stopped and wetness trickled down my leg as my ankles then my wrists were cut free. I fell to the dirt and what felt like a messed-up sheet as the man spat down at me, "I never should have let you live."

But he wasn't done with me yet.

Now so weak with my body quaking and my wrists and ankles stinging from rope burn, I took the pain and penetration as he clamped onto my hips. I didn't try to fight back anymore, even as my mind screamed at me to do just that. My sundress soon became a torn mess on the ground beneath me while hot tears fell, a never-ending tap from my burning eyes, until his curses of "fucking slut" ended with a groan and he stilled over the top of me.

Shoved away, I fell to the dirt, whimpering.

I heard a jangle as his pants were pulled up and his buckle refastened. Cold swept over my bared skin, chilling my sweat—and his that covered my legs and back. Dress torn to shreds, I was completely naked.

The man tugged me up then and dragged me down a tunnel. I gave in to what was happening, using my mind rather than letting the stumbling of my feet over sharp stones between dirt distract me. If I wasn't losing my mind, if this was a nightmare— delivered by that child—then there was something to be taken from this horror. There was something I was meant to find out…or do.

I just didn't have a clue what.

TWENTY-FOUR

I awoke with a start, ratcheting upright and gasping air. Dust puffed up around me and I coughed as I frantically scanned my surroundings. Flickering light, a dark window…and creepy drawings scattered over the floor. Still in the attic. I was sitting stiff as a board on the little girl's bed. Her diary was right beside me, open on the page I'd been reading.

My heart raced at the figure that registered to my other side, my entire body jolting as a male's hand reached for me. My heart stalled as sweat sprouted across my face, back, and chest. But then I saw through the panic and fear. I saw his worried face. Air left my lungs in a rush. *"Jeremy."*

He was kneeling on the other side of the bed, watching me. That sadness from earlier was still in his eyes, but now it sparkled with something more. "You lied to me. You weren't asleep earlier." His face scrunched with a deep frown. "What happened?"

The look in his eyes seemed to beg for trust. But I hardly knew him.

I shifted uncomfortably, a blanket of dirtiness settling over me with the memories that flashed alive in my mind every time the light blackened. When Jeremy said nothing more, waiting patiently— hopefully—I wondered, can I *trust* him? At the same time, I'd been out of it, completely vulnerable, and he'd stayed with me. Waited for me to come to. My earlier paranoia surrounding him after I'd seen Stan's blood on his hand now seemed silly.

I felt my lips moving and saying what I wasn't sure I should. "I have blackouts. They started after my parents'...*accident*. Sometimes everything is blank, but other times I get lost in nightmares, in horrific scenarios that feel so real."

"But they're not?" Jeremy's tone seemed open to any answer I might give, as if either answer were expected and would be accepted without any judgment.

I threw my legs over the bed's edge so my back was to him. I pressed my knees together as more of what I'd just envisioned flooded back. I almost felt that stabbing ache between my legs again. Almost felt the wet hard kisses and nips across my skin. I shuddered. Had that poor child from the diary really endured that? Could I really have seen that event from her past...or was my mind turning to jello? "Sometimes I don't know," I answered honestly.

"The things I dream are so vivid." So horrific. I shook the phantom pains away, looking toward the open trapdoor. "You stayed with me."

An emotion I couldn't gauge contorted his face as his eyes became distant. "You fell so suddenly, and then you wouldn't wake up. I was going to go and get Katherine, but…but I couldn't leave. And then you woke up."

Patting my hands down Jeremy's hoodie to my pants, I retrieved the orange bottle of pills Doctor Bethany had prescribed. The little white pills clinked as I shook the bottle. "These are supposed to help with the blackouts and the nightmares, but since…" I stopped myself before I could elaborate on my time locked away on suicide watch. I didn't want to go there, not now. Not with *him*. "Since I started taking them"—*ever since I left the hospital*, I added in my head—"the episodes have only gotten worse."

I stared at the little orange bottle with its white cap, spinning it around in my palm. I stopped. One edge of the label was peeling off. There was another label beneath?

"Ah…" I stood abruptly and dusted myself off, squeezing my fingers around the bottle. "I need a bathroom."

Jeremy studied me, taking a moment to say anything. "There are a few throughout the house. Closest one is just down the ladder and further along the hall."

The same one I'd found earlier with Stan. Feeling a shudder coming on, I steeled myself and held it back. With a nod, I walked to the trapdoor and climbed down.

Jeremy was right behind me and when we were both on the ground, I noticed something about him. He was shivering ever so slightly, but with his bluish lips, I guessed it had to do with his outdoor search for Stan. "You're cold. You should go warm up downstairs by the fire." I didn't really want to be alone after my latest episode—I'm not sure they were all delusions anymore—but I needed a moment to think and sort things out without being under the magnifying glass of someone's watching eyes.

And I really did need to use a bathroom.

Jeremy hesitated but then smiled. "Would be nice to close my eyes for a minute, too. I'm beat. But…I can wait for you. I wouldn't want you to, ah…blackout again or—"

"No. I'll be fine." I shook my head and stepped backward, bypassing the ladder. "I'll be down soon."

I turned away but jolted back when Jeremy touched my elbow. It was too soon after that horrific nightmare. "Sorry, I ah… If you're not back soon, I'll come looking for you. Okay?"

Instead of being a demand, he seemed to be asking if that was okay. Like he thought I might object. But the offer made sense, since now he knew I could pass out without warning.

I stepped back, breaking his contact. "Sure. But I'll be fine. I'll be back soon." Turning away from him, I walked past the communal bedrooms with their cracked-open doors. I breathed a sigh as I heard him turn and his boots creaking as he made his way down the stairs.

Now completely alone, the flashing light bulbs made the hall with its peeling wallpaper even creepier. I grasped the bathroom doorknob and rushed inside, shutting myself in. Which didn't help. The lighting was no better in here, illuminating the pale tile that was grimy and growing mold. Worse than that, as I made my way further into the room, I began to see things that weren't real. They couldn't be. But in every short flare of light, something was there.

I froze and my eyes peeled wide.

An adolescent boy shoving a younger and smaller, dark-haired girl down. A ring of boys centering the room and chanting out taunts. The same girl with torn clothes cowering in the corner. And then she was on the floor, the shower pouring down over her bruised and naked body.

I shut my eyes tight, feeling like my heart was about to explode. *Not real. Not real. Not real.*

The lights were still flashing when I peeled my lids open, but there was nothing else—no one else. Only me and my heavy breathing as I tried to get enough air.

Sweat spiked all over me and I rushed into the second cubicle with a door, making it just in time to retch up a slimy yellow stream of croissants à la acid. It was all too much: the ghost sighting, the rape, what I just imagined in this bathroom.

Wiping my mouth, I hurriedly relieved my bladder. Then I hesitantly peered out of the tiny cubicle. No kids. No visions of things that weren't real. As I stepped out of the claustrophobic confines of the cubicle, I found my terrified face in the old mirror that was losing its reflective film above the sink. "It's all in my head."

I backed up into the door as my blood pressure continued to lower, my arms dropping to my sides to feel...the bottle. I pulled it from my pocket. Like I'd noticed in the attic, the sticker was peeling, the one with Doctor Bethany's name signed on the label along with my name, the drug, and the dose. I gripped the edge and peeled it back gently, revealing a mirroring sticker from the same hospital. This one was signed by my doctor, but the prescribed drug was different and the name—my name—wasn't printed on the label. No one's name was. Whatever had been printed on the label had been scratched off with something sharp.

But I swear I could just make out a capital K. I gulped.

K for Kasey.

A giggle echoed from right outside the

bathroom. A wave of goosebumps swarmed over my skin like nails down a chalkboard. "Kasey?"

Whipping the door open, I stalled as I glimpsed down the hallway with its eerie light show. There she was in her dirty, torn jeans, sprinting to the banister to race down the stairs. I gasped at what my mind reconciled. Her feet were bare…and not even a smudge was left on the dusty floor in her wake. *Ghost.*

A shock of mobility rushed back to me that I couldn't refuse. "Hey, wait!" I took chase and pelted for the stairs, seeing her messy dark hair as she swiveled around the first post on the ground floor and swung left to scamper toward the back labyrinth of halls.

The recognition that I was actually following a *ghost* slowed my chase, and I took the steps down more quietly but two at a time. When I reached the ground her shadow beyond the flickering opening to the back hallways made my insides squirm. My tongue tied in my throat and all I could do was raise a halting hand.

The girl turned and took off.

"Dammit."

Picking up the pace, I followed her. The narrow surroundings were darker here with more lights blown than illuminated and the air was thick. Passing closed doors and only a few open ones that revealed rooms of cloth-covered furniture, I turned the bend. The intermittent flickers that remained darker for longer than they lit up messed with my eyes. But she wasn't there. No one was.

Breathing hard, I pulled my phone from my pocket and used the spotlight. My jaw fell. Leading a path across the bisecting hallway ahead was a messy and smeared trail of blood. It was glossy and red. It was fresh.

"Oh, dear God."

A *thunk* further up forced my shaking legs to walk on. Staring only at the smears as if I expected them to disappear at any second, my heart was thudding so hard when I reached the end of the hallway that I thought it might explode. I was back at that same spot where that puddle of blood had been. *Stan's blood.* It was gone now, well almost. So much more smeared than earlier, now it really did look as if something or someone had been dragged through it…and then through the *wall*.

My stomach dropped as I planted my hands on the wall's wooden panels. It wouldn't budge as I pushed, and I almost sighed in relief—until I shifted to lean against it. A *click* followed the movement of the wall behind me.

I reared up and spun. Not a wall. A *door.*

In shock reaction, I shoved the barrier wide open, ready to call out for the others. My open mouth choked back as a puff of stale air filled my lungs. With what looked like old mattress padding

241

nailed to the walls, it was a tunnel.

The same tunnel the man had dragged me through after raping me in my nightmare.

My need to call for the others fled. I didn't know what was going on. Stan was gone, *possibly*. Jeremy knew too much about me, *definitely*. And if any of my nightmares had been real…someone was hunting me and they were linked to this child in some way. Which meant, I didn't know what was real and what was not. And most of all, I didn't know who I could trust.

Needing answers, needing to know if I was in immediate danger, I stepped into the tunnel—and shut the door behind me.

Moving swiftly down the winding path, I felt like I could walk forever—but then I reached the end. I gasped at the sight. The place I'd been tied up in. Even in the low light from my phone, I knew it was the same place. A hut of sorts. But that wasn't the worst of it. The erect platform was still there, rope hanging from metal loops at the top and bottom corners. I held my phone up high, lighting up the wood of the platform. Drips and smears of blood colored the dented and serrated surface. I stepped forward, hand reaching to touch—

I banged into something. A trolley. My phone's light swung and I stumbled back. "Oh shit!"

The old and rusted frame housed a variety of nasty and sharp weapons. They were rusted too, and more than that, they were stained with blood. Old blackened blood. And *fresh* blood. One large knife on the top dripped crimson from its tip.

To test my eyes I ran a fingertip along the length. It was wet and sticky. My finger came away red. *Real.*

Staring around, I felt like I was about to pass out. My eyes stilled suddenly. The same window I'd seen in my nightmare. The trees beyond were taller and wider. More snow covered them now, but none filtered down from the clouds. In the sinking moonlight, even with the glass dirtier than in my nightmare, one feature was unmistakable. Smears of blood, on the glass and on the sill. Like someone had been dragged out that way.

I gulped, my stomach dropping like it was quickly filling with stones.

Suddenly I knew what the little girl wanted from me. She was warning me. This place had been used. Today. By someone in this house. It wasn't Katherine, Brad, or Jeremy. Katherine was female and both guys were too young. The man I'd dreamed about was older, past his prime. I hadn't seen his face properly, his features. But the build of him, that quick anger in his eyes…

I choked out the realization, "It was Stan."

TWENTY-FIVE

Eight and a Half Years Ago

A man's loud voice made my head snap up from my diary. It had come from downstairs, calling out "Evelyn" over and over. My mother's name. The voice wasn't my father's.

Dropping my book, I jumped off my bed and searched out the window. My mouth fell open and I covered it with my hand. Father's truck space was empty. Two muddy tracks were cut into the grass, moving away from the house and along the lake before they turned left and disappeared into the trees. Another car waited below, the engine rumbling and smoke puffing out from the back.

The teacher's car.

Mother's shrill voice sounded from below. I ran to the grate and saw her yelling to get the kids out of the mess hall. The door swung shut behind the last to leave and the stampede of many stomping feet raced up the stairs.

Down in the mess hall, the teacher gripped my mom's arms as doors slammed shut to the bedrooms below me. His cheeks were red and he stared through his glasses into her eyes. "Evelyn, come with me. Leave now. You and Kasey. We can start our life together, away from him."

Mother shook her head, short dark curls swishing over scared eyes. "Tom, I can't. He'll be back soon." She pulled away and pushed him back. Tears wetted her cheeks in thin streams. "You need to leave. Right now. You don't know what he'll do if he finds you here."

"No more than he's already doing to Kasey. C.J. told me about the bruises. He said this has been happening for years—before that monster even knew she was mine."

I gasped as they kept on arguing. Father wasn't *my father. Tom Stewart was.* That's why he hates me.

"I won't leave Kasey behind." Tom's voice was louder now. The way he looked at Mom made me stare. "It's not an option."

My heart did a little jump as Mom went still. She wanted to leave me behind? With him?

"Evelyn, please. I made the call about the package that needed picking up. He'll be at least another thirty minutes. Grab what you need, or leave it all behind. I don't care. Just come with me. You and Kasey. There's enough time if you hurry."

245

Mom shook her head, then nodded, wiping away her tears. "Okay. Okay. I'll get Kasey." She touched his face and lifted on her toes to press her lips to his. "Wait here." Then she was gone, rushing away and through the door to the hallway. Her running steps up the staircase echoed loud and clear. And then the cover creaked open and the ladder slid down. I heard the bolt clatter and I ran to the trapdoor and helped it open.

"Mommy, is it true? Is he—"

"There's no time for questions. We need to go." She disappeared down the ladder, calling back to me, "Hurry up or I'll leave you behind."

Scared she would leave me I moved fast, climbing and almost falling down the ladder. I slipped on a rung and smacked my knee. But I didn't stop. I jumped from higher up, seeing Mom rushing down the stairs. My ankles hurt but I ran after her, holding the railing to keep from falling. "Wait, I'm coming!"

Mom pushed through the door to the mess hall and I burst in right behind her—and smacked into her back.

She'd stopped suddenly, and as I peered around her, I knew why.

Over by the other entry to the kitchen was Tom. Father was behind him. He was back. A big knife was held at Tom's throat right under his jaw. And the look in his eyes was the worst thing I'd ever seen.

A cry squeaked from Mom's mouth before she covered it with her hands. I didn't dare say a word.

"I see you are all conspiring behind my back." Father pointed the sharp end of the knife at Mom and me.

"You gave us no choice," Tom's voice was strong, but his eyes weren't as he looked at me. They were glassy. This was the first time he'd ever seen me. He shifted, trying to get away. Trying to get to me. "They're leaving with me."

Father yanked his arm back so the knife was on the teacher's throat again. "Oh, are they? You must be delusional. See, I have the power here. I always have. You are nothing, teacher. Nothing but a bug in need of squashing. So this is how it's going to go. Leave and never come back. My wife stays. Her little bastard does too. They belong *to me."*

"You don't own them." Tom still watched me, his smile sad as he looked over the bruises on my arms and the new one that blackened my eye. "Kasey is mine. The authorities—"

"Tom, no!" Mom's cry stopped at the furious look Father sent her. She shook her head and her body trembled as she dropped to her knees. Her hands clasped together. "I'm sorry. I didn't know he was coming. I didn't plan this." She was talking to Father, begging for him to believe her.

Tom looked shocked, maybe even angry as he stared at her. "Give me my daughter and you'll

247

never see me again. If your wife wants to stay, that's on her."

"And if I don't, what? You'll report me again?"

Father pressed the knife harder into the teacher's throat, but Tom didn't give up. He opened his mouth, but his words stopped as the knife cut him and blood oozed around the blade.

"I should have killed you when I found out. When I knew that you had forced yourself on my wife and spawned her little bastard. I warned you before, and I won't live waiting for you to make another move." Father's face was the scariest thing I'd ever seen as he locked eyes on me. "Say goodbye to your daddy, little bastard."

I cried out too late. The knife sliced sideways as the teacher reached up to save himself. He didn't make it. But Father hadn't cut his throat. He'd stabbed him in the back. The teacher's legs stopped working, and Father's arm around his chest kept him up.

I knew what father had done. I'd seen wounds on the backs of bucks he brought back here sometimes. "A stab into the right part of the spine will keep the animal still but alive," *he'd told me before making me help.*

I stepped out from behind my mother. "Father…please don't."

My—not my—Father smiled. "Why would I do anything for you?" And then pulled the knife free and stabbed it into the teacher's—my real dad's—heart.

Tom Stewart stared down at the knife sticking out from his chest, tears falling and collecting on the inside of his glasses. Blood was coming out fast, staining down his pale shirt as he choked and spat blood. His head bobbed a little, his eyes unfocusing before settling on me like everything else had disappeared. "Kasey...I'm sor—ry. I...love...you."

Tom's eyes rolled back and Father dropped him to the floor. The sound was horrid, a crack followed by a splat. His glasses shattered and then skittered across the floor to hit my feet. I couldn't move. All I could do was stare...at Tom's dead body. At my real dad's dead body.

"Evelyn, lock the kids in their rooms then come and mop this shit up." Father stomped to me as Mother got up and ran out the door. He grabbed my jaw with his huge bloody hand and forced my face up. But I kept my eyes down, staring as too much red leaked out around my—my dad. "Go get my hacksaw and find me out back. I'll be damned it I'm getting rid of all this shit myself."

I didn't move or talk, seeing in my head how he'd once torn a huge buck to pieces and made me watch. When the meat was stripped, the carcass was burned.

He pulled my face up harder. "Are you fucking deaf?" Father's eyes were locked down on me with *hatred.*

I shook my head fast. I knew what was coming for me after the cleanup. *I was going to be next.*

TWENTY-SIX

Still staring at the blood that marred this dingy hut and fearing who it had belonged to, I backed up a few paces. Then I remembered my phone and lifted it to my face. "Fuck." No reception.

My boots started moving of their own accord, running from the hut to follow the internal decision I'd already made. I had to warn the others. I had to find them, all of them…if it wasn't already too late. The thought that they were injured or worse made me want to retch. No time. They were unaware.

Keeping up speed along the uneven trail, I knew Stan was up to something horrible. He hadn't left. He was after me, maybe even all of us. The image of all those deadly and stained weapons sent a shiver through me. The blood had been fresh. What if I was already too late?

An unsteady glow was visible up the long narrow pathway, revealing one edge of the door. The thought that he would open it as I arrived made my legs run faster and my lungs burn with ragged breath. Almost there—

My boot hit a rock and I went sprawling, phone flying and knees smashing the compacted dirt with force. I bit my lip to keep from crying out at the strike of pain and scrambled to pick up my phone. Hands patting the cold earth, I brushed over something flat and smooth. Holding it up, I found my phone with my other hand. The screen was cracked but still on, and the spotlight beamed to life. "Thank—"

I gasped and fell back onto my butt. The thin, flat object in my other hand was a photo. A Polaroid. The snapshot was taken of a dreary road that wound along between a border of tall trees and a sheer drop-off. Rain fell lightly from a gloomy sky.

My heart sank to my stomach and bile rose up. I choked it back down, my voice hoarse as I whispered trembling words, "It can't be."

Blinking over and over didn't change what I saw; it only flashed in my mind the next gruesome step in this scene. The one where our car plummeted over the edge and my parents, trapped inside, went up in a ball of flames. My face burned like I was inside the fire myself. Tears I hadn't realized I was crying carved cooling tracks down my face. There was only one conclusion I could make. "It's all connected. The accident. Me surviving. Winning this trip I never entered. The explosion that caused the avalanche. And being stuck here."

Nothing had been by chance or poor luck. It was all a methodically laid-out plan.

Sensing the danger of our situation even more than a minute ago, I shoved the photo into my back pocket and pushed up. My knees were grazed and hurt like they were bruised. My hands were sore from the many falls and injuries I'd sustained already. But I couldn't stop now. I had to act. "God help us."

Pocketing my phone too, I reached the door and slowly inched it open. I had to find the others before Stan acted—before it was too late. Moving as quietly as I could in my chunky boots, I rounded a bend and reached the open door to the room Brad and Katherine had been in. I didn't go inside. The room was empty—the bed a mess of tangled sheets and blankets. My stomach churned at the thought of what might have already happened.

Deep down I hoped I was being delusional, that I was seeing and dreaming things that weren't real, that the dodgy medication was playing with my mind. The nausea that swirled like a tornado from my stomach up to my throat told me I wasn't. It promised horror and pain—and a death like I'd dreamt when my body was dismembered limb by limb.

Clutching my stomach, I moved on, following the golden flicker of dancing flames among moving shadows. Peering into the communal room, I breathed a sigh of relief. Brad and Katherine weren't there, but Jeremy was. I looked behind me, making sure no one was creeping in, and then I slipped inside.

Stretched out on the central sofa, legs elevated on one arm, Jeremy's steady breaths were calming. His hands were folded over his chest, and his eyes were closed. Fast asleep.

I reached out to touch his shoulder, but stalled at seeing something poking out from under the cushion he slept on. Words left my mouth on a whisper, *"A newspaper."* Hand reaching, I stepped forward—and knocked his backpack over. A black Zippo lighter fell out and bounced across the floorboards. The sound was loud and made me cringe. But Jeremy didn't even flinch, and after a quick look and listen around, I heard and saw no one approaching.

Confused at the Zippo when he'd been using matches, I picked up the lighter and grabbed his open pack, ready to shove the thing back in and make a move—

I froze like a person who'd suddenly been turned to ice. Another object was on top of the wadded-up clothes that spilled from Jeremy's backpack. My heart pounded like a drum, and my hand shook violently as I bent and reached in to pull out—another Polaroid.

"No." I tried and failed to steady my breathing

as I stood, my eyes so wide they began to burn. When I looked to Jeremy, he was still out of it. But my eyes didn't stay on him. They couldn't. The photo in my hand was turned around, only the back black edging surrounded by white of it on display. But I had to see it. I had to know the truth.

Slipping the Zippo into my pocket, I used my free hand to steady my shaking one. My hand holding the photo turned slowly until it was facing the right way. I gagged and covered my mouth, stopping my scream before it could peel free. My feet were moving without thought, stepping back and away from Jeremy.

I looked away from the photo clutched between my thumb and fingers and back up at him. The guy who'd seemed so understanding and had kept me safe while I was out cold. The guy I'd felt suspicious of, but had come to trust the more I had gotten to know him. It couldn't be. But if this photo I held was his…

If Stan hadn't left, then they were working together, because…

I forced my wide eyes back to the photo. The nausea I felt was constant now, my gag reflex twitching and ready to force an evacuation.

This is what they had looked like right before they burned. In their smashed-up car with broken windows. Dad was unconscious, or maybe he was already dead. Mom was still alive, her eyes wide open and mouth gaping like she was screaming in horror.

As I looked closer, bringing the photo almost to my nose, I saw a reflection in-between the mud on the only unbroken side window at the back: a figure, hooded and with one arm up. Holding a flaming black Zippo? This was the second before she was burned alive. This was the moment of her death as I watched, paralyzed on the ground.

A tear fell as I looked up at the guy still sleeping soundly on the sofa. Sleeping like he didn't have a care or even a regret in the world. Like he was innocent. But it all added up. The newspaper. The lighter. And the photos. The evidence was damning proof.

Jeremy killed them in cold blood. Jeremy was my nightmares come to life—and my life was next.

I backed out of the room, staring ahead at Jeremy and unable to look away. One step. Two. I spun to take off running—and slammed into Katherine. Breath knocked from my lungs and I swallowed down my scream before it could escape. My heart was about to beat through my ribcage, but a quick glance over my shoulder revealed Jeremy still fast asleep.

"Where have you been?" Katherine hissed under her breath, a look of pure relief crossing her concerned face. "I've been looking—"

"Shh!" I covered her mouth with my hand,

forcing her to step back down the hall and away from the communal area. A few steps further away from our would-be killer I dared to whisper, "We're in danger. It's not safe here."

"I know." At Katherine's just-as-stealth whisper, I stopped to look at her. Her complexion was pale, her eyes a little wide and glassy. She glanced sideways into the room her and Brad had been in. "Brad's missing. I can't find him anywhere."

I thought of the fresh blood I'd seen in the hut and shuddered. He had been immobile, easy prey. Was it already too late for him? How could he disappear without anyone even hearing a sound? I eyed Katherine, my paranoia well deserved in my opinion. "Where have you been?"

"I went hunting for that bottle of gin when you never came back. But when I was returning from the kitchen I heard a sound. I followed it down a narrow hallway and found a bathroom. It was empty and I was about the leave. But then the door slammed shut and I couldn't get out."

I narrowed my eyes. "Then how are you here now?"

Katherine shrugged. "I guess I dozed off after a while, but when I woke up the door was ajar. I came straight back here. And saw this…"

She moved into the room and I followed, puffs of dust swirling from our hurried steps. I covered my mouth as she pulled back a dusty blanket from the bed. Large red stains pooled over the dirty sheets. Blood. Bucket loads of it. "Oh shit."

"And that's not all." Katherine held out a piece of paper—no—a photograph. It was old, not a Polaroid. A group shot filled with kids and two adults. One adult was a woman with downcast eyes and tightly laced fingers. The other was a man, with the same build and soulless eyes I'd seen in my nightmare. The same man from all the group shots I'd found with Jeremy under the stairs. Katherine pointed to one of the kids. "That's Bradley—our Brad. He was named Connor then. He was an orphan here. Before the place shut down seven years ago."

My mouth gaped as I saw the resemblance. The cocky smile, the mischievous eyes. A slingshot was held loosely in one of his hands. It was him. And now he was…

I gasped at the sight of another boy, one with blond hair and cornflower blue eyes. *Jeremy.* He'd said he was adopted…but I'd never even thought and he'd never said it. He'd been one of the orphans from this orphanage too.

I touched Katherine's arm, and her eyes met mine. "I found a secret hut filled with weapons. There was blood too."

Katherine dropped the blanket and made for the door. "We have to find Jeremy and leave."

I caught her arm to stop her. "No. We can't." At her questioning look, I held out the Polaroid of my parents. My heart shattered as I beheld my mom's face. "My parents died in a car crash. This crash. I was told it was an accident. But I never believed it."

Katherine shook her head, eyes searching frantically as her breath quickened. "I don't understand…"

"I found this in Jeremy's backpack. He took this photo—right before he set my parents' car wreck on fire."

She gasped and covered her mouth. For a second I wished I'd taken one of those sharp weapons from the hut. But there was no time now. There was only one thing we could do, one way to escape this.

"We have to leave. Now."

Katherine nodded, and we crept from the room. I peered inside the communal area as we passed, and my heart stopped. The sofa was empty. All of them were.

"Jeremy's gone. He was in there a moment ago." I threw glances all around, back up the hall, into the room where we'd sat before the fire that was now dying out. He was nowhere in sight.

Katherine rushed to the front door and threw it open. Icy wind and snow rushed in. With this house and all its corridors, if he was downstairs, Jeremy would feel the temperature change. She ushered me on. "Let's go!"

I instantly missed my thick ski jacket as we rushed outside. Wind batted my face and hair and ate straight through my ski pants and Jeremy's hoodie I still wore. But there was no time to turn back. No time to prepare.

We hit the snow at a dead run—and sank like stones. Our first steps were ankle deep, then knee high. We kept on, skirting the house and heading for the thick line of trees that seemed impossibly far away. The moon was edging the horizon, its light fading to a chalky white as a soft glow kissed the edge of the sky. Katherine ventured out further and I was right behind her, nearing a little wooden cabin that seemed to grow out of the sloping gradient under a copse of pine trees. I squinted in the almost nonexistent light, seeing no door, but rather, a single window on the side. And sunken boot-made steps? "Katherine, hold on a—"

Katherine sank up ahead of me with a shocked cry.

Swallowed up to her waist, I grabbed her flailing arms and tugged. "I've got you. Just hold on." I heaved, but there was no give, every time I got an inch, more snow would sink around us. I was sinking too. Snow now lapped at my thighs.

"Cassidy, this isn't working," Katherine's voice was hollow, terrified. "I'm stuck."

But I wasn't giving up. Jill was gone. Brad probably was too. I wasn't leaving Katherine behind. No way. Releasing her arms I plunged my fingers into the soft snow, using them as shovels. Despite the cold sting, sweat sprouted across my forehead and too soon my digits were half numb and so cold they felt like they were on fire. I didn't stop; I kept digging.

"It's working." Katherine began to wriggle upward, laying her torso flat over the top layer of snow and inching her trapped legs higher.

As she began to pull free, I saw something. "Wait!" Katherine paused in her escape and looked at me. I stared into the hole I'd dug around her and reached down to flake away snow from beside her boot. What I'd seen was unearthed suddenly, almost blue from being frozen. "Oh my God."

"Is that…?"

I gulped and blinked hard. This wasn't my imagination. What I could see, the bluish flesh and wrinkled skin…she could see it too. "A man's hand."

And then I saw what I had been trying to make out on the cabin window. Smears of blood on the glass…and dark patches beside, *yeah*, definite boot prints leading this way in the snow.

Katherine's legs propelled up and out of the hole like they were spring loaded. "We need to go. We need to go. Oh God." She scrambled, struggling to pull her flattened body along the soft layers of snow. "Jesus, Cassidy. Didn't you hear me? Why aren't you moving?"

Still staring down at the hand that was no longer

visible with the snow that had fallen in, I hesitated. Wind continued to whip my face and flailing hair, but I didn't move. "We need to know who that is. We need to see his face."

"Cassidy, someone is dead down there!" Her voice had risen and she reined the shrill back down to a whisper. "You need to listen to me. We can't stay here, okay? We'll be next if we don't go."

But I wasn't listening. Shifting closer, I began to dig. "I'm not leaving until I know."

Katherine cursed *"God help us,"* but didn't leave. Instead, she joined me, speeding up the reveal.

When my hand's clawed something harder and yet softer than the small grains of ice, I pulled back quick. My skin crawled. This was it. My whole body stiffened as I reached into the hole, into the shallow grave. I brushed the white dusting away, seeing a nose, then forehead, then open dead-fish eyes. *"Stan,"* I gasped in wide-eyed horror. "He never left. He never made it out of here. The blood puddle *was* his." And it was from much more than a busted nose.

"If he's dead and Brad's missing…" Katherine's lips pinned shut and her chest undulated like she was about to throw up.

I finished what she couldn't say, "Then there's only Jeremy left."

TWENTY-SEVEN

"Come on. We have to go. We have to go now."

Katherine yanked on my arm, but I felt numb. Dazed. I couldn't stop staring at Stan's open, unblinking eyes. His frozen expression was one of shock—of fear.

"Dammit, get up! I won't die here too. We should never have come here. The evil of this place didn't die with them."

My head whipped up, and I stared into her wide, scared eyes. "What does that mean? What do you know that you're not telling me?"

Katherine shook her head. "I…I can't. I can't go back. We need to go. We *need* to leave."

She was in shock. I probably was too. Hers manifested in panic, but my own seemed to have stripped the fear right out of me. Inside I felt the urge to act. Looking out into the snowscape that stretched out over the lake and then rose up around us, I knew we'd never get through the snow alive. We'd be buried like Brad had been before Jeremy and I dug him back out. My heart jumped at the memory. Jeremy had saved Brad then. Why bother if he wanted him dead? I saw in my mind how he'd heroically jumped into the frozen-over lake. He'd risked his life to try to save Jill. He'd almost drowned himself. But that had all been a ploy, a ruse to earn trust.

I blinked, knowing there was no escape from this. "We can't cross the snow. It's not possible. Stan never made it. Brad would have died sooner if I hadn't helped dig him out. There's no way out of this."

"You can't mean that. We can't stay here, Cassidy. Jeremy is still in there. He's probably watching and waiting for us to come back in so he can take us out too."

"We don't have a choice…"

A quiet vibration reached my ears. Katherine heard it too. I pulled my phone from my pocket. A low battery warning was lighting up the screen. But that wasn't all. "I have service. I have service!"

But as I looked closer, I saw there was one bar and only one bar. The battery icon was blinking red.

"Call 911." Katherine grabbed the phone before I could. Her hand shook as she dialed and held the phone to her ear. The light in her eyes died and she dropped her hand. "The bar is gone—wait, it's back!" If the cell tower had been hit by the avalanche, they mustn't have had it all fixed to go yet. She tried again, but the call failed. "I…I…"

Legs still buried, I snatched the phone and held my arm out as far as I could. The bar was back, but I didn't try to call. The battery could be gone at any second. Instead, I sent a text to the cell number from the lodge. *'SOS. Fernie Orphanage. He's going to kill us all. Send cops. Hurry.'* I hit send, crossing my fingers as I watched the green bar along the top slide left to right. There was a *zoop* as the bar hit the other end. *Message sent.* The single bar of service bleeped off before a *beep-beep-beep* killed the battery.

Would they see the message back at the lodge? How long would it take to get here, if they even could through the snow?

"Ca-ssidy…"

A child's ghostly voice whispered my name on the breeze. I turned to the sound and let my gaze travel up the tall wooden exterior of the orphanage—to the attic window. Yellow light flashed up there, backlighting an ominous figure standing behind the glass. A dark hood kept their face shadowed from view. But they were watching us. *He* was watching us. *"Jeremy."*

"Oh no. He knows we're down here. He's seen us." Katherine's hand on my arm was freezing cold and shaking like a leaf. "We need to…"

Snow started to rain down on us, hard and blustery. My lower half was close to frozen, still partially buried. My top half shivered from cold. He knew where we were. We couldn't stay out here. And even if we did and he didn't brave the whiteout that was blowing in over the mountain, we'd get hypothermia and freeze to death. I made a decision then; one I hoped would keep us alive until help showed up—*if* help showed up. "It's him or us. We need to kill him before he kills us. We need to kill Jeremy."

"No. Cassidy, *no*," Katherine choked out as I fought my way back through the sinking snow to the open front door. "If we go in there we'll die."

I called out over my shoulder, not slowing down even a bit. "If we stay out here we're dead too. He'll get bored of waiting eventually." Now I did throw a solemn look over my shoulder. "Nowhere is safe. Not until we make sure it is ourselves."

I continued on, and Katherine called after me as I reached the door. "Okay. *Dear God.* I'm coming!"

I kept watch as she fought the deceptive layers of powdery ice back to the house. There were no noises. No movement inside the communal area either. As soon as she reached me, I tugged her inside. We ran down the wide entryway, finding that dead end with a sharp turn to the left. I shoved the hidden door open. "Wait here."

"What? No!" Katherine's brown eyes were too wide in her narrow, middle-aged face. "I…I…"

I gave her arm a reassuring squeeze. "I'll be

right back. Just keep a lookout. You don't want to see what's down here anyway. Believe me."

She threw a glance down the dark passageway and shivered. "O-okay."

I didn't stick around, spinning and sprinting down the tunnel, managing not to fall with the intermittent light that skittered from behind Katherine. When I was only a few feet from the hut, where light was all but scarce, I finally slowed. But I hadn't needed to. No one was inside. Which made me kinda glad at the darkness. I didn't want to highlight the blood smears on the window, or the fresh spatters that coated the torture trolley. The memory of it all was already enough to make me shudder.

Ready to get the hell out, I snatched a bloody knife from the trolley…and a machete. Then I was back up the tunnel in a flash.

Katherine yelped and jumped as I reached her. She paled at the sight of the used weapons. "Is that…were they used on…?"

I handed her the knife. "I think so. *Come on.*"

Carving a quiet path through the back hallways, I easily remembered the trail that brought us out to the main stairs. The treads creaked and groaned under our boots, but as my eyes darted I didn't see anyone—didn't see Jeremy—coming our way. Was he waiting like a lion in his lair for us to stumble into our doom? Fear threatened to crash over me for a moment, but adrenaline and the ingrained need to survive kept my feet climbing.

On the second floor, the ladder was still extended. The trapdoor was wide open as if in invitation. Horrible yellow light flashed down through the hole, and in my head I imagined that spine-chilling music they always played in horror movies. But this wasn't a movie; this was real life. My life. Knowing what I had to do was morbid and terrifying. But what choice did we have? Kill…or be killed.

Clutching the machete harder, my arm shook. I nodded to Katherine, not daring to say a word before my eyes trained up on the opening. *This was it.*

Heart pounding in my throat, I began to climb. Each step was measured, silent. When I was almost at the top, I paused, trying to still my nerves, trying to breathe. *Dammit, breathe!* Kill or be killed. It was now or never. There was no other option.

From where I stood, I could see parts of the attic in every split second of illumination: the raked ceiling, the far-off wall above the window, the terrible drawings I now knew that little girl had created. I listened again for movement, for sound. There wasn't even a breath. If I was slow, he'd attacked me first. Maybe he was lurking just out of sight. Waiting. Maybe he'd already left and was stalking up from behind.

A quick scan below at Katherine and back to the

stairs revealed we were alone. For now. And if he was up there waiting…there was only one way to find out.

Swallowing my thudding heart that wanted to break free of the cage of my ribs, I launched my body up. The machete clattered on the ground as I shoved myself upright and twirled. No one advanced. Jeremy didn't attack. With both hands trembling on the machete hilt, a breath of relief filled my lungs.

"What's happening? *Cassidy?*" Katherine's voice was small, a terrified whisper.

I called down to her in an equally as quiet voice. "He's not up here." I turned back around to the window I'd seen him standing at, the one he'd been watching us through. The lights pulsed on, revealing the empty space, before dousing again. I stepped closer as the pulse returned—

And came face to face with that concealing hood and an unhinged smile.

Hands gripped either side of my face. There was a creak from the ladder. And then his head connected with my eye with blunt force.

Blackness overwhelmed me and I lost consciousness before any other sensation could register. But then a gentle white light crept in. Another sensation registered too. A frightening and aggressive sound that made every muscle in my body tighten to the point of snapping. A man's screaming voice.

With my hand and forehead on the chilled glass of the window, I stared down at the lake that was beginning to crust in from the edges. That horrible man was down there. And with the sudden light outside, one thing was clear. It had never been Stan. This man was bulkier, angrier. He towered over a cowering woman who trembled before him. Spit sprayed from his tight lips as he spoke. "You *fucked* him."

He struck the woman and she cried out as she fell to the frosty grass. Her head remained down, her black hair hanging over her face as she wept.

"You fucked someone and passed your little bastard off as mine. You think I didn't know she wasn't mine, you fucking slut? You think I couldn't tell?" He grabbed the woman by her woolen cardigan and hauled her up. Her hair cascaded back, revealing a puffy, black eye and split lip. "Why do you think I hate her? Why I always hated her? *You* did this. *You* made me this way." He spat in her face. *"You disgust me."*

He raised a hand as if to punch her this time, but stalled as the woman cringed.

His fist remained in the air. The threat in his eyes was clear. "If I *ever* find out who…if I ever see him, I promise you…" He brought his lips to her ear, but the words weren't a whisper. They were loud and clear. "It will be his last day." The man shoved her back down and stalked inside.

Unable to move, I stared, my sight growing distant as tears I hadn't realized I'd been crying trailed my cheeks and dripped from my jaw. My breath had fogged up the glass, removing the scene below from sight. Now I knew why this poor little girl had been punished. Why she was hated. A mother's mistake that she paid the price for over and over again. A mistake that, in the end, she died for?

As I blinked my eyes clear and leaned back, the steam over the glass shrank. My reflection came into view. My almost black hair, my pointed chin, my forest-green eyes...

I blinked and stared.

The face looking back at me wasn't mine. It was that child's—of maybe six or seven years—with her short hacked hair and saddened green eyes...with one damaged pupil.

TWENTY-EIGHT

KASEY

I waited as Katherine climbed up into the attic. At first her face was full of relief, but then she saw me. Something in my eyes must have given my intentions away, or it could have been Cassidy lying limp on the ground behind me. Or the machete I held up. She cried out and spun to the ground, clambering to get out of this hell.

She wouldn't get far. No one left here alive. Not anymore.

I clawed into her auburn hair and yanked her back. She cried out. The knife fell from her hand and clattered to the ground. I held her back to my chest and trapped her shoulders with one arm.

"No. Please, no!"

I shoved the machete deep into her side. Her whole body tensed and her scream cut off. There was a patter as crimson leaked from the cut and collected on the floorboards at our feet. The flashes of light made the drops glisten.

"W-why?"

Her voice was a gargle. They always asked that. Why? Like there had to be some greater reason to end a life. Well, I guess I agreed with that. This kill wasn't purely for fun. I whispered in her ear, "See no evil. Speak no evil."

I slid the machete free, red coating the rust-speckled length, and twirled her to face me. She stumbled so I snatched her neck to keep her up.

Face to face her wide eyes searched mine, seeking the answer she hadn't pieced together. Then I saw it. Recognition. "You?"

I let go of her throat and smacked the machete butt into her chin. She collapsed with a thud, lids fluttering as more red leaked from her side. Consciousness was fleeting. She wouldn't feel much of what I was about to do. And, for some reason, that was okay.

"I sh-should h-ave come back," she rambled, the words slurred and mushing together. "I knew. I—I saw... I...I'm s-sorry. P-lease..."

I dragged in a deep breath and held it. Dropping the machete, my fingers found the knife she'd been holding. "I am too." With my exhale, I sliced the sharp edge across her neck. She gurgled and spluttered, pupils growing larger by the second. Then I jammed the tip into her eye socket and cut around before withdrawing. Her eyeball popped free, hanging from the connecting nerves and veins in her skull.

She stopped moving—stopped breathing—as I sliced the second eye free.

Tipping back on my butt, I pulled a folded piece of paper from my pocket. Blood from my hands smeared across the white sheet that was tattered from its age and the many times I'd unfolded and refolded it. Katherine's hand twitched with dying nerves. But it wasn't her hand that I needed.

Moving to Cassidy, I snatched up the teddy bear on the ground and shoved it under her head. Then I pressed the paper into her palm and closed her fingers. "Now you'll know."

~

Almost Eight Years Ago

All the kids were gathered in the mess hall today. All except for me. Something was going to happen, and I desperately wanted to know what. Even if I couldn't join in. Mom had ordered every one of them to dress in their finest clothes. She'd even helped brush their hair and kept watch during their bathroom time to make sure teeth were scrubbed too. Now they were all lined up side by side, backs straight and shoes polished.

For the first time in so long, I had seen it all from outside the attic. Father was out on a trip to town, and C.J. had stolen his key before he left to unbolt the padlock from the trapdoor.

Now I hovered at the top of the stairs after a quick peek inside the mess hall and a wave to C.J.. I couldn't be seen. Mom wouldn't punish me like Father would. She never laid a hand on me. Not even to hug me anymore. But I always knew when she was mad, when I'd done something to upset her. The plates of food she snuck up for me once a day would stop. There'd be no glass of water for days, either.

I thought about the glass I hid between my mattress and the wall. I couldn't remember when the covers had last been changed, so it wouldn't be found. I just had to top it up a little on the days I was brought a drink.

Mom's voice made me sit up straighter. "Please do come in."

She was inviting someone in from the front door. The clip-clop of shoes was loud as they neared, and then I saw another woman down below. She was very pretty and had long wavy hair that was golden and brown at the same time. "I am very pleased to finally have some interested couples." She pressed down her buttoned jacket and plain black skirt before following Mom inside the mess hall.

I knew I shouldn't, but when I couldn't hear their voices through the door and walls, I crept down the stairs. Just outside, it was still hard to hear. So I peeked inside, holding the door open a crack with my bare toes. Two lines of kids stood before the long blackboard. The woman was walking up and down in front of them. She smiled and looked over each one as if shopping for the right candy. C.J. saw me and gave a straight smile, shrugging his shoulders.

"So, as you can see, we have some lovely children to choose from. A prospective couple would be lucky to have any one of these little gems. They are all so well mannered and well behaved."

The woman stopped in front of C.J. and touched his face. "You seem like a sweet boy. Are you ready for a new family?"

My throat closed up and I accidentally jerked. The door I leaned into creaked, and the woman and my mom turned around.

"Who is this?" The woman asked as she walked towards me.

Mom caught her arm before she reached me. "No one. She's not one of the orphans." She scolded me. "Kasey, leave."

I wanted to leave. I needed to. Staying would turn into more days without food. But I couldn't move.

When my mom tried to turn the woman around, she held up a hand. A frown wrinkled her pretty face that had been happy and without a single line. She looked from my face to my arm on the door.

I knew what she was staring at. One of my green eyes was surrounded by black from Father and his punishment yesterday. My pale arm had a mash of colors from yellow-green to purple-black. The old bruises never faded all the way before a new one was given.

"What happened to her?"

Mom's face turned red. She looked back at the line of kids then to the woman. "She had an accident yesterday. A little too much roughhousing with one of her friends. Connor?" She walked back to the tallest boy in line, and I felt sick inside when he looked at me in that horrible way. "You saw Kasey fall yesterday when she was running down the stairs, didn't you?"

Connor stopped looking at me to smile up at my Mom. "Yes, Mrs. Whitmore. I told Kasey not to run on the stairs, but she didn't listen."

Mom breathed loudly and walked back to the other woman. "Kids will be kids. And it is hard to keep watch of so many at once. These things happen sometimes. But as I said, she is not one of the orphans." The look she gave me felt like one of Father's knifes. "She is mine." She held out a folded piece of paper from her cardigan pocket. "See for yourself."

"Oh..." The woman didn't seem convinced, but she took the paper and looked it over. She turned to the other kids, her hand moving like she was counting them. "Yes, all the children are accounted for."

As the woman looked at me again, I wanted to whisper, "Help me." But if a cop wouldn't do anything, why would she?

The woman smiled at me. "Are you okay...Kasey? Is that what happened?"

I couldn't say it. My mouth and tongue wouldn't move. The way Mom looked at me kept them still. And then I nodded.

"See? She'll be fine. Go on, sweetheart. Go to your room and play. I'll be up there soon." I slipped backward slowly, hearing my mom continue to speak as I ran upstairs. "Come, Katherine. Now, where were we? Oh C.J. He is a lovely boy, really he is."

TWENTY-NINE

I gasped as I came awake, heart still hammering in its cage. Rubbing my sore, gritty eyes, my contact scratched from prolonged use. What I'd seen in my dream, the child's reflection in the window... I thought of the man in the hood, of how my own pupil had been damaged either during the *'accident'*...or in my imagined recollection after the car had gone up in flames when that boulder had been dropped from above my face. If that hadn't been a dream, if it was real...was the killer trying to turn me into that poor child, all grown up?

Something soft was under my head, and as I reached up I realized it was...the teddy bear?

The memory of being knocked out flooded back in a rush.

Ratcheting up, my head swam with rushing blood. The world tilted around me, the attic's dirty walls and window rising up before slamming down into place. I panted for breath, knees to chest as I scanned up and around frantically, seeing everything like I was looking through water.

Alone. No one was here.

But I'd thought that before.

My eyes refused to stop scanning, expecting that ominous hood to pop up at any second, to appear out of thin air. But it didn't. And I couldn't reconcile that I was still alive. Why not kill me when he had the chance? My throat constricted when the answer came to me. The sadistic bastard wanted to enjoy the chase and the kill...while I lay awake and helpless, knowing there was no way to survive or escape.

My mind slowed with morbid expectation and my vision cleared. In the crisp clarity I noticed a change, something more than the soft glow of dawn through the attic window that meant a good chunk of time had passed while I was knocked out. A lapse of time that meant a new day was here, a new day where I was officially a year older.

The lights were out. The trapdoor was shut. And leading from where I crouched—was a thick trail of smeared blood.

I stopped breathing. My mind raced. My blood rushed too fast for me not to be moving, but as I tried to stand, I came back down. Something crunched under my palm and I jerked away like I'd been stung. But it was only a crumpled piece of paper.

Looking around again, I dared to snatch it off the

floor. My hands shook, seeing a blood-smeared handprint as I unfolded the page. My eyes bugged as I read what was written…a list of names. Jill Smith: Bigmouth orphan. Connor (AKA Brad Miller): Sadistic shit of a kid. Stan Blunt: Ex-cop. I gasped out the last name, *"Katherine Reynolds: Social worker."* I instantly remembered her waiting down the ladder.

Inching closer to the trapdoor I stopped before pulling the barrier open. All these names…they meant something. Every single one of them, either in first name or title, had been in the child's diary. The orphan girl who'd ratted her out for playing and being a kid. The horrible orphan boy who had targeted and bullied her. The cop who'd ignored the proof of a child locked in the attic. And the social worker that was meant to help forgotten kids with a fresh start in a family that would love them, and who had accepted as an accident the clear abuse she'd seen on the one kid who wasn't an orphan.

I dared to look back at the list. My name wasn't there. Neither was Jeremy's. Because he was the one doing all of this. But why? Who was he? And why was *I* here? I wasn't an orphan. I wasn't part of this.

I put my palm over the trapdoor and closed my eyes. Katherine had to be long gone. Unless she'd somehow gotten away. Then I saw something that caught the growing light through the window, something that had moments ago been bathed in shadow. The machete rich with blood. Guess I knew where the trail had come from. Against the damning odds, I hoped the blood wasn't Katherine's, that she'd somehow turned the tables on Jeremy and lured him away.

I swooped the weapon up. "Guess it's just me," I whispered, voice strangely steady like my grip on the handle. If I wasn't locked up here, there was no way I was staying. I had to get out. Help had to be on its way, it just had to. And if it wasn't...I was thinking that freezing to death might not be so bad after all.

I swung the trapdoor open and clapped my hands over my mouth to trap my scream inside. A gory message was painted on the back of the wooden door in thick crimson. *See no evil. Speak no evil.*

After what I knew from the child's diary, I didn't need clarity to know what the message meant. No one had stuck up for that child. No one had spoken out and saved her. They'd all left her here...*to die*.

There was no light flickering below. Either the fuel had burned out, or the power had been cut.

Seeing no shadows moving below, I began to climb down. It was much darker down there than up in the attic. There were no close-by windows to lend much of any light. The light through the attic wasn't strong enough to reach down here. I stepped carefully, then reached my leg down off the last rung to touch—

I jerked my leg back up and dropped the machete. It clattered down, the loud bouncing on the wooden floor making me cringe. My foot had tapped something soft. Something still. I stared down, seeing the dark crumpled body beneath the ladder. *"Katherine."* It had to be her. The size and shape looked too thin to be Brad or even Jeremy.

I crept down, making sure I stepped over her quiet body. The ground was tacky as my boots made prints in her blood. She was face down, but as I bent closer to her unnaturally twisted body, I saw the horror. The blood had come from her side and her neck. Her eyes were gone. *Gone.* And her jacket was cut open, revealing her bare back and a message carved into her flesh. *"One left."*

"Cassidy!"

My whole body convulsed at the sound of Jeremy calling my name. *One left.* I was it. And now, as I heard loud footsteps growing nearer from downstairs, I knew he was coming to finish what he'd started.

An ingrained sense of preservation kicked in like a rocket and I propelled myself at the banister, ready to run down those creaking steps.

"Cassidy!"

A tall shadow grew below, coming through the opening from the communal area.

I slammed back into the hallway, lungs burning

as I sucked air. I shot a panicked glance left. There was no way I was getting trapped up in that attic. I looked right—and stared. The door down the end, the one that had been locked...had a key poking out of the keyhole.

The stairs creaked and I ran without looking down. My hands shook as I twisted the key. *Click.* I turned the knob and smashed my shoulder into the barrier before falling inside.

"Cassidy!"

Jumping up, I slammed the door shut and relocked it. Backing away, I tried to breathe. I tried to think.

"Shit!" The voice was muted but clearly his. He knew I'd found Katherine's body. "Cassidy!" *Bang. Bang.* The door vibrated, a fist bashing into it. The knob jiggled, and then came more banging. "Cassidy, open up!"

I backed up as he banged harder. Each hit made me jump. And then I was against the wall. I looked around frantically. Layered with dust was a desk, a reading chair, shelves of books... I flinched. And a bear hide with a stuffed head staring at me.

A long creak made me jump and whirl. In my panicked observation I'd shifted sideways—and pushed open another door.

One final bang hit the door I'd come through and then there was silence.

Heart thudding in my throat and stomach doing

backflips, I snatched out my phone. And then remembered it was dead. I squinted into the darkness, making out a long flight of rickety stairs. My free hand clutched around my throat and I glanced back at the door. He was either retrieving a weapon to break down the door, or he'd be coming around to this secret stairway. There were no good choices. Only chances of survival I had to pick from.

A subtle creak on the stairs back out in the hallway made my mind up. He was coming back.

An idea came to mind and I rushed over the bear hide to a grimy window. When I pushed the pane up, it shifted almost with ease. Frigid air swept inside, so cold against my perspiring skin. From here I could see the ground over the lower level.

Nearing footsteps stomped down the hall, and I jumped out, disturbing the layer of thick snow to the edge. I could make the jump. But I'd never get far once I was on the ground. There was only one way out of this.

And it was with someone's death.

Though I'd known before running to the window what my plan had been, my body shook as I forced my way back inside. This was only a diversion. If he got into the room it could, at best, buy me some time if he thought I'd escaped out that way.

Kicking the white crusts off my boots outside the window, I moved quickly but quietly. Once I reached the secret stairs, I flung myself through the door. I tried the key I still held and it locked behind me. Now I picked up the pace. Running in-between tripping, I used the railing to keep from falling and made it to the bottom of the stairs. Another door. This one had no knob. No keyhole. I held my breath and listened, hearing not a sound on the other side. Then I pushed.

A waft of earth blew past my face as well as something else. A scent that was thick and somehow metallic. I knew where I was at once. For all of its horrors, this place felt common to me. Almost like I'd been here a thousand times before. The tunnel.

Instead of making my way to the exit, I found myself walking toward the hut. My weapon from earlier was long gone. I must have dropped it when I found Katherine. And I needed a weapon, something dangerous enough to save me. Dangerous enough that I could wield...and kill Jeremy with.

I slowed as I reached the mouth of the hut. The change was unmissable and I gasped, hand covering my mouth before I could scream. I wasn't alone. *"Brad."*

Bathed in the dull pre-morning light he didn't move as I inched closer. He couldn't. He was strung up to that erect table, hanging limply from the ropes. His head was tipped forward. I didn't need to see his face to know he wasn't breathing. His chest didn't move. There was no sound of breath.

I stepped closer, using my sleeve to wipe a circle

of dirt off the window. I gagged at what the extra light revealed; the reason the bed he'd been in had been saturated red. Blood covered Brad in various places. From his arms, thighs... Vomit spiked the back of my throat. He'd been dismembered, his manhood cut clean off his body. The missing piece, looking like a giant dirty slug, lay on the ground, covered in blood and caked in dirt.

I staggered, my head airy, and caught myself on the trolley. My palm rested over the hilt of a thick knife. "Oh God."

"No. Not God. Just *us*."

Every hair on my body prickled and I froze. Mobility rushed back quick, and I whirled around, knife in hand—coming face to face with that dark hood. A punishing grip caught my wrist and twisted. The knife I held pierced my side.

"It's time to end this, *Cassidy.*"

My eyes widened as the knife slid out and was driven all the way back in. Blooming heat swamped my side as black ink dotted my sight. My knees were about to give out with my consciousness. But I could only think one thing.

That voice wasn't Jeremy's. It was a woman's.

~

I came to groggy, but as memory flood back my blood raced. My torso shot up and I bit back a cry, my hand flying to my side. My fingertips came away glossy red. I'd been stabbed. But I was still alive?

Head snapping up, I expected to see that hood staring down at me, waiting for me to come around and finish me off. But there was no one among the lingering shadows. She, whoever she was, was gone. *A woman?*

As I struggled to stand, I saw the knife I'd been stabbed with. She'd left it behind, as well as the trolley full of weapons. My mind ran wild. Was she working with Jeremy? Were they in on this together?

I didn't have the answers. All I knew was that I was a sitting duck down here. Cornered. I had to get out.

Moving through the pain and away from Brad's corpse, I stumbled up the tunnel. When I reached the door and heard no noise, I inched the barrier open and peeked out. The coast was clear. And now I had to make a choice. Stay and fight whoever she was as well as Jeremy. Or try to make a run for it.

Sneaking out to peer around the bend, the sight of sunlight through the windows beside the front door gave me hope. I didn't know how long I'd been out for, but with the sun rising the layer of snow wouldn't be thicker than earlier. It had to start disintegrating. It would be slow out, but if I stayed on top, crawling on my stomach, I could make ground. I hoped.

Keeping hold of the knife—because despite my hope, I knew there'd come a time when I'd need it to survive—I crept toward the door. As I neared the room Brad had been in—before being killed—I paused, peering in to make sure no one was inside. Clear. Then I crept on and did another check when I reached the communal area.

But this time something stopped me.

Just inside the doorway was a sheet of paper with rough edges along one side. A page from a book? I looked back down the wide hallway and through the room that was no longer lit by orange dancing flames, but instead smelled of sooty smoke. No one was around. Snatching the page up, I lifted it to my eyes. Instantly I recognized the paper size and handwriting. This was from the diary, an entry about the girl's only friend. C.J. About how horrible life was without him. My eyes bugged at the short message she'd written to him. *I miss you, Cameron Jeremy Peters.*

"Oh, my God."

Jeremy hadn't been on the hit list I'd woken to in the attic. But he had been part of this all along. The child's only friend. The one she'd written about. The one who'd left her. Alone.

Jeremy—C.J.—the kid who'd left her was back. He'd returned us all to this place…to exact revenge for what had happened to his friend. The girl who'd had no one else in the world but him. The girl who'd died.

Unless… I thought of my pupil again and how the leaking circle of black resembled what I'd seen in the reflection on the window. Did Jeremy want me to be her? Had that still been him in the hut just before, putting on a woman's voice? The thought terrified me even more somehow. He was crazy, delusional. *Twisted.*

I thought again of the child I'd seen. The ghost. The whispered voices. What if I'd imagined those things because of my tainted medication?

What if…that tortured girl wasn't dead?

"Stop!"

A man's shout brought me out of my head at once. I raced to the front door and stared out through the glass. *"Jeremy,"* my voice escaped in a choked whisper. He was outside across the snow, sunken to his knees as he limped back. His hands were held out in front of him, palms flat, fingers outstretched. Free of any weapons.

"Please, you don't want to do this."

Even from here the look on his face was clear. He was terrified. As I threw the front door open, I saw the shake in his voice matched his expression.

And that's when I saw them. A few yards ahead of Jeremy, who was backing up to the lake's snow-sheeted edges, was someone—and they were wearing a black hoodie. Their back was to me; I couldn't see their face. But I couldn't miss what was in their hand. Red with glossy wetness was a knife. Whoever was under that hood was going after Jeremy. They were going to kill him. He wasn't the killer? My forehead creased as I stared in shock, eyes trained on that knife. Identical to—

I looked down sharp and fast. In one hand I held the diary page. My other hand—was empty. My weapon was gone.

THIRTY

"No!" An overwhelming sense of protection took hold of my entire body. I stumbled out into the snow, tripping, falling, sinking, and clambering to get back up. I was unarmed and powerless. The stab wound in my side stung like hell. But a fear like I'd never felt before, of losing Jeremy, refused to release me. Refused to let me stop or even plan.

The next time I looked up I was so much closer to Jeremy than I'd expected. My heart felt like it had been shocked by defibrillators. I searched for the hooded person. But they were gone. Almost like they'd never existed. Jeremy was still there, his hands out as if to hold *me* back.

"Kasey, please. You know me." He backed up, wincing as one of his knees buckled. He was hurt? That fear in his eyes hadn't left as he stared at me. The blinding sun now clear over the mountain horizon only intensified his expression in all its strained lines.

I knew that name well now. The girl who'd been a prisoner and who I'd thought died here. Or not? She was alive? I looked around again, seeing the open front door and my messy sunken steps. Further along, there were messy tracks on the roof leading away from the upper-level window. A hole in the snowy ground below painted a picture. My diversion had worked. And Jeremy had fallen—*that's why he's limping.*

I completed a full optic circle. All around there was nothing else but trees and reflective white. The glare pierced my eyes and I blinked tears back to keep my vision clear. The hooded person was Kasey? But she wasn't here. How was she not *here?*

"Put down the knife," Jeremy said in a tone that was somehow stern and pleading at the same time. "Kasey. Put it *down.*"

Again I scanned for that hooded figure. But then I stopped.

Looking down, I knew it was there before I saw it. My fingers were curled too tightly, the feel of the hilt hard in my palm. I was holding the knife that was smeared red—the one that had stabbed me. The one I'd been missing moments ago. The one that had looked identical to the weapon I'd seen that hooded person clutching before I ran out here.

"I—"

My voice cut off, seeing more than what I clutched in a vice grip. My sleeve was black. The jacket, a thick snow jacket, I had on was fully black. Somehow I'd missed it a second ago, but I couldn't ignore it now. Either edge of my vision was blocked, cut off—by a thick hood.

My breath started coming faster. My lungs ached, feeling like I was suffocating. I patted my chest then stopped. My hand came away wet with crimson. Blood. It covered my black jacket like a blanket, too high up and too much to be from the slice in my side. The world began to spin, white dots springing into my vision as I gasped for air. "What's happening?"

Jeremy still had his eyes trained on me. Only me. He never looked away, not even for a split second. His hands remained raised as if trying to calm a Grizzly. "You don't want to do this Kasey. Please drop the knife. Let me *help* you." There was a sheen to his eyes, a build-up of tears. Sadness resonated in them even more than his fear. "Don't kill me, Kas."

As if his plea for life had brought it on, a sudden swirl of images swarmed my mind. It was like the diary entries I'd read had come to life suddenly. I could see the events playing out behind my eyes with the turning of each page…

Jeremy sneaking up to the attic with a stale bread roll and a glass of water, and him talking about escaping one day as he watched Kasey eat. The many times he'd sent a smile up through the grate, letting her know she wasn't alone up in the attic. When he'd helped her sneak out to go skiing with him. My mouth parted now as the memory of a rush of cool freedom batted the girl's face on an obstacle-laden slope. I saw over and over how Jeremy had stood up to her father when they'd been caught being kids. Sometimes he'd stood in the way, only to be thrown aside. Other times he'd batted the burly man with his small fists—and been backhanded. Once he'd run, screaming for the girl's mother to help. Then he'd been forced by her hands to watch as that man batted Kasey's face black and blue and red. He'd never left when that horrible man had dunked her in the frozen lake. He'd stayed and rushed in to save her the moment the man left.

He had been her only friend, the only one who had ever stood up for her. He had protected her with everything he had. He was injured and punished, but never as much as she was. Still, he never let her down.

Looking up at Jeremy, I saw in his face that young boy. The same one I thought I'd imagined while skiing. The same one I thought I had imagined when Jeremy was trapped under the lake's icy surface. The fear he'd had on his face back when they were kids was there now. But instead of being propelled at that monster, it was propelled at me. *At me?*

Something stirred in me, more than the

confusion of what I was seeing in my mind. My heart faltered as I was transported in my mind to another time. To almost eight years ago. With small hands pressed against the warm glass of the attic window, my eyes were set down at the ground. It was bright and sunny outside with chirping birds that flittered amongst spring blossoms, a perfect day— except for the knot of dread that invaded my stomach. Perspiration stuck my clothes to my skin, making it feel like I was in an underwater furnace. My eyes stung from the sweat beads that dripped into them. I didn't wipe them away. I just stared.

I couldn't breathe.

There was movement below. A younger version of Katherine was leading a young boy outside to a black car. No. Not just a boy. *Jeremy.* My mother and father appeared next, his arm tight around her shoulder. They were speaking, but I couldn't make the words out. Not that I needed to. I knew what was happening. This was the day Jeremy had been taken away. He'd been adopted. Somehow I remembered everything leading up to it. After squealing to the cop that turned a blind eye, Jeremy had been sold as the best kid when the social worker had come around. My mother had made sure he was picked. And then he was. A family wanted him. Today was the day.

C.J. was leaving the orphanage. He was leaving Kasey alone and unprotected. Her only friend, her only light in the black world she survived in was leaving her for good.

No. Not her. *Me.*

I felt that truth in the way total despair flared through me now. I was that little, tortured girl. The one everyone else had ignored and left in the hands of that monster. The one who'd lost everything— because he'd left her. Jeremy had left *me.*

Fresh pain struck me as if I'd plunged the knife I clutched, here and now, into my own heart. I felt like I was breaking. Like I was dying. Nothing had ever hurt so much as that moment from almost eight years ago. Not the beatings. Not the burns. Not the weapons as they cut and sliced and stabbed. Not even being raped. *Nothing.*

My voice shook as I spoke. "You *left* me."

"Cassidy?" Jeremy's voice was hesitant. His brows rose. "Please, Cassidy. I had no choice. You know I didn't. I never wanted to leave you."

Kasey? Cassidy? The two intermingled in my mind, too intertwined to be one or the other. "I'm…?" I knew the answer and I couldn't stand it. The pain. The memories. What all of this meant. It was too real. Too raw. *Too much.* "No."

I shook my head, fast at first, then slower. With every movement I felt like I was shaking the past away, shaking the agony away. New sensations overrode the pain, and I let them loose to flood into me. Heat burned inside my chest now, boiling my blood, turning my face and eyes hot. I felt like I was on fire. Anger ignited in my heart like it was stuffed with hot coals, the snowflakes that fell doing nothing to cool the burning rage. I glared at Jeremy, my grip on the knife squeezing with strangulation.

"You. Left. Me."

THIRTY-ONE

Seven Years Ago – To The Day

The moment the Monster—he had never been my father—left for town, I scurried over to the trapdoor. C.J. was gone. I'd already lost count of the days since. Had it been months or a year already? Maybe somewhere in-between. Even without him to sneak out to or get in trouble with, my punishments hadn't stopped. And they'd changed. Now the Monster stared at me with more than hatred. The look that now burned in his eyes when he had me alone made me feel dirty all over. What he did to my body after that look made vomit spike up the back of my throat even now.

Today had been the worst so far. "A celebration," he'd called it...for my birthday. Now I was a teenager. "A woman," he said.

I kicked at the trapdoor with the heel of my shoe that was two sizes too big and had a hole in the toe. Sharp stabs of pain shot up my leg, but I kicked again.

I couldn't rid the "gift" he'd given me from my thoughts. He'd touched me before today, had grasped the small swells over my chest and pinched the pink tips. Mouth on my own and then my neck, I'd felt his hand between my legs. I'd felt his fingers press up and inside. He'd made me touch him too.

I screamed out when I kicked the trapdoor again, anger at our secret time today refusing to fade from my mind.

Today...the worst so far.

All that had come before, and then the next step.

Strapped to the board, powerless to fight back. He'd made me wear a sundress—my first special gift—fit for a young woman. He'd torn my underwear right off my hips. Then his pants had dropped, his belt clanging as it hit the ground. I remembered his smell, the musk, the sweat. His skin below his hips had been damp, sweating with readiness. His mouth on mine had been hard. His body pressed into me after that. He grabbed between my legs, and the smile that pulled at one side of his mouth was sinister and full of want. "You're mine. I own you." He shoved up into me and heat and pain bloomed like I'd been stabbed. I choked back a cry. A stray tear slid down my face. His eyes never left mine. His smiled broadened. He retreated. Then he shoved into me again. And again. And again.

I kicked the door again, sweat and tears flowing.

300

A loud crack made me pause. The latch that held the padlock on the opposite side…I'd damaged it. As a wave of triumph overcame the disgusting dirtiness, I kicked again and again, imagining he was sprawled on the floor, imagining it was his face I was denting and cracking. One of the wood planks splintered. There was a pop of metal. And then a thud. I gasped as I stared. Had I done it? Was I free?

My sore fingers, nails stuffed with dirt, gripped the edge of the door and lifted, higher, higher. I flung the thing wide open. The cover was open; the latch was down on the ground. I kicked the hanging ladder, and the extensions slid down on their rails.

I was down those rungs faster than I'd ever been and darting for the head of the stairs. Voices carried up from below, drifting from the mess hall to me. The other kids were having dinner. And I didn't want to get caught by any of them. Without C.J. here, most—especially Connor—would love to call out to my mom to tell on me for trying to escape. I wasn't going to stay here another day. I couldn't.

I'd rather die.

Continuing down the hall, I pulled a thick brass key from my pocket. Father had been distracted on our way back up here from his hut. Him keeping me naked had helped. Staring at my dirty chest, he hadn't noticed my hand slip inside his jacket pocket before he locked me away.

I unlocked the door to his study, a room Mom

wasn't allowed inside. I darted in and locked the door behind me. The narrow stairwell beyond the side door to the left was dark, but I didn't need light to get down. Only losing control over the memories of every trip I'd taken down this way could stop me now. I counted the treads to distract the images and the memory of how hot his breath had been on my skin. One, two, three… By the time I reached sixteen I was in the tunnel, ready to hook a right and make that last sprint through the fake wall and out the front door.

I was so close.

A shuffling froze my first step to freedom. I wasn't alone. Someone was down here; they were in the hut. But I'd seen him leave the house. I'd seen him drive away. He'd been on his way to get whiskey; I'd heard him tell Mom he needed a drink after celebrating my birthday. I cringed. His last words to Mom had been, "Clean up the mess."

"No," my voice was choked. It couldn't be. She didn't know. But I had to prove my fears wrong. She couldn't…could she? In the shoes and socks C.J. had helped me hide in the attic so long ago, my footsteps were quiet. I stopped suddenly when a figure— smaller than the Monster—ran into me at the entry to the hut. Her shock matched mine as she stumbled back, her black hair a mess and arms full as a flashlight fell from her hand. "Mom?"

"Kasey, what are you doing down here? You

know what will happen if he catches you."

I stared down at what she held in her arms. Wadded up material that had this morning been pure white with bright yellow flowers. My sundress. The one he'd ripped from my body after cutting me down after the first "gift" to take me from behind in the dirt. Neatly on top of the dirty stack, which included the sheet from the ground I'd been forced to my hands and knees on, was the Monster's wallet. My fingers curled so tight that my bitten, dirty nails cut into my palms. With the flashlight she'd dropped half on her foot and tilting up at us, the blood smears on the torn dress and sheet were dark...a tale of what had happened.

I stumbled past my mother, catching myself before my shaking legs could drop me. There was a clatter, and I blinked at the many rusty and bloodstained tools on the trolley I gripped. "You knew?" *Thirteen years of hell, and I'd never blamed her.* Never. *But now...* "You knew what Father was doing to me? That he was hurting me?" *My voice was almost too quiet to hear. Almost.* "Touching me?"

"It was your own fault for angering him. If you'd just accepted your place and been good..." There was a slight pause as she huffed air. "Now go back to your room and think about what you're going to say to your father when he gets back. He will not be pleased that you came down here."

My mind went blank at her words. The shock and pain I felt suddenly didn't exist. It felt like I was standing outside my own body, like I wasn't me, like I was someone else, watching from a distance. And that person, the one watching, wasn't weak or scared. They were angry—angry as hell.

Any trembling in my legs stilled as my hands swept over the sharp weapons on the trolley. My voice as I spoke was emotionless but strong. "You're as bad as he is. Maybe even worse." I turned slowly, facing the woman who had birthed me into this world of lies and pain. The woman who should have loved me—who should have protected me. "You were my mother."

Her face was a mix of annoyance and confusion. I'd never even raised my voice to her before. I'd only ever begged to be loved. Now I'd never do either again.

Her mouth opened to speak and I pulled my arm from behind my back, slashing the knife I'd grabbed across her throat. Her eyes went wide as red spurted and swelled, coating my face. Her hands came up to cover the long slice, and more blood spilled through her fingers like a waterfall.

A beautiful red waterfall.

Her lips moved, but she could only gurgle. I kicked her in the guts, knocking her down onto her back. Standing over her, I watched as a pool of red grew around her head and shoulders. "You were never my mother. I hate you."

Her scared eyes got really wide and then…she became still. The shock on her face froze as a wheeze of air slid out from her neck. I didn't feel bad. I didn't feel upset or scared. I felt in control.

Bending down beside her, I checked her pockets. I found a ring of keys in her cardigan. There was a spare for the car, but the car wasn't here. Snowmobile. I smiled and snatched them up.

I was back up the tunnel in a rush, the flashlight's beam bobbing along the padded walls as I ran. My plans changed with each running step.

I'd killed her. My mother.

Escaping wasn't all I needed to do now. I needed to disappear. And I couldn't do that without money.

Stopping before the fake wall that would take me to the front door and outside, I pumped my legs back up the narrow stairs. In the study, I ran for the desk, tripping over the head of the bear rug before getting to and pulling out the drawers. Papers. Envelopes. Pens. "Cash." I smiled as I clutched a stack of bills folded with an elastic band around them. "Now move your butt—"

"KASEY!"

Paralyzing ice attacked my bones at the voice that'd screamed my name. It had traveled up the stairs from the hut. The Monster was back—because he'd forgotten his wallet—and he'd found her. My *feet moved before my brain could catch up. He'd kill me now. He'd seriously kill me!*

"I need the police. Right now. My daughter's murdered my wife."

I heard his enraged voice as I escaped out the study door with the key and ran for my life. The stairs flew past and the communal area littered with toys that tripped me up did too. The faces of kids poked out from the mess hall before disappearing back in with looks of fear when the Monster shouted my name again. Then I was out the door, the blast of freezing wind like a slap to my face.

The car was furthest away. I could see it even though the sun was behind the trees. The snowmobile was closer.

But I didn't get far.

The snow ate my legs like living ice monsters, each step taking my legs down lower and lower, trying to eat my big shoes.

"Kasey!"

The Monster shot out the front door, his face bright red. I'd never make it. Not to the snowmobile. I needed to run. Head whipping right, the lake was frozen over, a thin layer of white hiding its dangerously thin top.

"You're dead, you little bitch!"

I didn't stop; I kept moving, fighting the snow to move to the right. The laces tied to my ankles kept my shoes on. And the closer I got, the less my legs

306

sank.

And then I hit solid ground, my shoes leaving prints on the lake's frozen top as I ran for my life. My legs moved faster than they ever had before, aching more with each step. I'd never really sprinted in my life. I'd never been free to. The further I got, the more I felt him gaining on me. He was on the lake now too. Splinters started to strike out beneath me. The ice was thinner in the middle. If I wasn't fast enough and light enough, I'd fall—

A punishing hand caught my arm and ripped me back. I flew through the air, landing on my butt with a crack of ice. I scrambled up quick, but he was right there. And then he had hold of me, squeezing so hard I felt like my arms would break.

"I ought to kill you for what you did, you little fuck. But you don't deserve death. You're going to suffer locked away. They'll give you shock treatment. They'll drug you up." His anger flared into something even more terrifying. "And then...I'll openly accept you back...where you belong. You will pay for what you've done. Every single day...for the rest of your miserable life."

I shook my head. He wasn't lying, and I knew he could get people to do what he wanted. The cop. The social worker. My mom. I'd never leave here alive. Not in the end. And I couldn't do it. I wouldn't. Not for another day. Another minute. Another second.

I whispered my choice, "I'd rather die." Then I

stomped my big shoe down, hitting the patch I'd fallen on.

Splinters cracked loud like thunder, striking out like a frosty star. The Monster lost his hold on me as jagged pieces drove up. And then we both fell. I tumbled backward as I twisted, grabbing a large jagged piece that hadn't broken off.

The Monster spun too, broad hands reaching out—and missing the edge. He plunged into the icy water, head submerging—one, two—before popping back up. He gripped the edges, breath coming out in quick white puffs. Each time he grabbed, the ice broke away. The layers were too thin here.

He couldn't get out.

"Kasey!" He paddled in the water like a dog, head coming up then going under. His clothes and boots must have been heavy. And he was big, getting tired as he grabbed and slipped off the breaking edges. "Kasey, help me out."

His hand came out of the water, dripping as he reached for me. I stared, not moving an inch as he snarled and grasped the slippery, breaking edges again.

In my head, I saw the day I'd almost drowned. The day he'd walked away while I struggled to keep my head above the water. If C.J. hadn't been there, I would have died back then. Maybe that would have been better. At least all the days since then wouldn't have happened. Today—my birthday gift—wouldn't have happened. But I couldn't change that now.

Seconds turned into minutes of him splashing and panting as more and more ice broke in his grasping hands. Still I didn't move.

"Please, Kasey. I'll let you leave." His eyes were wide now, his head surfacing for only seconds at a time. "I won't bring you back here. I promise."

I looked around and saw the house. It was getting darker out here and there were lights on inside. Kids' faces filled the windows. They were watching, all of them. Even Jill and Connor.

They'd tell on me. They'd say it was all my fault.

Almost in a trance, I shifted closer. But then that strange sensation came back, that out-of-body feeling of not being me. I was a watcher too, someone who'd seen it all and was okay to take control, to direct my actions. My hand reached out slowly, getting closer and closer as he dipped below and resurfaced again. Relief flashed in his eyes as he reached for me. He could almost touch me now.

Almost.

My fingers curled into a fist. "Goodbye, Father."

He roared and snatched out with his bluish fingers. I cried out and turned to run—and then I fell. The Monster had my ankle, squeezing so hard the bone ached. And then he tugged. Not to pull himself out, but to pull me in too. To drown me.

I screamed and clawed the ice. My nails bent and broke as he pulled harder. Bloody smears

309

followed my fingers. And then icy wet attacked my foot. I shrieked and kicked out over and over—until I hit something hard. Spinning up to sit as my leg came free, I saw the blank look on his face and the blood smeared from his nose.

He sank below the water, his blue hand the last thing I saw as I gasped for air. This time he didn't come back up, only bubbles did, popping on the surface. A slow smile crept over my face.

I was free.

~

One Year Earlier

I sat on a hard metal chair in a white sterile room. Handcuffs tied my wrists to the cold metal table. Screws kept the table legs bolted to the gray linoleum floor. I'd found that out the hard way the first time they locked me in here. My fight had died soon after that first day, at least on the outside. No matter what they said, I knew I was never getting out of CWC. Years had passed like an eternity, but somehow I'd transitioned from a scared adolescent girl into a fully grown woman. At least on the outside. Now I sat somewhere deep in my mind, rehashing the events of my life that had brought me here, that had damned me to this new kind of torture. I'd thought the attic and the Monster were bad, and they had been. Now I was free of that and in a whole other kind of hell.

"Tell me again what happened that day, Kasey?" Doctor Bethany sat across the stainless steel table, hands clutched gently. Her posture was straight like her red hair. The black-framed glasses on her nose needed pushing up. "What happened to your mother?"

"Tell her we didn't mean it," a little voice inside my head begged. The child I'd left behind that fateful day. My innocence. "Tell her we're sorry."

I shut the voice down and a smile crept over my lips. Remembering how the blood had pooled out of her was now a fond memory. Something I was proud of. But that wasn't what the doc was asking. She wanted a full re-cap. Again. The actions, the reasons. She wanted me to respond with remorse and guilt like a "normal" person would. But I'd never been normal. And I never would be.

A flash of me strapped to a thinly padded bed entered my mind. The leather cuffs were always tight. And if you thrashed too much, another strap of leather pinned you down by your forehead too. And then the needles came. The drugs to make me "better." All they ever did was make me sick, tired, and angry, amping me up to a point where I needed to explode. Punishments were readily handed out for acting out. Apparently breaking two orderly's noses, splitting a forehead or two, and leaving deep bite marks that drew blood was a no-no. They should have just stopped *fucking with my brain*—which they didn't appreciate me screaming at them, either.

"She died," I said finally, voice flat and unaffected by any emotion.

At the raising of the doc's brows, I was tempted to add, 'after I gleefully sliced her open with one of his rusty blades.' But that and any variance of that hadn't gone down well in the past. I absently tried to reach for my temples, feeling a jolt of memory. Shock treatment was a bitch. It scrambled my brain and left me like a zombie for hours and sometimes days. It never "fixed" me. Because there was no fixing me. I wasn't broken. I had escaped and survived. I would never feel guilt over my actions against her, and especially not *him*.

"How do you feel about her death today?"

"Sorry. We're sorry. We didn't mean to hurt her."

With a shake of my head, that little pleading voice washed away. I looked at Doc Bethany but said nothing. I'd never lost a battle of the minds with her—or my former self—and as she finally sighed and looked away, glancing out the window with thick, close-crossed wire to the greenery outside, today wasn't going to be any different.

"You drowned your father, didn't you, Kas?"

My nostrils flared and I gritted my teeth. C.J. used to call me that.

I spat as I spoke, "The man you call my father? I

312

wish I had. I wish I'd held his head under and felt the life drain from his body as he fought to breathe and gulped water. Better yet, I wish I'd had the chance to gut him like a fish, to watch his innards slip free of his abdomen and spill onto the white snow with a splat."

I knew my reaction would award me another treatment, but I didn't care. Those quiet moments in my mind weren't all bad. I was left alone for days. Left in peace. In solitude. A padded cell with nothing but the past to stew over.

Doctor Bethany's expression dropped with defeat. Her shoulders slouched with a sigh. "I am sorry you feel that way. Believe it or not, I don't want all of this for you. Those drawings on the walls—they show a different side of you. A child who was hurt beyond comprehension—"

"Hurt beyond repair, doc. You know it and so do I. So stop wasting your breath. I can take whatever you can throw at me." No matter what they did, it was never as bad as what I'd already endured. "You won't break me."

"I'm trying to save you, Kasey. I'm trying to give you hope for a future other than this. Nerve damage runs deep. You have to feel the pain, to let it all in before you can start to heal."

I closed my eyes. The words were all good and well, but it was no use. I'd shut that part of myself down that day. The last day of horror. To kill my *mom I'd had to. To watch that monster die, that old part of me had needed to die along with him. I would never be that vulnerable child again. Physical pain couldn't penetrate me now any more than those memories could. They were just a stepping stone. A driving force to hold my focus on my plan for the future. On my revenge. My escape. Her innocence, now locked away, would never see the light of day— until I needed it to. It was all in the details now. The time was near.*

Letting myself think back, I saw that last day from years ago like I was there now. The snow glistening as the moon rose and grew in luminosity. The deep holes my stumbling steps had made. Me on the snowmobile, flooding the engine as sirens and flashing lights blared through the quiet, night-darkening trees. The cop's—Stan's—belated return, and the gun he fired to take me down when I tried to flee. The last thing I saw as the asshole cuffed and shoved me into the back of his cop car was the lake...and the memory of that blue-skinned hand sinking down to the depths.

My smile grew wider, flashing my teeth. "Nerve damage is all I have. Wounds heal, doc, but scars are forever."

Doc Bethany nodded up to the burly male guard siding the only exit, his hand resting deceptively on his stun gun. He shifted, and I didn't create problems as I was unlocked from the table and escorted back to my cell. When the door closed behind me, I laid down in the middle of the concrete floor and stared up at the ceiling, crossing my arms over my chest. The chair I had a long time ago was gone. But I didn't need it now. The names I'd carved into the ceiling while balancing on the back of the bolted-down chair were still there: Stan, Connor, Jill, Katherine, C.J. The main players who failed or abandoned the little, lost girl I had once been.

A calmness settled over me and I breathed deeply. "Don't worry. I haven't forgotten all of you. I'll see you soon...in your worst nightmares."

THIRTY-TWO

The girl I'd been, this Cassidy girl without a clue of true deep and destroying pain, melted away. What was left was the real me, the person I'd had to become to survive. There was no little girl who'd lived in horror left inside. I was the new Kasey. The improved Kasey. And I had a job to do. It was time to finish this.

Once and for all.

Grip tight on my knife, I stalked forward. My feet and legs sank, but it didn't stop me. Nothing would. Not anymore.

Jeremy backpedaled in front of me, tripping in a sudden hole to land on his butt before twisting to get back up. "Cassidy, listen to me. *Please.*"

The sun that broke through overhead clouds flared across his strained face with its handsome lines that were consumed by fear. I blinked at the reflection off the white snow as pins stabbed my retinas. Still I kept forward, mouth twisting up at the sides, lips parting with a cold smile. "There is no Cassidy. It's just me. And I'm not leaving until this is done. Until you pay."

"Kasey," Jeremy choked out. He continued back, his falls diminishing as the surface of the snow hardened. Then he was on solid ground. The lake. Limping back, his hands stayed up as if they could hold me back. I was only a few feet in front of him. "Kasey, you don't want to do this."

When I looked at him, I saw that boy. I saw that day he left me—and the fleeting glance he'd sent up at my window. He hadn't begged to stay. He hadn't shed a single tear. My smile widened. Jeremy saw the threat in my eyes, the challenge. The promise.

As he turned to make a run for it, I leaped forward. Chest connecting with his back, the knife sank in deep, finding resistance as it hit bone. A rib. Jeremy cried out and spun sharply, throwing me and the knife I clutched back to the ground. A crack rang out where I hit, but the layer of ice held its form.

I watched in fascination as Jeremy pressed a hand to his side. Blood leaked out between his tight fingers. His face paled as he stared at me. He didn't run, even though I made no move to rise and take chase. "I know you're still in there, Kas. That innocent girl who only ever wanted to be loved. What you're doing is killing her. She'd never want this. She'd never do these things. I know she's fighting to break free; she's fighting to stop you

317

before you kill him. Before you kill *me*. Can't you see *me*? Don't you remember C.J.? It's still me, Kas. I'm still here."

My fist on the knife curled tighter. Jeremy's blood stained past the hilt and smudged over my knuckles. The anger inside wouldn't let me hear him, wouldn't let me feel anything for him except rage. "You left us. You left *her*. You broke your promise."

Jeremy shook his head. "It wasn't my choice. Your father made sure I was gone. My new family lived across the country. And that's no excuse. I could have tried to escape, to get back to you. But I didn't."

I hissed and crawled onto my knees.

Jeremy's hands came up again in surrender, in a form of pleading. "Kas, I wanted to. I did. I thought about it every day and especially at night. I couldn't sleep, and when I did, I dreamed of what he was doing to you."

I rose to one knee, desperate to pounce. To end this. "Poor, poor you. And here I was, actually going through that hell. Living your nightmares out."

"I know! It killed me because I knew. But listen, I had no choice. I couldn't come. Your father—"

I jumped to my feet. "That monster was never my father!"

"I know. I do. I didn't mean— He, he said if I ever spoke of anything he'd hunt me down. He said if I ever came back, Kas, please…" His eyes were pleading. His hands shook. "He said he'd kill you."

His last admission hit a note. For the briefest moment I wanted to feel something for him. I wanted to remember. But as the good images came back, so did the bad. All the years of torture at that Monster's hands. I gritted my teeth. "Then you should have put me out of my misery."

Jeremy screamed "No!" as I drove the knife down into the ice. A crack erupted, splitting a jagged line down the white-dusted crust and through Jeremy's feet. The ice beneath me gave way, but I anticipated it and rolled sideways as the ground tilted up like an iceberg and bobbed.

Jeremy wasn't so prepared.

Two large cuts of ice beneath each of his feet tipped at his weight, becoming vertical. He scrambled to reach solid ground as he fell, but he caught the cuts of ice as they drove up instead. They acted as slow-sinking floatation devices, steadily failing to hold him up. And then it was just him, treading water as he gripped for the edges that cracked with each attempt.

My knife was gone, but as I ambled slowly closer, I knew I wouldn't need it. The water was freezing. Like it had been all those years ago to the day. My Birthday. For every second he grabbed for the edges while his body remained submerged, he was being frozen from the outside in. Soon his limbs would turn to putty, losing their momentum. His brain would know what was happening; his lungs would keep up the pace, the warmest internal organ aside from his heart that would want to race but slow with the sluggish return of chilled blood.

Soon enough the splashing and grasping at flimsy edges stopped. Jeremy treaded water, breath slowing from his abandoned struggle to pull himself free. His voice shook, his lips now blue but turning gradually purple as he spoke. "I never wanted to leave you. Not ever. You were my everything too. I had no one else. He forced me, Kas. It was set up after I tried to tell that cop about what *he* was doing to you. And then I heard the news." He stopped to take a few breaths, each one becoming more labored than the last. "I heard what you did, Kas. I knew you'd gotten out. But then there was nothing. Nothing in the news. No clues. It was like you disappeared. I've been looking for you all these years. That's why I enrolled at the University of Calgary. I thought if I could find you anywhere it would be back here. With winter coming, I planned to find out if I was right. But then I won this vacation…"

More breathing, and I saw his arms moving with more rigidity below the surface. Those toned muscles were gradually becoming frozen solid. It was getting harder for him to keep his head above water.

"I would n-never hurt you, Kas. And I never abandoned you." Now his voice was failing. "You were my b-best friend. My...world."

I stared without moving, feeling like I too was being frozen from the outside in. His teeth were involuntarily chattering now. He made another attempt to grip the edge as I watched. The ice broke and this time his head disappeared below the black water. Something in me twitched, a sensation I didn't want to let in. Fear. Then his head bobbed back up, and he gasped in a ragged breath before spluttering.

His eyes watered as he looked at me, his expression so much like that little boy. He looked as lost as he had those times he'd tried to protect me and been powerless against a stronger force. "D-don't kill me, Kas." His teeth chattered, the words broken and slurred. "D-don't let me d-die. N-not here. N-not w-where...you...k-killed him. Plea—" His words bubbled as his mouth slipped below the surface. His head followed right behind—and didn't bob back up.

In the quiet aftermath my focus started to shift, frost melting away as the bright sun shot higher. It blinded me before revealing a scene as if I'd somehow been transported back in time, back to the attic. I saw the day Jeremy had been dragged away from me and what had really happened—not what I'd distorted in my broken psyche. He'd been screaming, begging for them not to take him. Locked in the back of the social worker's—*Katherine's*—black car, his hands had pressed into the window with desperation. His cheeks had been wet with streaming tears, the glass foggy from his cries to stay.

"You did fight for me." I barely heard the words leave my mouth, but I couldn't deny their truth. That old memory—the one of him leaving without a care—had been manufactured to feed my hate, to make him my enemy. But it hadn't been real. What I saw now was.

An empty hole of resettling water.

I sniffed and touched my face. Tears were rolling down my cheeks, steady and cold, slowing as they began to freeze toward my chin. *"C.J."* His name was a croak from my mouth as sudden pain almost floored me. The girl I'd become these last few weeks, the one who'd relived so much horror, the one who understood both sides of who she was and had been, broke free. Kasey had used me to plant evidence on Jeremy, to make him the villain. But he never had been.

And as Cassidy I couldn't stand by and let her kill him. I wouldn't.

Rushing forward, I slid to my knees. More ice splintered away, and I inched back to keep from toppling in. I thrust my arm down into the icy water, receiving a blast of hot as the freezing cold penetrated my sleeve and attacked my arm. And then our palms connected and our fingers gripped for dear life. I panted as I hauled, scooting back as more and more ice gave way.

His pale face broke the surface and water sprayed from his mouth. Jeremy didn't let go and neither did I. When the ice no longer cracked before my knees, I caught his elbow in my other hand and pulled with all my might. Every muscle in my body sang as I heaved and we both grunted. He planted his other hand on the ice, and when it didn't give out, I gave one last tug as he pushed up.

I fell as he pulled free of his watery death and landed on my back—a second before Jeremy fell on top of me.

Panting for breath and clutching his side, Jeremy rolled off of me. His teeth chattered. His eyelids fluttered against the bright sunlight streaming down the mountain at us. The blood leaking from him was slow and watery, once again staining the white of his jacket red between the black-and-gray pattern. But it would speed up as his body warmed itself from the inside out.

I didn't move from beside him as my breath gradually regulated itself back to normal. Too many things were swirling through my mind. I knew the truth now. I'd been burned, cut, touched...*and raped.* The memory was enough for me to feel his hands on me now, enough for me to feel him press up and take away my virginity. The last of my innocence. I was that tortured girl. The same girl who'd killed her parents in cold blood.

The woman who'd returned to the place of the crimes against her.

More memories swarmed back like an angry plague in my mind, filled with blood and gore. I held my hands up to shield my eyes from the blinding sun—and saw rivulets of dripping blood. I blinked hard and rubbed my palms together, but even when I reopened my eyes, the fresh thick blood was there.

"I—I killed them." My voice was small, a ghostly sound as brutal images inundated me. Stan. My fist clenched as I remembered driving that knife into his gut. I'd dragged him down to the hut. I'd strung him up. The taste of acrid smoke filled my mouth. I'd burned him. I'd tortured him. I blinked again and saw those pliers and the second I'd sliced his tongue clean out of his mouth. As it fell, the knife sliced across his throat and cut off his screams. "I killed Stan."

Next I was in that downstairs bedroom, perched on the bed. I held a pillow over Brad's face as he thrashed. And then he stopped. I'd suffocated him to within an inch of his life. Then I'd disabled him, cut the nerves to keep him paralyzed—and cut off his penis. Payback for trying to rape me, for molesting me countless times before that day. "And Brad."

I saw Katherine up in the attic next, with her gentle and concerned expression. I'd cut the look clean off her face. First the machete buried deep into her side. Then I sliced open her throat. Her gargling as she died didn't deter me. I stabbed into her eye and cut one out after the other as she went still. "And Katherine." The message on her back was a clue, a promise that I wasn't done with my rampage.

You're still not done. C.J. is still breathing.

"I'm not done?" I sat up fast, and my clothes expelled water. My thoughts raced, the horror and reality of where I was compounding the chill I felt at hearing that voice so strong in my head.

Jeremy was upright now too, his wet hair being blown to frosty waves as he shivered. He still clutched his side but had scooted back across the ice to put some distance between us. The look on his face was filled with caution as he watched me without blinking. Clouds shifted across the sun, darkening the valley and shadowing Jeremy's expression. His voice was a warning as he spoke, "Cassidy, don't l-let her back out. Hold on to your control. D-don't let her win."

"Her?" I studied his face, feeling the old love and care I felt for him begin to war with my bubbling anger.

"You're n-not that person. You're n-not Kasey anymore. S-she did this. Not you." He struggled to his knees, grimacing as fresh crimson leaked out between his fingers that clutched his side. "Don't g-give in to her. Be strong. You al-ways were. F-fight it."

The more he talked, the more that rage inside me flared. I was alone then, and I was alone now. *If he'd ever truly cared he would never have left you. All of this is his fault. He needs to pay. He needs to die.*

The sun broke away from shifting clouds and the glare intensified. Jeremy struggled to stand and I followed the movement. Something gleamed as I rose, sending bright flashes of light into my eyes. It wasn't too far away. The knife. I thought it had fallen into the lake, but there it was. *Ready and waiting.*

Jeremy saw it too, saw the way my feet began shifting in that direction. "Cassidy, K-kas, stop! You saved me. You d-didn't let me drown."

Yeah, but you should have. Now it's time to finish this, once and for all. Letting him live means he won. You'll never escape this. He betrayed you. Kill him.

"No." I shook my head even as I bent to swoop up the blade. "I don't want to."

You have no choice. A siren blared in the distance. Coming here? I remembered the text I'd sent. The SOS. *See, they're coming for you now. Kill him and disappear, before it's too late.*

My resolve was swallowed as panic of being locked away took over. All the torment at this place and the institution I'd been trapped in overcame that sliver inside that urged me to stop. To not do this.

326

My resistance failed and my heart went from fast to slow and steady. "Okay."

"Okay?" Jeremy's voice shook. He was still shivering from the cold and from being soaking wet. He took a rigid step back, groaning as his knee failed. Still he remained standing. "Cassidy?" His expression fell with morbid realization as he stared at me. *"Kasey."*

I nodded, sauntering closer and closer, leaving icy footprints with each calculated step. I pointed the knife in his direction.

"No, w-wait. Stop!" Jeremy stumbled back. His legs weren't cooperating, not with the freezing wet or his fall injury. He went down to his knees. He didn't try to get up. He didn't retaliate. Instead, his hands came together, pleading. "I don't w-want to leave you. D-don't make me leave you."

I froze with the knife to his chest, the point pressed into his jacket right over his heart. Staring down at him, I saw the eyes of that boy. The one who'd kept me safe, who'd battled the Monster and tried to save me time and time again. Now as a tear trailed down from his eye, I saw again his wet face as he cried to stay while bashing on that car window.

I saw his true fear at leaving me behind.

The same fear spiked in his eyes as the sirens blared louder and red and blue flashing lights broke through the trees to the left. "You fought for me, every single day until they sent you away." I didn't look over to see how many cars had arrived. I didn't listen to the words yelled from the megaphone. All I could hear was my own heartbeat in my ears. All I could feel was the hilt of the knife I held, and the resistance I felt as I twisted my wrist—to point the blade at myself. "I don't want to hurt you."

"Kas, no!"

Jeremy leaped up—too slow.

I drove the knife in deep and twisted. A cry peeled from my throat. My chest bloomed with heat and crushing pain. My lung—I couldn't breathe.

Jeremy caught my hand and his arm came around me, catching me as I fell. "What did you do, Kas? What did you do!"

Staring up, the sight of his face faded in a blur of tears. "I'm sorry, C.J.. I'm…so so-rry." A chill struck the heat from my body as fast as if I'd been drowned in the lake myself. My ears rang as darkness cloaked my vision from the edges, growing inward to turn him and everything else into black emptiness.

Now it was over. Finally.

THIRTY-THREE

I existed between alive and dead, the nightmare taking form in perfect sequential order. First I was in that sterile white room, being spoken to by Doc Bethany. My night in solitude after another bout of shock treatment had left me weakened. But that wasn't stopping me. Not today.

Through the unbreakable window spanning vertically out from beside the solid door, a young woman with long dark hair was being helped down the corridor by her doting parents. They were both dressed in fine clothes, the man a suit, the woman in a dress and dripping diamonds from her neck, ears, and fingers. Wealth. They clutched their daughter's shoulders, holding the University of Calgary jacket in place as they ushered her on. Suicide watch. Again. This wasn't her first time. And for a girl that had it all. Parents who loved her. Money. Privilege. Yet she valued none of it. Appreciated none of it.

"To help with your nightmares and the

blackouts."

I faced the doc as a white-capped orange bottle of pills was pulled from her white coat pocket. It made a tic-tac sound as she unscrewed the lid and tapped one free before placing it in front of me. She slid a paper cup of water over the cold metal table. She knew better than to offer it from a glass.

"I hope they will give you the relief to be able to see that what you did and how you feel is not okay." She raised her brows at me. "Take it now."

Her clipped tone left no question to what she was getting at. *Take the pill or have it shoved down your throat.* Or injected—if I decided to bite an orderly again.

I complied, chains that tied my wrists to the table clanking as I shoved the pill into my mouth. Then I swallowed the water—keeping the pill tucked up against my gum. I opened my mouth like a *good* little girl.

After that I was escorted back to my cell. The metal cuffs were released from my wrists and then the door opened. I smeared my mouth quickly and walked in without drama, brushing my hand over the metal plate in the doorjamb as I passed. I smiled at the guard, hiking up my nondescript hospital shirt to flash skin as I licked my lips and jogged my brows. "See you later."

His face reddened and he pulled the door shut with a glare, leaving without noticing the lack of *click* when the door hit the jamb.

I smiled and eased back onto my bed. From below the metal frame's leg, I pulled the small photo I'd stolen from one of the doc's files and unfolded it. As I stared at the face of that dark-haired beauty who had it all, her features began to change, eyes glowing greener, lips becoming a touch thinner but mouth wider, and oval-shaped face becoming slightly more square until the face staring up at me was my own.

"All in good time."

Tucking the memento away, I waited. The sun set slowly through my tiny barred window. The sounds around the psychiatric hospital became quieter, the rattling of med and food carts, guards' booted strides, and mutterings from sad visitors all diminished. Only the sobs and intermittent screams of the insane remained.

I slipped off the bed, the safe foam mattress not even creaking as I stood. Then I was at the door, pulling it inward, and stepping out into the abandoned corridor. First order—clothes and meds. Then—freedom at any cost.

The moment I started running, the scenery changed from sterile and light flooded to a secluded corner in the library of Calgary University. I'd just finished typing 'Thanks lover,' and attached an uploaded polaroid of *her*—wearing a ponytail and doing a high kick in preppy cheerleading clothes—that I'd planted a kiss to with red lipstick. Clearing the computer's history, I was at the printer ending a tall shelf of books, and snatching up a warm printed page on bomb making. I slid a smile to the pretty girl staring blankly out the window.

Tomorrow we'd meet *officially*.

With a blink, my location shifted again, this time to a bus stop outside the university. The smell of commuter car fumes filled my nose as morning traffic whizzed by, and a gentle breeze swept my long hair back from my face. The long metal bench I sat on was hard, my backside numb from waiting. In my hands were colorful flyers for an all-expenses-paid holiday to the Fernie Alpine Resort. There were five all filled out. Katherine, Jill, Brad, and Jeremy. The *lucky* winners. I smiled down at the envelopes I held. Each had one of their names printed on the front with their address and a postage stamp. The fifth one was for Stan. Even without entering he was in for a trip like nothing he'd ever experienced—no one would give up a free holiday. Especially not a guy like him who was so easily bought off.

A bus pulled up with a gush of air and squeal of breaks. The same young woman stepped out, her trusting bluish-green eyes brightening and her lips forming a smile from the sadness they'd been curved down with a moment ago. "Hey, Kasey! We have to stop meeting like this." She laughed a little then took a sip from her Starbuck's cup. "So what do you think of the campus so far? Will you be staying here?"

I'd let her run into me a few weeks back, after following her movements around and out of school. Like the other days, a long sweater covered her arms and hid her wrists—her scars. Her smile was a mask. It had become a late morning thing to say hello and get to know each other—at least on the surface— after her quick return trip for a caffeine hit.

I smiled back at her. "I think I will. Was going to enroll for next semester." Winter break was almost here. The time had almost come. "Hey, Cassidy, you going away for winter break?"

The kids with money never stayed.

She shrugged and wrinkled her nose. "Yeah, I guess. Going off campus at least. My parents are picking me up next Saturday morning. At the crack of dawn. My dad doesn't believe in waiting for sunrise. Not when the whole day is waiting."

Two days time…and I was ready. "You don't sound too excited to go." I tried to sound interested.

"Family cabin out in the middle of nowhere. No TV. No Internet. And dad wants to take the long scenic route. That Kananaskis trail that's twice as long." She rolled her eyes.

I gave a little laugh. *Perfect.* "Well, enjoy it while you can." At her frown, I covered. "I mean the break. Boring or not, it's still time off school, right?"

"Yeah. I guess so." I seemed to have hit a nerve, and her sparkling eyes cast away momentarily. "Well, I'll see you next semester?"

I smiled and nodded, and she waved as she walked away, taking the path up toward the university's front building. My arm moved off of the sixth envelope I held. Cassidy's name was written in bold pen. No address for this one. I'd be hand delivering it. But first…

I went from sitting to standing, walking down a winding road. Spitting rain fell. Water splashed up the back of my jeans with each booted step. My hoodie kept me warm from the waist up—kept me hidden too, making me blend into the dreary landscape of soaked gravel, grass, and trees.

Suddenly I was running and crouching, staring at beaming headlights, my fist tight on thick metal that strung out along the road with spikes. The car flew by, breaking for the slippery hairpin corner, but not enough to miss the road trap. There was a *pop-pop-pop* and a fading squeal of rubber as the tires locked up, and then the car flew past, narrowly missing me as it fishtailed and catapulted over the edge and down the ravine.

I made quick work of packing the spikes back into my backpack and then I slid my way down the slope. By the time I reached the bottom, the loud bang and crunching of metal had ceased, and I was covered in mud. The rain kept on, and I hoped the sky would open up soon and wash away my presence. But first…

I dragged the unconscious young woman from

the wreck and then created a gas leak with a rag and lit the end with *his* black Zippo. The car went up fast, a cry from inside dying as the flames engulfed the living.

And then I was standing over her—over Cassidy. The real Cassidy.

The skull-sized bolder in my hands was heavy. Too heavy to keep hold of. And then it didn't matter. My hands released and the rock fell—right on top of her face with a wet crack.

Sudden trees shot up all around me. My hands and clothes were drenched in blood. The feel of hot flames caressed my face as the putrid smell of her burning body and head full of hair curled up my nose.

Everything had gone to plan. The removal of the body from the crash site to stash it for later in the trunk of my hidden—*stolen*—car. The stepping in as the girl thrown from the wreck—the sole survivor of her doting and rich parents. A single child with no other family in the whole wide world to deny my identity. I'd done it. Now all that was left was to take her place.

To become her.

Suddenly sitting behind the dresser in my new dorm room, the feel of hot flames from the barrel dissipated along with the smell of her burning limbs. I stared at my reflection, at the misshapen pupil staring back at me. A photo was beside my hand—of my parents. The ones I needed to make proud. More photos were stashed in albums, and as I'd gone through them earlier, each time I'd see that girl her face had morphed into mine, the memory of the outing, vacation, or special occasion burning a new memory into my mind. Creating a new me. The wastebasket beside the dresser was filled with blackened remnants now, the smell of burned paper still detectable despite my open window where fresh air ruffled white-and-yellow curtains.

I kept my focus trained on my eye as I inserted the contact lens. Then I tapped out a pill from an orange bottle and swallowed it down. Imprinting the false memory of my release to cover my escape had already taken shape, so much so that even the quiet me wondered if any of it had ever really happened as I locked those raw truths deep down inside. Giving my control over fully, I saw a new me. The mask of innocence from unknown horrors, and the guilt of causing my parents' deaths that could never belong to the real me.

To my reflection I said, "I'm Cassidy Lockheart, daughter of Jean and Phil. And I will survive."

THIRTY-FOUR

I blinked, feeling like my lids were weighed down by lead. Voices registered, soft at first, far away, but growing closer as consciousness returned. Light hurt my eyes and they watered as I blinked faster, levering up on one elbow, feeling unable to shift to use both.

Definition crept back in, and my eyes darted. On the floor, *the padded floor*, there was nothing around me. No furniture. No sheets or even a pillow. The walls were just as white as the floor, just as white as the ceiling. Padded, the lot of it. No window in sight and only an outline for the door—also padded. The glary light above—was it behind a metal grate?—refused to let my eyes clear, attacking them with bright splotches.

"Wait out here," a female voice directed as the door opened. Voices got louder as a woman in a long white coat entered. Screams and tortured cries peeled out from behind her, cutting off as she closed us in.

Out of instinct and confusion, I tried to move. Searing pain struck through me at once and I looked down. *Straightjacket?* I began to hyperventilate.

"I'm glad you're awake finally. Your self-inflicted injuries were quite extensive."

I knew that voice. My mouth went dry as I blinked fast, daring to let myself register who stood before me. She held a clipboard and pen, her hair tied back in a bun and black-framed glasses perched on her pointed nose. "Doc Bethany?"

I wondered manically if everything I thought had happened had truly been a nightmare. Had I manifested all the horror inside my head? Been stuck in nightmares that seemed so real I'd been trapped until right now? But the pain I felt, the locations of more than one deep sting below the straightjacket—it was where I'd been stabbed in the hut, and where I'd stabbed myself out on that lake to stop Kasey from taking over. To stop her from killing Jeremy. But if I'd dreamed that? Had I tried to kill myself to escape my nightmares? Is that why I was locked up here? Why I was restrained without anything to use against myself?

The doctor's mouth was parted. She studied me but stayed by the door. "You remember me?"

I did. Of course I did. And out of all the mess of my memories, I knew when she'd felt the most real to me. "You're my doctor. You helped me."

"Did I? And how did I help you?"

I wished she'd said my name, called me Cassidy. Just that small title would lower my heart rate and the fear that was pounding through me. "You made me realize there was life for me after my parents died. You made me see that my nightmares weren't real, they were just my way of processing the horror of losing them."

Doc Bethany's eyes fell. She sighed deeply and shook her head. "I see I have Cassidy here. The medication shots must be taking effect."

I wanted to clutch my stomach as I bent sideways and held back the urge to heave. I was going to be sick. *Medication shots?*

"To keep Kasey dormant. To make sure you are not a danger to yourself or anyone else."

"No." I shook my head as tears welled and fell, leaving small round spots on my white straightjacket and equally as white pants. "It's not true. She's not real. Tell me she's *not* real."

"You remember, don't you?" As my lower lip quivered, she scribbled something down on her clipboard. She sighed again. "I'm sorry, Cassidy. I know this seems unreal, unfair even. But we can't risk a repeat event. You killed four people this time—almost five. The medication is suppressing your dominant personality now, but we will never know if it will be enough. If *she* will take control again." The doc came closer now, kneeling just out of reach. "It is a risk I can never take. Kasey will never leave this place again…and neither will you."

Good. Let her think that.

I sucked in air as she straightened and stepped back. I stared up at her, but that voice hadn't been hers. Sudden memories of all the heinous things I'd committed with my own hands tied my tongue and my thoughts. Those horrific images were a part of me now, a part of Cassidy, the persona I'd stolen. A persona that felt so real to me. Every time I blinked I saw one: blood, gore…I heard the screams, the begging… A never-ending loop of horror. I didn't want to be let out of here. I didn't want Kasey to come back—was that really her voice in my head? I wanted to die. To have everything wiped into nothingness as I ceased to exist. To not be stuck here living out a permanent sentence for Kasey's murders. The murders I let her commit every time I blacked out.

You can't escape me. None of them can. I still need you.

"Now I know this is against protocol…"

Doc Bethany's words interrupted my shock at that repeated voice only I could hear and stalled my intention to beg for death. She reached for the door handle as I struggled to get to my feet without the use of my hands. "No. Wait!"

Too slow and uncoordinated, the door opened before I could stop her. There was a tear from my straightjacket that was swallowed by cries beyond the door as I fell and rolled back onto my butt. Stabs of pain ripped through my side and my chest and I tried to breathe.

And then I saw him.

My heart pounded as I stared up at the guy who stepped inside and shut the sounds of torment out once more. Exactly the same as that day on the lake with his dusty blond hair and cornflower blue eyes full of sadness, hope, and fear. A crooked smile adorned his full lips, and his hands were buried in the pockets of his jeans. When he stepped closer, there was a bunching of his brow as if he were in pain.

Because I'd stabbed him. Right in the gut.

"Hey, Kas…Cassidy?"

I couldn't speak, but I could hear her loud and clear in my head. *We're both here. We're one in the same. And we're not done with you yet.*

I squeezed my eyes shut, my hands behind my back fiddling as I tried to shut her out. But it didn't work. The meds weren't doing enough. I could feel her inside me, feel her taking over with every second that ticked on. And her threat was real. I couldn't see the details, but I felt her intentions welling with a hot rage inside of me.

The horror wasn't over.

"After what Jeremy went through, what he said you did, I thought maybe he could help. Given your history, he might be the only person who can."

I shook my head up at the doctor. "No." I sent a pleading look at Jeremy. "You need to leave. Now. Jeremy, *please*."

"No. I won't do that." Jeremy came closer and knelt before me. When he reached up to touch my face, I flinched, but then relaxed as warmth and gentleness made contact from his hand on my cheek. "No matter who you are, no matter what you feel about me, I'm not going anywhere. I made a promise when we were kids, and I'm not breaking it. You're not alone. I will always be here. I'll never leave. And I'll never give up. I know you, Kas. You're my best friend and you've survived so much. It's not your fault he broke you. I hope one day you can believe that. I hope one day you can see yourself the way I still see you now."

When my thoughts stayed quiet, I almost breathed a sigh of relief. Tinking from my fidgeting hands even stalled. Maybe Jeremy was the answer. Maybe his love could fix me.

But I couldn't take that chance. No matter how much I wanted to. Guilt aside, I wouldn't let Jeremy pay the price. Whatever Kasey had planned for him, I couldn't let her do it. I wouldn't. And the only way to stop her for good was to stop me too. To end me. Find a way to slit my wrists, pick a fight with the most dangerous patient when I was let out of this padded cell to get shived. Whatever it took to kill Kasey and escape the torment that drowned me at everything I'd done, I would find a way. I would stop this sick cycle. I would stop *her*.

I looked back up at Jeremy, ready to say whatever it took to make him leave and never come back. "I think one day I could see myself through your eyes." The words that came from my lips did so without my permission. Unable to stop myself, I shrugged and shifted my legs, motioning for his help to stand.

Oh no. Stop! This was bad. Really bad.

"Jeremy, keep your distance," Doc Bethany warned.

Jeremy already had a hold of my arms and was hauling me upright. "It's fine. She's fine. I trust—"

Kasey took complete control with a grunt as she tore one arm free of the straightjacket's buckle. Her shoulder—my shoulder—rammed into Jeremy and drove him back into the wall. Freed hand around his throat and squeezing, our restrained hand twisted enough to jab fingers into his stab wound.

His hand to hold me back flew to the pain as the doctor screamed and bashed on the door. "Kas, Kas—*stop*," Jeremy choked out. But his plea was as useless as my own as I screamed for Kasey to let him go.

Her sharp voice spoke fast as Doc Bethany dropped her clipboard and rushed over. She grabbed at me, trying to pry us off. *Even think about ending us again and I'll take Jeremy out too. I'll kill him. I swear to God. It may not happen today, but one day, I promise you, it will. And the next time* nothing *you do will save him.*

My head snapped back, connecting with something hard. There was a cry and the doc fell, clutching her face.

The door belted open then too, and guards flooded in. A shock of voltage attacked my back and my neck. Our death grip on Jeremy relinquished and we fell, the padded floor cushioning the landing.

Lying sideways, I heard Jeremy spluttering. His back was to the wall and his knees were bent. The voltage had taken his legs out too. The doc, with a coating of blood on her face, was helping to pull him up as more voltage pinned me down. A sharp sting came next as an orderly's white shoes came into my field of vision.

In the distorted shaking of my sight, I saw the malevolent plan behind Kasey's threat. Fooling everyone to lessen security. Another escape. But this time we weren't leaving. Well, not at first. The guards with their happy stun guns and the orderlys with their shock treatment and painful, numbing injections would experience what they dished out. And once they were all quiet and still, it would be time for list three. All the boys who'd stood by and watched—*or worse*—as Connor molested that little girl time and time again.

And then Jeremy will be lucky last—should you

try to take us out or stop me in any way.

The shakes dulled as damning calm overtook my body. Kasey receded into the dark shadows of my mind as my breathing slowed and I stared around. I saw the guards first, three standing in wait of my possible reanimation. Behind them Jeremy and Doc Bethany were back by the door, him red-faced, her bloody and clutching her clipboard, and both still catching their breath. The orderly beside them waited with another uncapped injection.

"I…" I coughed, getting my voice to work through the tears that streamed from my eyes and clogged up my throat. "I tried to…I didn't mean—I mean, it wasn't me. I'm sorry. Jeremy, I…"

"Kas, I know. It's…"

Doc Bethany pulled him back when he started to walk toward me. "It's time you left."

Jeremy's face hardened, his jaw clenching, but he nodded down at me anyway. "I will be back. You can't scare me off."

"No, don't—"

My throat constricted like it was wrapped by tight invisible hands. At the same moment Jeremy replied, "I'm not leaving you. Not now. Not ever. I *will* be back.

Doc Bethany forced him from the room as I was held down for my next shot. My voice died with the last of my mobility, leaving me alone as everyone left, and staring up at the padded ceiling—with only

345

her. And her psycho logic and hunger for revenge that if I tried to escape, by way of death, would kill the only person in this world that truly mattered to me.

I was out of options and unprepared. This new plan wasn't new at all. Returning to this horrid place was all part of it.

So I only had one choice. Kasey and I both deserved death, painful and slow. We were two parts of a horribly twisted puzzle that was now glued together. But I couldn't give up. I wouldn't. From this day forward I would fight for control. Fight to be the me I needed to be. Fight to be free of the homicidal urges inside. I had to. For Jeremy, for everyone else on that chopping block, I would become that innocent girl again. I would regain control over Kasey and stop her next rampage. And I would keep him—the one person I could never let down—alive.

Even if it killed me.

THANK YOU FOR READING!

Dear Reader,

Thank you for reading *Nerve Damage*. If you enjoyed this book and have a moment to spare, please post a review. It doesn't have to be long—one or two sentences would be amazing!

The more reviews a book has the more Amazon is willing to put it in front of potential readers. As an indie author, I don't have a big publishing company promoting my work, so every little bit helps and I'd love for my audience to be a part of it. I read every one of my reviews and completely appreciate the thoughts and opinions of all my readers.

http://bit.ly/reviewnervedamage

Thank you, J.L. Myers.

CONNECT WITH J.L. MYERS

If you want to stay updated about my latest book releases, join my VIP list!

Visit : www.bloodboundnovels.com , enter your email address and you'll be the first to know when my next book is released. You can unsubscribe at any time and your email will be kept 100% private.

Come check out my series and author pages on Facebook. I'd love to hear from you:
https://www.facebook.com/author.jlmyers

Come say hi on twitter!
https://twitter.com/BloodBoundJLM

Connect with me on Goodreads
https://www.goodreads.com/author/show/7178370.J_L_Myers

Want to read more from J.L. Myers?

Visit her Author Page for a full list of her currently published books at: https://www.amazon.com/J.L.-Myers/e/B00DK4P0EO/

12468295R00208

Made in the USA
Middletown, DE
16 November 2018